"*When a Secret Kills* was a fabulous read! Eason is a master at romantic suspense with the perfect blend of suspense and romance. I gobbled up the novel in two days and promptly ordered the first two books in the series. Highly recommended!"

—*Colleen Coble*, author of the Rock Harbor series and the Hope Beach series

"*When a Secret Kills* by Lynette Eason is a fast-paced romantic suspense with compelling characters who pull you into the story and make you care what happens to them."

—*Margaret Daley*, author of *Scorned Justice*, the Men of the Texas Rangers series

"Clear the runway and fasten your seat belts. This novel captures the reader in the first line and doesn't stop until the end. Eason has created a suspense-packed story that captivates the reader. The suspense never stops!"

—*DiAnn Mills*, author of *The Chase* and *The Survivor*

Past Praise for Lynette Eason

"*When the Smoke Clears* is a story about reconnecting with friends, facing the past, and falling in love—with a bit of murder along the way. I highly recommend my friend Lynette's stories, and I love this book. It will keep you guessing until the very end."

—*Dee Henderson*, bestselling author

"Eason does an amazing job of setting the bar high for romantic tension, as well as offering a deep dark secret that may or may not ever come to light."

—*Suspense Magazine*

"Balancing skilled action writing with quality characterization is difficult for many writers, but Eason does both well."

—Crosswalk.com

"This plot-driven third entry in Eason's Women of Justice series is sure to appeal to fans of romantic suspense as well as readers who like Joel C. Rosenberg and Ted Dekker."

—*Library Journal* on *A Killer Among Us*

WHEN A SECRET KILLS

Books by Lynette Eason

WOMEN OF JUSTICE

Too Close to Home
Don't Look Back
A Killer Among Us

EBOOK SHORTS

Gone in a Flash

DEADLY REUNIONS

When the Smoke Clears
When a Heart Stops
When a Secret Kills

DEADLY
REUNIONS
BOOK 3

WHEN A SECRET KILLS

A NOVEL

LYNETTE EASON

Revell
a division of Baker Publishing Group
Grand Rapids, Michigan

© 2013 by Lynette Eason

Published by Revell
a division of Baker Publishing Group
P.O. Box 6287, Grand Rapids, MI 49516-6287
www.revellbooks.com

Printed in the United States of America

Library of Congress Cataloging-in-Publication Data
Eason, Lynette.
    When a secret kills : a novel / Lynette Eason.
        pages cm — (Deadly Reunions ; book 3)
    ISBN 978-0-8007-2009-4 (pbk.)
    1. Christian fiction. 2. Mystery fiction. I. Title.
PS3605.A79W45 2013
813'.6—dc23
                                                            2012050049

This book is a work of fiction. Names, characters, places, and incidents are the product of the author's imagination or are used fictitiously. Any resemblance to actual events, locales, or persons, living or dead, is coincidental.

The internet addresses, email addresses, and phone numbers in this book are accurate at the time of publication. They are provided as a resource. Baker Publishing Group does not endorse them or vouch for their content or permanence.

Published in association with Joyce Hart of the Hartline Literary Agency, LLC.

—■—

To my awesome Revell team.
You guys are amazing.
Working with you is a joy and a privilege.
I pray God's blessings on each of your lives.

—■—

But those who hope in the LORD
    will renew their strength.
They will soar on wings like eagles;
    they will run and not grow weary,
    they will walk and not be faint.

—Isaiah 40:31 NIV

PROLOGUE

"Are you crazy?" Jillian Carter stared at the man seated across from her, momentarily distracted from watching those who entered and left the restaurant.

"No. I'm serious." Jeff Lindler's dark eyes flashed with good humor as his lips lifted in a lazy smile. "I think it could work."

"Marriage? But . . . we're best friends." And she used that term loosely although he was one of the few people she trusted. But he still didn't know her. Not the *real* her.

"And you don't want to marry your best friend?"

"I . . . I . . . ." Jillian snapped her lips shut. "Well, yes, of course, but I just don't think of you like that. I . . . don't . . . think I do anyway."

Tenderness filled his eyes and he clasped her hand. "Will you try? Give us a chance? We make a great professional team, why not a great marriage? You know I'm crazy about you."

Did she?

For a moment, she was tempted. Oh so tempted to give in and forget the past, to simply live in the moment. "Jeff, I don't know what to say." She did notice that he hadn't said he loved her. Crazy about her? Sure. She was crazy about him too, in a best friend sort of way. But not crazy in love with him like she'd been with—

"Say you'll think about it." He leaned back and studied her while she looked at him with new eyes. A reporter for KSWB, he was the one person at work she'd let in to get to know her. And that was still at a very shallow level.

"Jeff, I'm sorry, I'm not looking for marriage or romance or—"

His lips tightened and the tenderness slid into hurt. After a moment he tried again. "You are the most mysterious person I've ever met. You're also the best investigative reporter I've ever worked with. With all of the stories and leads you've ferreted out, you could be a household name. And yet, you choose to let me have all the glory. Why?"

"The truth is very important to me. I don't care how it comes out, just so it does." She eased up on the intensity in her voice. "And besides, glory looks good on you, Jeff. Natural."

"Stop trying to flatter me and tell me what's going on with you. I've known you for four years and you won't let me any closer than friends. Come on, Julie, what gives?"

Julie. Julie Carson. The alias she'd been using for ten years.

And the reason she and Jeff would never be anything more than friends. She took a sip of water and plastered a concerned look on her face. A look that had gotten more than one subject to open up and tell everything she knew. "What do you mean? I share almost everything with you."

"Yes. Everything to do with work." He slapped a hand on the table and she jumped. Customers nearest their table cast them sidelong glances. "But nothing about what's going on inside you. What is it you're hiding from? What keeps you looking over your shoulder every time we go out? Who are you afraid of?" He leaned in. "Let me in."

Jillian closed her eyes and drew in a deep breath. She'd had no idea he'd been so perceptive, so in tune to her fears. When she opened her eyes, he stood.

"You can trust me, Julie. I love you."

Now he said it. Three words she'd longed to hear. Just not from him.

"You don't even know me," she whispered. "No one can know me."

His brows drew together and he shook his head. "I don't believe that."

"We've never even kissed. How can you say you love me?"

He leaned over, cupped her chin, and placed his lips over hers. Stunned, she could only stare at him when he lifted his head. He smiled. "Trust me. I mean it. Now give me the keys. I'll pull the car around while you pump the mayor for more information on those corrupt real estate agents."

Jillian spied Mayor Jacobs to her right. "No, I'm not in the mood."

"Get in the mood. This is the perfect time. He hates me, but will spill his guts to you if you turn on that southern accent you do so well."

She jerked. "Southern accent?"

"It comes out when you get mad or want to be charming. Now go use it."

Jillian sighed, wondering how the man could just turn his feelings off like a switch. She didn't want to talk to the mayor. She wanted to go hibernate for a week and process what had just happened between her and Jeff. Instead, she said, "Fine." She handed Jeff her keys and crossed the room to stand in front of a man in his midsixties. He had his gray hair styled and combed to the side. Sharp green eyes watched her approach.

Jillian forced a smile. "Hello, Mayor Jacobs."

"Hello, Ms. Carson." He lifted his glass in a mock toast. "Loved the piece you did on my daughter's equestrian award."

This time Jillian had no trouble producing a genuine smile. "She's an amazing rider. I enjoyed the afternoon and the interview." Jillian paused and slid into her reporter personality. "I was wondering if you could—"

The glass window behind the mayor exploded. Jillian screamed as the floor shook, knocking her feet out from under her. She landed hard on the tile, the mayor fell beside her, eyes wide open, mouth slack. Screams of terror echoed through the restaurant. Jillian felt the sting of cuts, saw a gash on her forearm, and felt the air whoosh from her lungs.

Scrambling to her feet, she grabbed her cell phone and clicked it into video mode. Terror rushing right along with the adrenaline surge she always got when she smelled a story, she shot a quick glance at the mayor, who struggled to his feet, eyes dazed. But he was alive.

Then she saw the cause of the explosion and all thoughts of any story vanished.

The burning remains of her car greeted her stunned gaze. "Jeff!" Stumbling, shoving past other panicked customers, she forced her way to the exit and burst outside. "Jeff! No! Jeff!" The heat of the flames kept her back as horrified disbelief and grief hit her at the same time.

SUNDAY

1

Would he try to kill her today?

Probably.

Jillian shifted her carry-on bag and walked through the jetway into the airport, her eyes scanning every face she passed. Yesterday, she'd called Serena Hopkins, one of her best friends from high school, and gotten an earful on events in her hometown the past two months. Serena had warned her in no uncertain terms that Jillian was a target.

Jillian had almost laughed out loud. She'd been a target for the past ten years.

She fingered the healing scar on her forearm as she thought about Jeff. The grief threatened to smother her and she shoved it off with a vengeance. There would be time for grieving later.

Knowing they'd tracked her down after ten years of hiding not only scared her down to her bones, it told her two things.

They were getting desperate . . .

. . . and it was time to fight back.

Serena had had to back out of picking her up due to a last-minute meeting called by her boss and an unexpected autopsy, but she'd promised someone trustworthy would meet Jillian at the baggage claim.

Someone trustworthy?

Or someone who wanted to see her dead?

No, she could trust Serena.

Jillian picked up the pace and followed the flow of the crowd, staying a little to the side and yet trying to blend in. Baggage claim crawled with people, and she swallowed hard as she tried to scan each face, be alert to anyone who seemed too interested in her.

She hitched her carry-on up on her shoulder and shoved her glasses to the top of her head. One finger reached up to twirl the brown strands as she let her eyes rove the area for a familiar face. Uneasiness clamped down on her stomach as she made eye contact with a tall man leaning against the terminal wall. He offered her a small smile and straightened.

Jillian frowned and turned, indicating her disinterest while keeping him in her peripheral vision just in case . . .

He came toward her and Jillian tensed, moved to the side, and dropped her carry-on to the floor beside her. All she had to do was defend herself long enough for security to grab him.

And then a pretty blond woman dashed past her and into his arms.

As they kissed, Jillian wanted to wilt into the floor. Releasing a harsh sigh, she felt her adrenaline ebb. Grabbing her carry-on from the floor, she looked around again and, seeing no one she knew, headed for the restroom off to the side. She needed to calm down. To think. Convince herself she was doing the right thing. Again.

She entered the bathroom and took her spot in line. After a short wait, she rounded the corner and stepped into the first stall, just vacated by an elderly woman.

Hanging her bag on the hook on the door, Jillian leaned her head against the wall and closed her eyes for a moment. She was so tired. When her phone buzzed, she groaned. Serena? Or Meg?

Just thinking about Meg stiffened her spine. She was doing this for Meg. A glance at her screen told her nothing. She didn't recognize the number. She frowned and felt her tension build. Who would have her number? Had Serena given it to someone?

Probably the person who was picking her up. Her tension eased slightly as the call went to voicemail. She'd check it in a minute. As soon as her pulse slowed a little more, Jillian sent a text to her friend. *Who's picking me up?*

Reality started to sink in. She was home. Back in Columbia, South Carolina.

And she was here to right a wrong, to face her past, and to put a killer behind bars. So she and Meg didn't have to live in fear, constantly watching over their shoulders, Jillian wondering if this would be the day they'd die.

Beautiful, full-of-life, nine-year-old Meg.

Did *they* know about her yet?

Just the thought of the people after her finding out about Meg sent waves of nausea through Jillian. If they knew about her, they'd find her and use her.

And that's why failure wasn't an option. One by one she heard people leave the restroom. Time to get going, to face the past and step into the future. Jillian grabbed her bag from the hook and stepped out of the stall, senses alert.

Movement to her left. A flash of something metal coming toward her. A woman's scream distracted her for a brief second, then instinct and training kicked in. Jillian ducked and spun, using her carry-on as a shield. She felt the knife rip into the bag as she stumbled back. The bag hit the floor and she crashed into the sink.

The attacker paused for a split second, then came at her once again, dark eyes cold and determined. She read the mission there.

Kill Jillian Carter.

With a scream of fear and outrage, she used the sink behind her as leverage to lift herself from the floor. She kicked out and gave a hiss of satisfaction as her foot landed against a hard stomach.

———

Colton Brady stepped into the airport baggage claim and looked around. The flight had landed ten minutes ago. Serena said Jillian would be waiting on him. She'd be in disguise as a brunette and she was about ten pounds heavier than the last time he'd seen her.

Ten years and two months ago.

But he wasn't counting. Really. He wasn't.

He was just doing a friend a favor.

A scream echoed through the area and Colton froze, determined the direction of the sound, then rushed toward the women's restroom, pulling his weapon as he ran. He flashed his badge at the two TSA officers and one airport police officer also attracted by the scream and rounded the corner into the bathroom.

His brain registered the facts.

A man attacking a woman. A woman fighting for her life. A cop in front of him.

"Police!" the officer yelled.

The woman froze. The man didn't.

The knife arched downward.

Three shots from the cop a breath of a second before Colton's finger tightened.

Blood blossomed on the attacker's chest and he dropped like a rock.

Colton held his fire, raced in, and kicked the weapon away. He handcuffed the wounded man's hands behind his back, then rolled him away from the woman. She sat up with a shaky grunt.

"Is he dead?" She scooted away, grasped her carry-on, and stood. Flecks of blood covered one cheek. A whole lot of it had pooled on her right shoulder.

Colton leaned over and checked the man's pulse. Weak and

thready. "Not yet." He looked up at the hovering airport police officer. "Get an ambulance."

The officer holstered his weapon and radioed it in. Colton had his doubts that the attacker would live long enough to benefit from the help.

"Are you hurt?" Colton asked the woman.

"N-no. I don't think so. I managed to block the knife, but . . ."

The fine tremor in her hands and the shallow panting breaths told Colton she was on the verge of either hysteria or collapse.

Then she surprised him by hitching the carry-on over her shoulder and shoving her tinted glasses up onto her head. She marched to the sink, grabbed a handful of paper towels, and started to scrub the blood from her face.

Once again he felt his heart slam into his lungs. Jillian Carter. She had been beautiful as a blond. As a brunette, she took his breath away. He wanted to pull her into his arms, kiss her senseless—then demand what she'd been thinking when she'd disappeared from his life ten years ago. Either that or send a fist through the wall, releasing all of the pent-up anger he'd thought he dealt with years ago.

He did neither.

"He tried to kill her. He just attacked her . . ." Shock stood out on the white face of the witness to his right. "I saw him but I . . . it just happened so fast." She looked at Jillian, her trembling increasing with each word. "I'm so . . . so sorry . . . I—" Her eyes dropped to the man on the floor, whose breathing was shallow and labored, and Colton saw her shudder.

Jillian shook her head. "It's all right. You couldn't have done anything."

Colton motioned for a uniformed officer to usher the woman from the bathroom. "Why don't you get her statement?"

The officer swallowed hard and nodded. "I called 10-99. Everyone's rolling."

It was going to be a madhouse. TSA, FAA, and the FBI were no doubt already on their way. TSA was in the process of shutting down the airport and screening every person in the building. Colton gathered his composure and walked over to Jillian. He took the paper towel from her trembling fingers and said, "It's been a long time."

As though in slow motion, her eyes lifted to meet his in the mirror. Tears trembled on the edges of her lashes and his gut clenched. Then those brown eyes narrowed. He stared, trying to see past the contacts that covered the blue eyes she'd been born with. Her tears faded. "Ten years."

"I've been counting," he said as he wet the towel a little more and wiped up a few spots around her nose that she'd missed. "Did you get any in your eyes?"

"No."

Good. He made a mental note to check with Serena about blood-borne diseases on the dead man. No need to mention that to Jillian right now.

She hitched her carry-on up again and nudged her glasses farther atop her head, then twisted her fingers together.

"That's how I knew it was you," he murmured.

"What?"

"You used to do that same maneuver in high school. Shrug your backpack up higher on your shoulder, then push your glasses on top of your head."

She went still and fear flashed across her face. "I did?"

Colton frowned at the fear. "Yes."

"Sir?"

Colton looked up and away from Jillian's puzzling expression. "Yeah?"

"We need to secure the crime scene."

Jillian stepped away from the man who'd tried to kill her, and Colton followed her from the bathroom.

Colton rubbed a hand through his hair. "Looks like Serena will be making a trip to the airport after all."

Her throat worked and he wondered what was going through her head. But instead of saying anything, she let out a sigh, looked at the blood on her shoulder, and grimaced. She asked, "Were you my ride?"

"Yes. I was on my way to church when Serena called me about an hour ago. I called your cell phone, but you didn't answer."

"Of all the people—"

Colton had to strain to hear her words, but he gathered she wasn't happy about his presence. Tough.

She shook her head. "I guess we have to stay here, give a statement or whatever." Her eyes jumped from one person to the next, her shoulders stiff, posture on guard.

She was watching, ready for an attack from any side. Colton felt the first stirrings of sympathy for her. "Yes."

Jillian dipped her head, hiding her eyes. Her hair slid over her shoulder to cover her face. She dropped her carry-on to the floor and sat on it. "Fine."

"Do you have a different shirt in your bag?"

She looked up, surprised. "Of course."

He wanted her out of the open. Even though the bystanders had been ushered out of view of the scene, he wasn't sure someone wouldn't try to grab a few pictures with a cell phone. "Why don't I clear the men's room and you go in and change? You'll feel better. Keep the bloody shirt, though. It's evidence. I'll get a bag to put it in."

With a grateful glance at him, she nodded. The men's bathroom, right next to the women's, had been cleared. Colton waved her in. Five minutes later, she returned and placed the shirt into the bag he'd found and now held out to her. She leaned against the wall, closed her eyes, then slid to the floor, her carry-on bag pulled against her stomach. He gave her another couple of minutes to gather herself, then stood in front of her. "Why don't you tell me what you've been doing the past ten years and why you're back now?"

Jillian groaned and dropped her face into her hands. "Go away."

Anger shot through him and he sank to his knees as he placed a hand beneath her chin to jerk her face up to his. "Oh no, Jillian Carter. I'm not like you. I don't run away when the going gets tough. I've waited ten years for some answers. You're not leaving my sight until I get them."

2

Jillian swallowed. Hard. Colton's green eyes had a look in them she'd never seen before. One that said he'd grown up and hardened in the past ten years.

A look that said he'd suffered when she'd left without a word.

A look that said she was going to give him answers whether she wanted to or not.

Unfortunately, she couldn't do that. Yet.

Before she had a chance to figure out what to say, the airport doors slid open and more law enforcement descended upon them. Uniforms already swarmed the area, but this new group she knew.

She breathed a sigh of relief for the reprieve. Colton wasn't so happy. He shot her a look that said they weren't finished and turned to fill in the newcomers.

Jillian registered the faces from her past.

Hunter Graham, Chad Graham, and Katie Isaacs. She thought she might know a few more, but her befuddled mind couldn't find the names. She'd worked so hard to forget and yet at the same time couldn't—she'd known *he'd* try something.

And he had.

Colton's leadership skills stood out as he spoke. She took a moment to study him. Same shaggy blond hair, green eyes, and square chin. The dimple in his cheek still peeked out even when he frowned.

"Jillian, is that you?"

She looked up to see Hunter Graham staring down at her. He'd broken away from the group and squatted in front of her. "Yes, it's me."

"Boy, do you look different. What are you doing here?"

Jillian sighed. "Coming home. Unfortunately, I can't seem to go anywhere without trouble following. Sorry about that."

"So I've heard." He paused. "Alexia and Serena will be glad to see you."

Jillian gave a humorless laugh. "I'm not so sure about that. Knowing me put them in danger. And it's still not over."

"We caught the guy after Serena, but not Alexia." He paused. "Is that why it isn't over?"

"Yes. No. Maybe."

"Well, that clears it up."

She grimaced. "Sorry. There's just a lot you don't know."

"Then tell me."

"I will." She looked around. "Just not here."

"Right." He looked over his shoulder and she followed his glance.

Serena made her way through the airport doors. Jillian wanted to rush over and give her friend a hug, but it wasn't the time for that. Serena caught her eye and gave a slight wave, the expression on her face saying they'd have a talk later. Jillian nodded and Serena stopped to sign in to the crime scene. After she slipped on gloves and booties, she stepped into the bathroom.

Jillian's eyes slid to Colton as he talked to Katie. She was nodding and waving an arm as she responded. "She's very animated, isn't she?" Jillian said. "Has she changed?"

"Animated is one way to put it. And no. She hasn't changed a bit."

Jillian grimaced. "Wonderful."

"Aw, Katie's all right." He studied her. "You *really* look different."

"I know." She'd be explaining why later. She let her eyes slide back to Colton. "You trust him? Is he a good cop?"

Hunter's brows lifted in surprise. "One of the best. And yes, I'd trust him with my life."

"Even though he's related to Frank Hoffman?"

Now Hunter just looked puzzled. "The senator? Sure. Frank's a good man. Might even be president one day."

The thought turned her stomach. "Right."

He studied her with a questioning look. "Why do I get the feeling you disagree about the good man part?"

Colton turned and walked over to them. "Jillian, are you ready to give your statement?"

She shuddered. "Sure." From the corner of her eye, she saw the airport police officer who fired the shots talking to Chad Graham. He rubbed his eyes and shook his head. Grief stood out on his face, and Jillian felt guilt and regret well up inside her. This was all her fault. If she'd stayed in town ten years ago and gone to the authorities, told what she saw . . .

No. If she'd stayed, she'd be dead. And so would Meg.

This time she wasn't going down without a fight. Part one of her plan. Find the evidence to convict Frank Hoffman, and stay alive while doing it. Part two? Find a way to tell Colton about Meg without endangering her daughter.

Colton helped her to her feet. "Come on. They're taking statements in a room down the hall. I need you to walk me through what happened." He motioned for Hunter to join them.

In silence, Jillian walked beside Colton down the hall. Hunter followed. Colton led her inside the room and she sat at the table. A video camera had been set up to record her statement. He turned it on, pulled out a little green notebook, and said, "Okay, tell us what happened in as much detail as you can remember."

Stuffing down her emotions, she said, "I got off the plane and came down to baggage claim. When I didn't see anyone I knew, I went to the bathroom. When I came out of the stall, the woman screamed—he was . . . there." She hated the shakiness in her voice, but couldn't seem to control it. "He had a knife and he tried to stab me," she drew in a shuddering breath and forced the words out, "but I was able to throw my carry-on bag up and the knife hit that instead of me." She swallowed hard, remembering the paralyzing fear. She was extremely grateful she'd allowed a friend to talk her into several years of self-defense training. They'd just saved her life. "I kicked him in the stomach, but he managed to tackle me. I think that's where Colton and security came in and," she grimaced, "shot him."

Colton nodded and snapped his notebook shut. "I have a laundry list of questions. Let's start with, Have you ever seen this man before?"

"No. Never."

"Was he on the plane with you today?"

"I didn't notice him, no."

Colton sighed and scratched his chin. "Did you notice anyone following you?"

"No, Colton, no one. And it's not because I wasn't looking."

His lips puckered, and memories of their long-ago summer together washed over her. Beneath the table, she curled her fingers into fists.

He asked, "What about who knew you were flying in today?"

"No one." She swallowed hard. "I told no one." Except the people who had Megan, but she couldn't say that. And she knew without a doubt they hadn't been the ones to say anything. No, whoever had known she was on that flight was right here in Columbia, South Carolina.

"Who's after you, Jillian? Who wants you—and Alexia and Serena—dead and why?"

She sighed and closed her eyes as she tried to find a way around her answer. But she couldn't. Opening her eyes, she said, "Your uncle, Senator Frank Hoffman, wants me dead because I saw him murder a man ten years ago."

3

"What?" Colton jerked and nearly dropped the notebook as he registered her words.

Jillian lifted her chin, eyes clear, determination etched, shoulders squared. "It's true. I saw him do it."

"I don't believe you." He heard the frigid tone in his voice, saw her flinch, then narrow her eyes.

"It doesn't really matter if you believe me or not. It's why I left that night and it's why I'm back now. To prove it. With or without your help."

What she was saying was crazy. And a lie. But why would she lie about something like that?

She pointed toward the door. "That man tried to kill me to shut me up." Her jaw firmed. "Well, it's not going to be so easy this time. I know it doesn't look like it, considering what happened in the bathroom, but I've had ten years to learn how to take care of myself."

Colton watched her eyes. They flared with truth and determination. A sinking feeling swirled in his gut. She believed every word she said. He shot a glance at Hunter, who'd been quiet through the whole conversation. But the frown pulling his brows toward the bridge of his nose suggested he was thinking. Hard. "Hunter?"

"There's something . . ."

"What?"

"Something I read not too long ago." He rubbed his chin. "It was when someone was after Alexia and we were searching for the guy. We had connected that whoever was after Alexia had something to do with the night Jillian left town. I researched all of the crimes and 911 calls that came in that night."

"What'd you find?" Colton asked.

"Something about a gunshot being reported in your uncle's neighborhood, but when authorities got there, all was quiet. The police did a drive-by, stopped at a few random houses to ask questions, but came up empty and just wrote it off to a car backfiring."

Jillian drew in a deep breath and asked, "And what was the date of that report, Hunter?" Colton could see that she already knew the answer to the question.

Hunter looked first at Jillian, then at Colton. The sinking feeling grew. Hunter said, "Graduation night. Like I said, it was the night you left town."

"And they covered it up. Somehow." Jillian fidgeted with the carry-on, the hole from the knife a visible reminder that someone had really tried to kill her.

But Uncle Frank involved? Colton shook his head. Impossible.

"Excuse me?"

Jillian jumped and Colton swung around to see Serena and Rick. He stood and shut off the camera. "What do you have?"

Serena gestured for Rick to go first. He said, "I've got his prints." He held up a device and Colton exchanged a look with Hunter. Rick caught the exchange and snorted. "Don't worry, I'm not going to force you to add to your limited knowledge at this point in time." However, a small secretive smile crossed his face. A smile that made Colton nervous. Rick didn't explain the look. Instead, he said, "I just came to tell you that your dead guy isn't in the system."

"Of course not," Colton muttered. "That would be too easy." He looked at Serena. "Your turn."

Concern knit her brow as she glanced at Jillian, then over to Colton. She said, "I've already talked to TSA and the FBI, but wanted to fill you in. Cause of death is pretty obvious. The three shots to the chest killed him. He bled out before the ambulance pulled in the parking lot." She looked at Jillian. "There was no ID on him. You know who he is?"

"No. Not a clue," she said. "I'm sure he's just a hired killer. Someone to do the senator's dirty work for him."

Colton looked at Jillian. "You can't make these kinds of accusations without proof. If you go public with that kind of thing, you'll ruin his career. Ruin *my family*. Is that what you want?"

He saw a deep weariness invade her features before she schooled them. Her brown eyes held his as she said, "I have no intention of making accusations I can't back up with solid proof. That's why I'm here, to get proof." Her gaze flicked back and forth between him and Hunter and Serena. "And that's why I've told you what I have. Now if I turn up dead, you'll have your motive."

Colton rocked back. The confrontation in the bathroom, seeing Jillian again, fighting memories of their past—and now hearing her talk as if his uncle was a murderer swarmed together in his mind. He looked around. "We need to talk. After I finish here, we have some serious catching up to do."

She lifted her chin. "Fine."

Hunter nodded and Colton made a mental effort to loosen his jaw before he shattered his teeth. He narrowed his eyes at Jillian. "Where are you staying? Your dad's?"

"No." She didn't elaborate. "Not there. I was going to get a hotel room and go from there." She paused. "My top priority is to put a killer behind bars and stay alive while doing it."

Serena smiled and spoke up. "You can stay with me until you figure out what you're going to do."

Hunter shook his head. "I don't think that's a very good idea, Serena. You've already been targeted and we don't know that it's over."

"Exactly." Serena hitched her chin much like Jillian had done moments before and looked first at Hunter, then Colton. "If she's with me, it'll be easier for you to keep us safe." She motioned to a man who hovered discreetly behind her. "Besides, I have a shadow. He can watch us both at the same time."

"Dominic might have something to say about that," Colton said.

"Wait a minute," Jillian said. "Dominic? Alexia's brother?"

"You and Colton aren't the only ones who need to catch up." Serena lifted a brow at Colton. "Dominic will agree."

Colton smiled. "Yeah, I guess he will if *you* ask him."

Serena nodded. "I'll ask him." She stepped the rest of the way into the room and rounded the table to gather Jillian into a quick hug. "Welcome home. Get your things. I'll show you where I live." She looked at Colton. "Once you're finished here, will you bring any luggage Jillian can't get to right now to my house?"

"Sure." Colton frowned as Serena led Jillian from the room. Neither woman paid attention to the man who moved to follow them, but he made eye contact with Colton and nodded. Colton nodded back. Dominic had hired someone to continue watching out for Serena. Anyone with Serena would receive the same treatment. Jillian was safe.

For now.

———■———

Jillian stepped into Serena's house and shut the door behind her. Serena's shadow stayed outside. She set the hard case box containing her weapon onto the table in the foyer. Getting it had taken some doing. But Jillian had followed all regulations for flying with a firearm. After TSA had searched everything except her large suitcase that hadn't shown up by the time she was ready to leave, they had returned her things. She set down her small suitcase and slid off her backpack, taking in her surroundings. "I'm impressed," she told her friend. "This is nice."

Serena punched in the code to deactivate the alarm. "I've done all right."

"More than all right." Jillian felt some of the stress of the last ten years ease as she looked around. "It's very peaceful. *Serene*."

Her friend smiled at the pun, then frowned. "I can't believe you carry a gun."

"Never let it get too far away from me. Thanks for doubling back at the airport and letting me claim it." She paused. "I didn't want to have to explain it to everyone."

Serena's eyes changed, studying her. "You're different," she said.

Jillian nodded. "Very." She softened her gaze. "I had to change, to learn to rely only on myself if I wanted to survive."

"You were so young," Serena whispered.

That brought a sad smile to Jillian's lips. "We're the same age."

Serena frowned. "I feel older."

Laughing, a short, amused chuckle, Jillian shook her head. "I don't know why."

"I guess because I keep picturing you as you were ten years ago. We've only spoken on the phone a few times in ten years. That's made it hard to know you, to know who you are now."

Jillian felt tears prick the back of her eyes. "I know."

"So why didn't you want to stay with your dad?"

Grateful for the change in subject, Jillian said, "Same reason I'm not sure I want to stay with you. I don't want to put anyone in danger."

"So it's better to stay with me since I'm already a target?" Serena asked with a teasing smile as she walked toward the living area. She gestured to the couch.

Jillian sank down onto the soft leather and sighed. "Something like that." Then she frowned. "I'm sorry I dragged you into this. I shouldn't have sent you that package."

"Ah yes, the package." Serena looked away for a moment.

It didn't take a genius to understand. "You read it, didn't you?"

"I did."

Jillian studied her friend. Guilt and some other emotion clouded Serena's eyes. "You felt you had to?"

"Yes."

Serena looked relieved at Jillian's understanding. But Jillian knew her friend. If Serena had read the information in the package, she'd had a really good reason.

Serena ran a hand through her thick black hair, pushing strands behind her ears. "We thought there might be a clue in there to tell us who was after me and why. I'm sorry, Jill, I wouldn't have read it if—" She bit her lip.

"It's all right." Nerves made her want to fidget. "Who else knows?"

"Just Dominic and me."

Relief crashed over her like giant waves. "Then Colton doesn't know?"

"That you and he have a daughter? No."

Jillian swallowed hard. "I'm going to have to tell him, aren't I?" Serena simply looked at her and Jillian grimaced. "I think I've known I was going to have to do that for a while now."

"She's nine?"

"Yes. She'll be ten on December 25th." She couldn't help the small smile that curved her lips. "My Christmas baby."

"Where is she now?"

"With a friend. A very trusted friend."

"If the people after you—us—find out about her, they'll use her."

Fear shivered through her. "I know. I've already thought about that, trust me."

Serena clicked on the lamp on the end table next to the sofa.

"We memorized everything about Meg and deciphered your crazy clues as to how to find her if we received word of your death and then destroyed the package."

"Good."

"I figured that's what you were doing. But you took a big chance on mailing that to me. What if it had gotten lost in the mail or worse—intercepted?"

Jillian winced and licked her lips. "I was desperate. I'd felt like someone was watching me, following me. I figured they'd found me and I had to give myself time to come up with a plan, but I had to make sure Meg was taken care of in case I failed. So I took a chance and prayed God would deliver it to you." She swallowed. "And that if it fell into the wrong hands, no one would be able to figure out what everything meant."

"Well, God got it to us, but someone knew about the package."

"So you said."

"My house was broken into more times than I like to remember. Thank goodness I had the foresight to hide that package really well."

Emotion clogged her throat. "Thank you, Serena."

Serena nodded. "Okay, enough about that. Let me show you the spare bedroom and you can freshen up, take a nap, whatever you need to do."

"You need to get back to work?"

"Yes, I'm the weekend shift this week, but don't worry, this house is now more secure than Fort Knox. Dominic had the security upgraded. Every window and door is wired. The fence outside is lined with motion lights and sensors. If someone even touches the fence, an alarm goes off. It's not sensitive enough to sound if the wind blows hard, but if anyone tries to climb over or come through it, you'll know."

Jillian swallowed hard. "I can't believe it's come to this," she whispered. "I need to call my dad and warn him that I'm back, that he might become a target." She gulped. "Everyone I love is in danger now."

Serena's brow wrinkled. "I think they must be getting desperate for some reason."

Jillian picked up the cordless phone and dialed her father's number. It rang four times, then went to voice mail. When his deep bass voice came over the line, Jillian's heart shuddered. With her mother dead, her father meant even more to her than she realized. She'd missed him. He was a good father. Confused by his only child and hurt by her lack of communication, but she knew he still loved her. At the beep, she found her voice. "Hi, Dad. It's been a long time, but I just wanted to let you know that I'm home and I need to talk to you. Um, I've got some pretty nasty people after me. Please be careful and watch your back. They might try to get to you to get to me." She paused. "I love you, Dad. Call me." She gave him her cell phone number, disconnected the call, and looked at Serena. "I didn't tell anyone I was coming home, but they found me anyway."

"You said they'd found you in California."

"They did." Sorrow pierced her as she remembered the explosion outside the restaurant, the death of a good man—and the raging terror as she realized her worst nightmare had come true.

But that story could wait. She'd kept Serena long enough. She stood and grabbed her suitcase and backpack. "Show me which room is mine and I'll get out of your hair."

"You're not in my hair." Serena led her into a beautiful room done in tasteful antiques.

"You've always wanted your own house to decorate. You've done a wonderful job. This room is gorgeous and peaceful. Something I really need right now." She gave her friend a quick hug. "Thanks for letting me stay."

"Of course. I'd be hurt if you didn't." Serena motioned to the door to the right. "Bathroom is there, closet is on the other side."

"Got it."

Serena hesitated at the door. "So, what's next?"

Jillian dropped to the bed. "I don't know—I really don't."

Serena nodded. "We'll figure it out. I have a date with Dominic after work so it'll be a late night. We're going to the evening worship service, then to dinner."

Jillian shrugged. "I don't sleep much these days. I'll probably be up when you get back."

Up and planning her next move.

4

Senator Frank Hoffman hung up the phone and leaned back in his leather chair as nausea swirled in the pit of his gut. He picked up the 1894 Colt Bisley from the desk and continued cleaning. As much as he loved shooting the old guns, cleaning them had become like therapy to him, helping him relax, get his thoughts in order. So he cleaned.

He rubbed the cloth over and over, in every crease and crevice. Then he attached a cleaning patch to the patch holder and ran the holder up the barrel of the gun. Mindlessly, he repeated the action, switching out the dirty pads for clean, while his thoughts taunted him.

Jillian was still alive and a professional assassin was dead. And not only was Jillian still alive, so were Alexia Allen and Serena Hopkins. How was this possible? How hard was it to get rid of three women? Three women who could ruin him. Or was it more than that by now? The longer they lived, the more the odds increased that Jillian would tell what she saw that night. If she hadn't already.

No. If she had talked, he'd be in custody. He had to get rid of her immediately.

Frank finished cleaning the weapon and turned to settle it back into place on the wall behind him. He turned back to his desk, his thoughts on his career and the certain knowledge that, if Jillian Carter didn't disappear soon, he would *have* no career to think about. Just visualizing such a thing struck terror into his heart. He'd worked so hard on keeping everything above reproach. His image, his private life, his physical health, his family appearances . . .

Everything. And now, in the length it would take Jillian to tell what she saw that night, he could lose it all.

Frank broke out into a cold sweat and looked at the calendar. Three months until election day. Campaigning was hot and fierce between the candidates, and Frank had no intention of losing—or going to jail.

Appearances. He had to keep up appearances.

And get rid of Jillian.

A curse slipped out.

"What was that?"

Frank jerked as his wife, Elizabeth, stepped into the room. Beautifully made up, she exuded poise and class. Exactly what he'd been looking for when he'd gone searching for a wife. The perfect political partner, one to inspire confidence in the voters; if such a woman would marry him, he must be worthy of their trust and their votes. "Sorry, I was just thinking about the debate coming up."

She arched a delicate eyebrow. "Well, if you plan to use that kind of language, you can pretty much kiss your career goodbye."

He rolled his eyes and stuffed down his impatience. "I think I can handle it."

Her shuttered eyes gave him a cool appraisal. "Be sure you do."

"Is there something you wanted?" He couldn't help the impatience in his tone.

She narrowed her eyes. "Carmen will be home next weekend. I do hope we can at least have one family dinner while she's here."

Carmen. His daughter. His troubled daughter who seemed to

be trying to make something of her life. Finally. "Of course. Friday night?"

Elizabeth gave him a slightly warmer look. "Perfect. Here or out somewhere?"

"Let's go out." Being seen in public as a family was always good for a few votes. As long as Carmen behaved herself.

"Wonderful. I'll tell Carmen." She turned toward the door, then looked back at him over her shoulder. "You seem more stressed than usual, Frank, is everything all right?"

Frank forced a smile. "Everything's fine. Where are you headed?"

"Girls' night out."

"Right. Well, enjoy yourself."

"I plan to. Don't wait up."

And then she was gone, her light perfume lingering behind. He smiled. He'd brought that particular scent back on his last trip to Paris. She'd loved it and seemed genuinely happy with his gift.

Current problems intruded on his pleasant memories and he frowned once again.

Rising from the black leather chair, he paced his home office. He thought he'd had the best people that could be bought on this. But they'd failed to take care of the problem. Time after time, they'd failed. Maybe it was time to take matters into his own hands.

Literally.

He lifted them, palms up, and stared at them. Smooth and white. Yet even now, ten years later, he could almost see the blood dripping from them. Blood he'd never actually touched but caused to flow nevertheless. He still couldn't believe he'd become a murderer. Never would he have envisioned himself capable of killing someone.

But he had, hadn't he? That night was such a blur. It had happened so fast. And it hadn't been premeditated, he reassured himself. It had been an act of fury, of uncontrollable rage. And the determination to let nothing get in the way of his plans. But it hadn't been premeditated.

He snorted. Like a jury would care about that now.

He continued to stare at his hands, then drew in a deep breath, curled his fingers into fists, and determined that, yes, he could kill Jillian with his bare hands as long as it meant he kept his secret. But hopefully it wouldn't come to that. That's what the help was for.

He picked up the phone and waited for the familiar voice to come on the line. "You need to get it done tonight."

———————

Nine-year-old Meg stomped across the field to the red barn that held her best friend. Texas Two Step was a brown-and-white paint horse who had become Meg's favorite confidant. She pushed open the door and walked to the second stall on the left. The horse nickered and shoved his nose over the stall door.

Meg reached in to rub his silky nose and feed him the apple she'd snitched from the kitchen table. While the horse eagerly crunched his sweet treat, Meg talked. "Mom left yesterday, Two Step. She said she had to go 'take care of some unfinished business.'"

She wiggled her fingers around the phrase like she'd seen done on television when quoting someone. "And she wouldn't take me with her." She frowned. "And now Uncle Blake's leaving. I know it's cuz he's worried about Mom." Meg sighed and Two Step nudged her hand. "Don't have any more apples, boy. Sorry."

Meg rubbed Two Step's nose again just the way he liked. "I've got to come up with a plan to figure out what Mom and Uncle Blake are up to and what's so important they couldn't take me with 'em."

"Meg? Are you out here?"

She jumped and Two Step tossed his head at the sudden movement. She clicked her tongue to settle him down and said, "Sorry, boy. Gotta go. I'll come see you after school."

Meg left the barn to find Grandma Jo almost to the door, hands on her hips. "Child, if you don't quit running off, you're going to add a whole new layer of gray to my head."

Meg did her best to look appropriately sorry. "I just wanted to tell Two Step good morning."

Grandma Jo sighed and shook her head. "Well, at least I usually know where to find you. Come on." She placed a hand on Meg's shoulder. "One day your sneakin' off is going to get you in trouble."

"Me? In trouble?" Meg practiced her angelic look and Grandma Jo laughed just like she knew she would.

"Get in the house and get your backpack, little girl. It's time for you to get to school."

School. Who cared about school when she had important things to think about?

Like finding out a way to go join her mom—wherever *that* was.

5

A knock on the door jolted Jillian from her light doze. She glanced at the clock and frowned as she realized her father still hadn't called her back. Swinging her feet to the floor, she reached for the gun she never left far from her fingers. Approaching the front door, she kept herself to the side and looked out the window.

Colton. Here to deliver the large suitcase that sat at his feet. Her stomach flipped a few times as memories rushed in. Sliding the gun into her waistband at the small of her back, she pulled her shirttail over it to hide it and let out a slow breath. She gathered her nerves, and opened the door. "Hi."

He stepped inside and set the suitcase in front of her. "We need to talk."

She shut the door. "Everything all right?"

"Not really. I had to tie up some loose ends on a couple of cases and delegate a few more so I can focus on . . . other things for now."

Meaning her?

The vague thought that she should be more cautious about being alone with the nephew of Frank Hoffman flitted through her mind. The Colton she'd once known would never have had anything to do with something like that. But what about now? Ten years was a long time. He could be anyone by now. And Frank Hoffman was family to him.

"Jillian?"

The reassuring weight of her gun rested against her back. "Sorry. Come on in."

Colton swept past her and into the foyer. She nodded him toward the living area. "Might as well get comfortable." Although she didn't think she'd ever feel comfortable in his presence again. How would he react when she told him about Meg?

Angry? Hurt? Definitely.

Demand to see her? Very possibly.

Which was why she couldn't tell him anything just yet.

Colton seated himself on the edge of the couch and she could see the tension in his jaw.

"You want something to drink?"

"No."

So he wasn't going to make this easy on her. Well, what had she expected? She didn't blame him. Jillian took a seat across from him on the love seat with the coffee table between them. She needed a buffer right now.

He clasped his hands in front of him. "Serena said you're an investigative reporter?"

"Yes."

"Are you here for a story?"

She frowned. "What?"

"You just accused my uncle, a prominent citizen of this state and a well-known politician, of murder." He smirked and the cold look of disgust in his eyes hurt her to the core. Before she could protest, he said, "That would make a pretty sensational piece if you were to come out with something like that. You would become a household name overnight."

Jillian closed her eyes and counted to five. Then ten. When she opened them, she said, "If I wanted to be a household name, I could have been one years ago. I don't care about name recognition. I care about getting my life back! I care about exposing a liar and a murderer. I care about the truth!"

"Then tell me the truth," he gritted between clenched teeth.

"I am!"

A muscle in his jaw jumped, telling her how hard he was working to restrain himself. "Tell me the whole story," he demanded. "Every last detail."

Jillian bit her lip. "Fine. Where do you want me to start?"

"June 6th, 2002."

Of course. Graduation night.

She wanted to fidget but refused to let herself. Rubbing her hands down her thighs, Jillian took a deep breath and looked at Colton. His usual happy-go-lucky countenance had disappeared to be replaced by a fierce frown and serious, hard green eyes. For a moment they simply stared at each other. Memories flickered across her mind. Memories she tried to forget. Memories that never should have been made.

"Wait. I need to say something first." He pinched the bridge of his nose and took a deep breath. "I owe you an apology and . . . I'm sorry."

She blinked. "Sorry? What for?"

A flush crept into his cheeks. "That night."

"Oh. Right."

He ran a hand down his face. "I'm getting ready to ask you to be open and honest with me. It's only fair I do the same."

She waited.

He swallowed hard and said, "I was wrong to . . . uh . . . let things get out of control that night. I could blame it on the fight with my dad or the feeling that I was getting ready to lose everything, but . . . the truth is, I was irresponsible and inconsiderate and I know it's a mistake we can't undo, but . . ."

Jillian listened even as her heart broke at his words.

Because they were so sweet and something she needed to hear.

And yet their mistake had produced Meg. Beautiful, adorable, sassy Meg. "I have to take some of that responsibility, Colton. I could have said no."

He nodded. "We were both wrong, but I've waited a long time to get those words off my heart. I've already asked God's forgiveness, but now," he cleared his throat, "I'm asking for yours."

Jillian's jaw ached with the effort to hold back her tears even as a question formed in her mind. If Colton thought that night was a mistake, would he think Meg was one too? Shoving that thought aside to address later, she managed to whisper, "You have it."

He closed his eyes and took a deep breath. "Thank you. Now," he cleared his throat and opened his eyes, "could you please tell me about graduation night?"

She nodded, glad to move past that difficult topic. Not that this next one was going to be any easier. "All right. I went looking for you that night, but you weren't in the gazebo."

His features softened a fraction. "I was having a hard time getting away from my dad. He wanted me to go to that party at Uncle Frank's and I had no interest in it."

"I know. When you didn't show up at the gazebo, I thought maybe you'd decided to go after all."

"No." He looked away and sighed as he ran a hand through his hair. "I was about thirty minutes late getting there."

"When you didn't come, I wasn't sure what to do." She gave a shake of her head. "It was one of the few times I wished I'd let you buy me a cell phone."

He studied her. "You were pretty stubborn about not taking much of anything from me."

She set her jaw and stared at him. "You know why."

"You didn't want me to think you were interested in me because of my family's money." He paused as his features softened. For a moment he reminded her of the boy she'd fallen in love with. He nodded. "I knew that. I never saw greed in your eyes."

44

His words shocked her. They were true, she just hadn't expected him to say it. "Well . . ."

The hardness returned. "Anyway, after you saw I wasn't there, what did you do?"

"I thought about just going on to the graduation dance, but I really wanted to find you. I needed to . . . I was—" She broke off and swallowed hard. She wasn't ready to tell him why she'd been so desperate to see him that night. "It was a pretty night, so I started walking and found a pay phone. When you didn't answer your cell phone, I called as many people as I could, but no one had seen you." Colton had been in her graduating class and they had been planning to skip out on the graduation party to spend time alone.

"I didn't have my cell phone with me anymore," he murmured. "My dad threatened to cut me off if I didn't start doing things his way, told me I'd have to make it on my own. I pulled the phone and my car keys from my pocket and threw them at him. Told him I didn't need him or his money. And then I went to find you."

"Only I had left by the time you got there."

"I figured that's what happened. I thought maybe you went on to the dance so I went over to the gym, but you weren't there either."

She shook her head. "I didn't get there until later, like ten o'clock."

"Why?"

"Because," she drew in a shuddering breath, "I went to your uncle's house. I wondered if you'd decided to go to the party after all, so I went home and got my mom's car and drove over there."

"I never went to Uncle Frank's house that night."

Jillian looked down at her hands. "And I wish I hadn't."

"Tell me."

His simple command somehow made it easier to go back in her mind, to voice the details she'd never forgotten yet never spoken about. "When I got there, it was loud. I could hear the band playing, the people talking. I looked everywhere for you."

He lifted a brow. "How did you get past security?"

"It was easy. I was already dressed for the graduation party."
She shrugged. "People were parking on the curb and checking in
at the gate. I simply followed along behind a couple. The guard
took me for their daughter."

"Huh. Uncle Frank wouldn't be too happy to hear about that."

"Once I was inside, I started looking for you. Even snuck into the
private sections of the house. When I realized you weren't there, I
went out to the pond to sit and think about what to do next. People
started leaving, but I waited because your parents hadn't left yet
and I hoped you would show up eventually."

"I was out looking for you. It never occurred to me to check
that stupid party."

Jillian couldn't stand sitting there. She got up and paced to the
window and looked out. The sun crawled down the horizon. She
turned back to Colton. "As the house emptied, I finally realized you
weren't coming, and I headed for the front door. As I approached
your uncle's office, he and another man were arguing."

"Who was he arguing with?"

Jillian licked her lips. "At first I couldn't tell. They were really
going at it. I stopped because I had to pass by the door to get out
of the house. I figured I'd wait until the other man left, then I
would sneak on out."

Colton rubbed his chin. "But that didn't happen."

"No." She shook her head as the memories slipped over her.
Turning back to the window, she stepped to the side and parted the
blinds to glance at the backyard. Quiet. Peaceful. A mirage? She
flipped the blind closed and rubbed her arms as a chill washed over
her. "Your uncle yelled that he'd worked too hard to have everything destroyed and grabbed one of those guns off the wall—"

Colton's gaze sharpened. "One of his antique collectibles?"

She waved a hand. "I didn't exactly have time to study it, but it
was one of those he kept on the wall behind his desk."

"Locked and loaded," Colton whispered.

"What?"

He looked at her. "It's always been one of his sources of pride. He keeps those guns in prime working order. I remember him cleaning them all the time."

"He leaves them loaded on his wall? That's crazy!"

"And dangerous. Nevertheless, he did it. Still does it as far as I know. And everyone knew it." He shook his head. "My dad used to harass him all the time about it. What happened next?"

"The man he was arguing with vaulted over the desk and knocked your uncle into the wall. They both landed on the floor, but the man was quick. He jumped up and grabbed one of the other guns, held it to your uncle's head, and said he'd have him arrested if he ever threatened him again—and if he ever pulled a gun on him again, he'd better be prepared to pull the trigger. Then he threw the gun on the desk, turned, and walked from the office. I hid real quick behind the door that led to the patio. Unfortunately, that's where the man went, through the sunroom and out onto the patio, and your uncle followed, furious and spewing threats. But he was acting . . . weird . . . too."

"Weird?"

"Yeah, like he was drunk. He was slurring his words and stumbling around."

Colton frowned and shook his head. "That doesn't sound like him."

"All I know is what I saw."

Jillian noted Colton's hard fists and white knuckles. He said, "Go on."

She rubbed her palms on her thighs and pulled in a steadying breath. She had to finish this. "They started arguing again. I peeked through the crack in the door and . . ." She bit her lip as the horror of that moment swept over her once again.

"And?"

"Your uncle said something insulting about your aunt, lifted the gun, and pointed it at the other man, who looked scared and said, 'I'm walking away. I suggest you do the same.' And then your uncle started to walk forward, made a weird sound, stumbled—and pulled the trigger." She raised a hand and covered her mouth. Behind her hand, she said, "He just pulled the trigger like he didn't care that he was taking a life." Confusion flickered as it did every time she thought about the next part. "And then they both fell."

"Both?"

"Yes. I didn't have a good view of your uncle from where I was hiding, but the man he shot fell immediately. Then your uncle cried out and sank to his knees." She closed her eyes tight, picturing the moment. "He still held the gun in his hand."

"He wound up in the hospital that night with a mild heart attack," Colton muttered. "I found out the next day. He had all kinds of tests run and came home late the following night."

Jillian raised a shaky hand to shove a lock of hair behind her ear. "The man your uncle shot was dead. At least he sure looked like it. His eyes—" She shuddered. "I'll never forget seeing that. I freaked. And ran." She looked him in the eye. "I looked back to make sure I was getting away, but your uncle had stood up, looked right at me. Then he lifted the gun . . ." She shivered and closed her eyes. "If I hadn't run when I did, he would have shot me too."

"I don't believe it," he whispered.

Jillian walked over to Serena's mantel. Then she looked back at him. After a long pause, she said, "Yes, you do."

His expression hardened. She couldn't read what lay behind his eyes. "I *can't* believe it."

"Then help me prove it didn't happen."

That stopped him. "But you just said it did."

"And you don't believe me." She lifted her chin. "So help me find the truth."

"Who was the man you say my uncle shot?"

Jillian froze, then bowed her head. When she lifted it, she said, "Governor Harrison Martin."

6

It seemed like each time she opened her mouth she delivered a punch that left Colton breathless. And shocked. He finally found his tongue again. "Governor Martin? Are you insane? Are you sure you have the right person?"

She snorted and crossed her arms. "I was quite sane . . . still am, thank you. And I knew exactly who it was. I voted for the man. He was my very first vote after I turned eighteen. Trust me, I recognized him."

Colton couldn't sit still a minute longer. He stood and began to pace from one end of the room to the other. And back. "I don't believe this."

Her sigh sounded weary and for a moment he wondered if she'd recant her crazy story. Then she said, "It really doesn't matter if you believe it or not. I'm here to prove it, with or without your help. I happen to be very good at finding the truth." She walked to the window facing the front of the house and parted the blinds once again.

Colton frowned at her skittishness. She sure believed what she was saying. "And that attack in the airport? That was someone trying to shut you up before you could say anything?"

"Yes."

Her simple answer made him antsy. "What is it?"

"I don't know." She looked around. "Where are Serena's animals? I didn't think to ask her when she dropped me off."

"Her fish died. The cat and dog are at the vet getting their annual checkups."

She lifted a brow at him. "And you know this how?"

"Serena asked if I'd pick them up when I was finished here. She and Dominic have a date."

Jillian looked out the window again, shut the blinds, and paced over to the glassed-in porch.

"What are you doing?"

"Watching. Waiting."

"For what?"

"For him to strike again."

Her flat certainty caused the first swirls of anxiety to kick up a beat in his gut. "Jilly, hon—"

She whirled. "Don't call me that!"

He flinched at the ferocity in her eyes, the flare of her nostrils—and the ready-to-fight stance. Colton held up his hands in a gesture of surrender. "Sorry." He kept his tone soft, soothing. "I'm sorry." The nickname had come easy, naturally, rolling off his tongue as though the past ten years had never happened.

Jillian spun around, keeping her gaze away from him, but he thought he caught a flash of tears before she could hide them. Colton sighed. Whether he believed her story or not, Jillian believed it. His mind almost couldn't process the change in her. She'd been a sweet teen, a little shy and reserved, but good-hearted. And she'd loved him with everything in her. He knew that then. He knew it now. But this woman before him wasn't the young high school sweetheart he remembered. Jillian had changed, and grown up strong—and suspicious.

Still facing the porch window, she asked, "What about Camille, where is she?" Camille Hughes, the teen Serena had taken under her wing.

"Since the attempts on her life, Serena felt like Camille would be safer with her parents."

She turned back to him, shoulders stiff, features composed. "Let's get out of here."

"Why?"

"I'm not sure why. I'm uneasy and edgy and I don't like it. Whenever I feel like this, something always happens."

Colton felt his frown deepen. "This place is tighter than Fort Knox. You're fine here."

"Mentally, I get that. My gut's screaming at me, though." She glanced back over her shoulder. "I want to check on something."

"What did you see?"

"Nothing. At least nothing really out of the ordinary."

But she'd seen something disturbing enough to want to check it out.

Colton shot to his feet and followed her to the front door. She punched in the code to disarm the alarm and they stepped outside. He watched her take in her surroundings. She bristled like a spooked porcupine. The hot, muggy southern night made sweat break out across his brow and in the middle of his lower back. The smells of honeysuckle and freshly mowed grass hit him. But nothing that triggered his internal alarms.

Something had set hers off, though. Jillian hurried around the side of the house. Colton followed, watchful, but not overly concerned.

Behind him, a loud boom rocked the house.

A scream came from around the corner.

Spinning, he lost his balance as the ground shook. He went to his knees, arms outstretched. The front door of the house landed beside him. Flames licked through the shattered windows.

Fear caught his breath as much as the smoke covering him. "Jillian!"

She appeared in front of a haze of smoke, blood on her forehead. "Colton! Are you all right?"

"Yeah." He grabbed her arm and pulled her away from the burning house. With his left hand, he grabbed his phone as neighbors stepped out of their homes to gape, phones pressed to their ears. He paused. The neighbors would handle the 911 call. He punched in Hunter's number.

Hunter answered on the third ring. Colton cut off his greeting. "Someone just blew up Serena's house. I need you out here now."

"On the way." Hunter severed the connection and Colton knew he was already calling in reinforcements. Hunter's unspoken questions would be answered soon enough.

"What was it? How did—" Jillian gasped and gaped.

Smoke billowed toward them. "We'll figure that out later. Right now, we're too exposed. Whoever did that wanted you dead."

"You think?"

"Sarcasm's not your best asset." He pulled her toward his truck. She stumbled along behind him. He opened the driver's door and she hauled herself up and into the passenger seat. Colton climbed in after her and slammed the door shut. "Hunker down. No sense in attracting a sniper's bullet if someone's holed up and watching."

But she was already hunched down, her eyes scanning the neighbors' windows.

Okay. Now he was concerned.

Twisting the key, he looked at her. "Someone means business about getting rid of you." Colton pressed the gas pedal and backed the truck from the front of the burning house. He pulled down the street and parked. Far enough away so he could watch the crowd gathering and keep Jillian safe if whoever had done this was still around and wanting to finish the job.

Shaking, she gave a humorless laugh. "That's what I've been trying to tell you." Her lips twisted. "They would have succeeded too, if I hadn't seen those birds." She looked back at Serena's house and Colton followed her gaze. Tears flooded her eyes. "And they don't seem to care if they have collateral damage."

Through the truck windows he'd left cracked, the faint sound of sirens reached his ears. "Help's on the way." He blinked. "Birds?" He pulled a handful of napkins from the center console and leaned over to press one to the cut on her forehead.

She replaced his hand with hers. "When I was looking out the window. A whole mess of them flew into the air like they'd been disturbed. I wanted to know what disturbed them."

"Disturbed birds? We're alive because you saw—" He shook his head. Unbelievable. "It could have been a dog or—"

"I know that," Jillian snapped. She pulled in a deep breath and said with less heat, "I know that. But for the past ten years I've been in the habit of checking every little thing that seems . . . off."

They had no more time to talk. Fire trucks screeched to a halt in front of Serena's house. Fire chief Hayden McDonald bolted from the truck and started yelling orders as hoses were hooked up.

Police cruisers pulled up and Colton waited for the unmarked cars to arrive within a few minutes.

He and Hunter had plans to make.

———■———

What was she going to do? Jillian watched the firefighters get to work on Serena's house and shook her head at the senseless devastation. The cut on her forehead stung, but it wasn't deep and had already stopped bleeding. The flames reached higher.

Oh, Serena, I'm so sorry! She paused in her thoughts, then prayed, *But thank you, God, we're still alive.*

Officers swarmed the area, an ambulance arrived, and the neighbors clustered in a tight group to watch the action. Panic started to close in on her and Jillian took a deep breath, reaching for calm in the midst of the chaos. She could do this. She'd planned and trained for this. God willing, she would accomplish her goal and survive doing it.

But at what cost? What about those who wanted to help her? Who placed themselves around her? People she cared about, people like Jeff back in California. Someone had already died because of her.

"Having second thoughts about coming back?" Colton's quiet question jarred her.

"Yes." She looked at the burning house and hardened her resolve. "Yes, but I know it's the right thing to do."

He studied her long enough to make her start to squirm. Finally, he said, "Then come on, let's go give a statement. And while we're out there, I want you to scan the crowd. See if you recognize anyone. Anyone suspicious."

She snorted. "It won't be anyone I know. Whoever did this was a hired killer. Your uncle's not going to do his own dirty work."

Colton's nostrils flared, but he held his tongue and simply nodded. "Still, I want you to look."

"Fine."

They climbed from the truck. As they approached, two officers stood outside the taped-off area, far enough from the house so as not to interfere with the work of the firemen. Steady streams of water surged from the hoses. Colton flashed his badge, gave his name to the officer, and together they walked to the fire trucks.

Jillian spotted Alexia, her firefighter uniform making her look like something from an alien movie. She'd removed her helmet and sweat ran in small rivers down the sides of her face. Marks from her mask still creased her forehead and cheeks. When she spotted Jillian and Colton walking toward her, her eyes went wide and she broke away from the chaos to meet them halfway. Alexia threw her arms around Jillian.

"You're all right?" Alexia asked.

"Yes. Scared and shaken, but alive."

Concern in her eyes, Alexia shook her head. "What happened? Was there a gas leak or something?"

"Not exactly," Jillian muttered.

Colton said, "I've called Hunter and a buddy at the ATF. He said he'd handle the case."

Alexia's eyes narrowed. "ATF. Someone blew up the house on purpose."

Jillian shivered. But of course the Bureau of Alcohol, Tobacco, and Firearms would get involved.

Colton gripped his phone. "I'm asking Dominic to help as well."

"The FBI?" Jillian asked. "But this wouldn't be an FBI case."

Colton lifted a brow. "It's an FBI case if someone requests FBI assistance." His jaw tightened as he looked at the house. "I'm officially requesting assistance. And besides, he's going to want to be involved in catching the person who did this to Serena's house." He looked at Jillian. "I think I'm convinced there's merit to your story. Parts of it anyway."

Relief swelled inside her as Hunter pulled up to the scene. She looked at the house being soaked by several high-powered water hoses, then back at Colton. "The part where I insist someone wants me dead?"

"That would be the biggest part." He shook his head and punched the touchpad. She heard him mutter, "I think we need to go fishing."

"What?" she stared at him, puzzled. Had she heard him right?

"I'll explain later." His attention focused on something behind her as he made a quick call to Dominic.

She turned. Katie and Hunter. Serena should be here soon, but thankfully, her medical services weren't needed at this scene.

Hunter caught her eye, then looked past her to motion to Colton.

Colton nodded and said, "I'll be right back."

"I'm going with you."

She could see the protest in his eyes and simply notched her chin higher. A sigh slipped from his lips, and without another word, he headed in Hunter's direction. Giving the burning house a wide berth, Jillian followed Colton around the outside of the fence that separated Serena's backyard and her neighbor's. She saw Katie standing next to a large playhouse.

Colton nodded toward the main house and asked her, "Is anyone home?"

"Nope. I knocked several times. Nothing. We've got uniforms canvassing the area, questioning the neighbors. Hopefully someone saw something."

Colton nodded and looked at Jillian. "Was this where you saw the birds?"

She thought about it, closed her eyes, and pictured them taking flight. "Yes." She opened her eyes. "I think they came from the tree, though. I was looking out the window and they just all scattered like something scared them. And that—" she shrugged—"scared me."

He looked from the playhouse to the tree. "I want the crime scene unit over here before we start messing with this area." He pulled his phone from his pocket and punched a speed-dial number. "Rick? Colton here. How far away is your unit?"

"Right behind you."

Jillian turned to see Rick.

Colton pocketed his phone. "Thanks for not wasting any time. If you're here, you must be short staffed again."

"I am. What do you have?"

Colton filled him in while Hunter and Katie discussed various possibilities about how the "bomber" had launched an explosive device from this yard without being seen or heard.

"How far do you think it is from here to Serena's?" Katie asked.

Hunter shrugged. "A football field length? A little less?"

"Yeah." She glanced up at the trees on either side of her.

"Let me get to work over here," Rick said. He pulled out a flashlight and got to work on the playhouse.

Jillian focused her attention on the action surrounding Serena's house. She caught sight of Serena making her way toward the cluster of officers in front of her house. Anger and frustration combined themselves with the anguish she already felt at her friend's loss. Jillian took a step to go back to the house and beg Serena's forgiveness, but stopped when she saw Alexia turn and throw her arms around Serena as she reached the group. The sight gave Jillian a measure of relief, knowing Serena had support right now. Jillian decided her begging could wait.

She turned back to listen to the detectives' discussion. For the last twenty minutes, the only chatter had been about the possible evidence being collected. She glanced at her watch. 8:02. They were running out of daylight. In less than fifteen minutes, it would be dark. And still the sweat pooled under the weapon at her back and in between her shoulder blades. She glanced up into the tree to the right of the playhouse and a light flutter caught her eye.

Rick finally stood and said, "I think we're good here. I don't know what I was looking for, but if it was left here, I've got it now."

"Did you find anything at all?"

"Maybe. I took prints from the playhouse, but I'm not holding out much hope. There's nothing to indicate anyone was here, really."

"Right. Thanks, Rick." Colton said.

Jillian heard him, but her attention was on the tree. Walking over to it, she looked up again, but couldn't see what had snagged the attention of her peripheral vision. Ignoring the law enforcement chatter going on behind her, her investigative reporter instincts kicked in. She climbed on top of the playhouse for a better look up in the tree, keeping her shirt pulled low over the back of her pants waistband. She wasn't ready for anyone to know about the gun yet.

"What are you doing?"

Colton's voice made her pause. She braced her hands on the limb that was now at chest height. "There's something in the tree." With practiced ease, she hauled herself up on the limb before Colton could protest.

"Hey, it might be evidence."

"Then give me some gloves."

"Jillian, let Rick or me do that."

"I'm already up here. Give me some gloves, please?" she insisted.

With a low growl and a mutter she was glad she couldn't understand, he grabbed a pair of gloves, then made his way up to sit on the branch beside her.

She stared at him in surprise. "What are you doing?"

"Collecting whatever you said you saw. If we wind up in court, my evidence isn't getting thrown out because someone other than law enforcement collected it."

"Oh."

"Right." He looked around her. "Now, what did you see?"

She swallowed hard and motioned. "It's some kind of material."

He looked where she pointed. "How did you see that? It looks like a leaf."

"I was looking in the tree, because I'm pretty sure this is where all the birds came from. I just saw it hanging there and thought it looked odd."

Colton reached around her. As he did, she could feel the heat radiating from him and smell smoke mingled with the musky scent she remembered from high school. In spite of the heat, goose bumps pebbled her arms and she gulped.

Then noticed something else.

The limb in front of her made a nice resting place for her elbows. Leaning forward, she had an excellent view of what used to be Serena's glassed-in porch.

7

Frank watched television news anchorwoman Kylie Wharton rise from the table. He stood too and she smiled as she gathered her purse. "It was a pleasure, Senator."

"Always, Kylie. When will the story run?"

"Probably on the eleven o'clock news tonight and the morning news tomorrow. That was a nice donation you made to the boys' home and our viewers eat that stuff up. Gives them a break from the crime that seems to surround us."

"I'll be watching." They shook hands and the pretty brunette gathered her purse and walked toward the exit as Frank felt his pocket vibrate. Without taking his eyes from her pleasing form, he took his seat again and pressed the talk button on his iPhone. "Hello?"

"She got out."

Frank sat straighter in his chair, the only outward sign of his distress. He gripped the edge of the table tightly to keep his emotions in check and forced a smile. "How?"

"I don't know." The tight words held frustration and fury. "She was looking out, watching. I could see her. Then she suddenly turned. I pulled the trigger and thought that would be it."

"But she got out."

"Yes." He cursed. "I don't know what made her decide at the last minute to leave the house, but she did." A pause. "Colton was there."

"What!" Frank's voice came out in a hiss, drawing him a few stares from the sparsely populated restaurant. "Hold on a minute. I can't talk about this here." He got up and tossed his napkin and a twenty-dollar bill onto the table and strode outside. Even this late, humid heat blasted him and it took a minute for him to catch his breath. He closed his eyes, refusing to believe Jillian was still alive. "All right, go ahead."

"Like I said, she's still alive."

"Unfortunately I got that part. Any witnesses? Anyone see you?" Frank's heart beat harder. "Did Colton see you?"

"No. No one saw me."

"What was Colton doing there?" Frank's brain scrambled for a reason as to why his nephew would be at Serena Hopkins's house with Jillian Carter.

A humorless laugh drifted through the phone. "I don't know. I was already in place, watching the house when he drove up. I didn't realize who he was until she screamed his name."

"I don't know what you were thinking, trying to get Jillian by yourself. This isn't what you do. If you try to handle this yourself, you're going to make a mistake. You don't do this professionally."

A slight sigh slipped through the line. "Not anymore anyway." He paused. "Look, I have to do it. If I keep using my contacts, the cops are eventually going to put it together. It's time to just take care of this myself."

Frank wasn't sure he liked that idea. "If you get caught, it'll come straight back on me. We can't afford that."

"I'm well aware of that," the killer snapped.

Frank's jaw tightened. "Well, I know people too. I'll see who else might be a good pick to help us out." He pulled a handkerchief from his back pocket and wiped the sweat dripping from his brow. "I've got to get out of this heat. Don't do anything else. I've got an idea."

"What kind of idea? You can't do anything that's going to get back to you. You have to keep your nose clean for this election. Both of our careers are on the line."

"Like you, I'm well aware of that," Frank snapped.

Silence on the other end. Then a low voice said, "No need to bite my head off. I'm on your side, remember?"

A sudden chill slid down his spine and Frank backpedaled. He needed this man. No need to make an enemy of him. "I know. I'm sorry. I'm just stressed." He slipped into politician mode. The apology sounded sincere even to him.

"I know," the voice soothed. "I get that. I'm going to take care of it."

So you've said for the past two months, Frank thought to himself. Instead of saying what he wanted to, he simply sighed. "Fine. I'll be working on something from this end. And don't worry," he hastened to reassure the man on the other end of the line, "I won't do anything without running it by you first."

"Good."

"But for now, stick with my nephew. Find out why he's with Jillian."

"Oh, don't worry, I'm keeping an eye on him. In fact, I'm watching him and Jillian right now."

Frank frowned at the man's tone. "Don't do anything stupid like kill him. That would just hurt the campaign."

"I don't know . . . a dead nephew, a grieving uncle. Might buy you some sympathy votes."

Frank swore and walked toward his car. "Leave him alone. Keep him out of this." He unlocked the door and slid behind the wheel.

"What if he won't *be* kept out of it?"

Frank took a deep breath and waited for the pain to subside like it always did. He was way too stressed. "What do you mean?"

"I mean it looks like he's planning to take a little trip with the girl."

Concern beat with a steady hum through Frank's blood. "Follow him."

"What if she's already told him what she knows?"

"He won't believe her." Would he? Of course not. "I can handle Colton, you know that. I'm the father he always wished he had."

"You're not competing for Father of the Year, our goal is to win the election. You better keep that in mind."

"I'm not likely to forget it anytime soon. Now you do your job and let me do mine."

MONDAY

8

"Fishing? That's your Plan B?" She had followed him out of his house and stood next to his truck, frowning. Colton thought about how cute she looked first thing in the morning, then reined in his thoughts and frowned right along with her, because he didn't need to notice that. He'd picked her up at the hotel, and when he asked how she slept, she'd answered with a shrug. "Fitfully." The Bible on her bed told him what she'd been doing when she wasn't sleeping.

"Yeah, it's a safe place for you to hide out for a bit while I check on some things."

"Check on what?"

He gave a sharp whistle and Jillian jumped. He smiled. "Sorry."

"What was that for?"

Colton nodded his head toward the woods. "I'm taking them with us."

Jillian turned and he heard her give a gasp as his two matching German shepherds bolted from the trees. Tongues hanging, tails wagging, they raced for him. Colton gave a hand signal and both dogs skidded to a halt and sat in front of him. He looked around. "Best alarm system ever invented. No one'll get close without these two setting up a howl. Or more likely a growl." He motioned her over and she walked around the truck to stand next to him. "Jillian, I'd like you to meet Bert and Ernie." She lifted a brow at him and

he shrugged. "I didn't name them. They're retired military working dogs. I adopted them about three years ago." He paused. "I
wanted Mr. Snuffleupagus too, but one of my buddies took him."

"Sesame Street?" Jillian leaned over and gave each dog a scratch
behind the ears. Instant love for Jillian had the dogs squirming for
her attention.

He defended the names with a shrug. "Military guys have a
weird sense of humor."

"Huh. Kind of like cops."

Colton's lips quirked. "Exactly."

Jillian shook her head. "People and their weird animal names.
First Serena with her Star Wars fetish and now you and Sesame
Street."

He snapped his fingers and waved a hand toward the truck.
The dogs responded without hesitation and hopped in the back.

Jillian looked at him. "Fishing, huh?"

"In a sense." Colton threw a duffle bag in the back of his truck.
"Just for tonight. Someone tried to kill you—and me." He tossed
in two sleeping bags and four pillows. "That tells me that my uncle
isn't behind this. He'd never do anything to hurt me."

"Come on, Colton, he had no way of knowing you would be
there last night."

Colton had whisked her away from the scene as fast as he could.
Their statements had been brief and to the point. One minute they'd
been in the house, the next they'd been outside and the house had
exploded. End of statement. They'd seen no one, hadn't noticed anyone hanging around the area, and Jillian hadn't recognized anyone
in the crowd. And she hadn't seen anyone who'd seemed suspicious.

But there'd been the birds.

Birds. Really?

Or had she set the whole thing up? He didn't want to think it.
Didn't want to believe her capable of something like that. Any
more than he wanted to believe that his uncle had anything to do

with killing the former governor. "But he knew you were going to be there. How?"

That stopped her. She stood, one hand on the handle of the truck, her eyes on him. "I don't have any idea. Staying with Serena wasn't planned."

"Then someone followed you from the airport."

She narrowed her eyes. "Then they're good because I was watching."

He barked a hard laugh. "And exactly how much experience do you have watching for tails?"

Jillian simply looked at him, drew in a deep breath, and said, "More than you might think, Colton."

It was his turn to pause. And he realized he knew nothing about this woman standing before him. Physically, she'd changed little except for gaining a few curves in all the right places. But on the inside? She was a whole different person.

Colton hung his head for a moment, then lifted it to scan his home. He'd moved into this house a little over three years ago after tiring of apartment living. Peaceful, set back in the woods on twenty acres, he had room to roam. Room to raise the horses he and Jillian had dreamed about back in high school. For the first time since making the purchase, he allowed himself to admit that he'd bought the place with Jillian in mind.

He opened the truck door. "Get in."

She slid in the passenger seat. "Where are we going again?"

"To a little place owned by Hunter's grandfather. I have an open invitation. I also have a key and go there often to just get away and relax." He could see the exhaustion on her features and promised, "A friend of mine, Jonah Gunter, does some moonlighting as a bodyguard. He's going to meet us out there and watch out for you. You need to rest without worrying about when whoever's after you is going to strike next. And I need to make some calls without worrying about *you*."

"I never asked you to worry about me, Colton." She grabbed the door, and slammed it shut.

Colton winced. He rounded the truck and slid behind the wheel. "I know. You never ask for anything, do you?"

Jillian hesitated and he wondered if she would answer him. Then she said, "No. I guess I don't. Not willingly anyway."

Colton cranked the truck and did a three-point turn. He accelerated down the drive, then turned left to head for the highway. "Which makes me wonder why?" He shot her a quick glance. "Who are you now, Jillian Carter?"

"Someone you wouldn't recognize." He almost didn't catch the low whisper.

"Why's that? What changed you so much?"

"I saw a murder ten years ago, Colton, and the murderer saw *me*. That changed me. I've been in hiding and now I'm on the run with the nephew of the man I saw shoot another man. I must be crazy."

Colton tensed, insulted and angry that whatever she thought she saw that night, she really believed his uncle was guilty of murder. She had been a scared teenager who'd bolted after seeing two men argue. And the governor had been alive enough to drive toward home instead of to a hospital. How could she believe his uncle could be involved in something like this?

Instead of venting his anger, he swallowed it, kept his eyes alternating between the road and the mirrors, and said, "Then let's work together to figure out what happened ten years ago."

"I thought we already agreed to something along those lines."

"We did. Only I want to talk to my uncle and see what he has to say about your accusations."

"Talk to him?" Jillian jerked forward against the seatbelt and half turned her body toward him. "No way! No, no, no. You can't do that. I don't have any proof, and if he thinks you're involved in some way . . ."

Colton glanced at her, then back to the road, then the mirror behind them. "But don't you see, Jillian? It's the only way. I'm going to drop you off at the cabin and then go see Uncle Frank."

"But you—"

"I want to know how Governor Martin died," he interrupted.

Jillian felt her frown deepen as she let him change the subject. "I told you. He was shot."

Colton shook his head. "I would remember that. I remember the man dying, but not much else. There was nothing sensational about his death—other than the fact that he died. I think it was a car wreck. He was driving alone at night on that curvy road our parents used to forbid us to drive on."

"Culver Park Road," Jillian said.

"Right. The paper said that's how he died."

She shrugged. "I didn't stick around to read about it in the paper." In fact, she'd done her best to forget all about that horrible night. Although, now that he said that, a little niggling of doubt tickled her mind. "I know it wasn't a car wreck, though. Can I see your phone?"

"Where's yours?"

"It just got blown up, remember?"

"Oh. Right." He handed her the device. "We need to get you another one ASAP. I'll get Jonah to bring you one—let me call him." She passed him the phone and he made the call.

When he handed the phone back to her, she accessed the internet and did a Google search. He glanced at her and saw the tip of her tongue peeking out of the corner of her mouth just like it always did when she concentrated on something. A pang of longing hit him. Longing for the past, longing for that graduation night to be different. If only—

Colton shut those thoughts and feelings down. No sense in wanting something he couldn't have. The only thing he could do now was work on the future.

"Okay, here it is."

Her soft voice pulled at him. "What'd you find?"

She read, "'Governor Harrison Martin apparently lost control of his car around three o'clock yesterday morning on Culver Park Road. He hit the guardrail and went over. The car caught on fire and the governor had extensive burns all over his body. The medical examiner reports that Martin died from a combination of the burns, smoke inhalation, and severe head injuries. He was declared dead at the scene.'" She finished reading and went still. Then she handed his phone back to him.

And just sat there. Quiet. Chewing on her bottom lip.

It made him nervous. "What is it?"

"It's a lie."

"How can it be a lie, Jillian? There would have been cops all over the place, an investigation, an autopsy . . ." He shot her a sidelong glance and turned beneath the arch of intertwined branches of two towering oak trees that signaled the entrance to the cabin on Lake Murray. "You're saying the medical examiner lied."

She bit her lip and narrowed her eyes. "I don't know how they did it, but they covered it up."

"A conspiracy theory?"

"No. A cover-up."

"Same thing. Basically."

She snorted and glanced out the window. He could almost smell the smoke coming from her ears as her brain worked. The gravel drive ended and he heard her gasp. "This is Hunter's grandfather's 'cottage' on the lake?"

"Yep."

"It's beautiful."

Colton studied the glass front. "Yeah, Hunter's grandfather bought it ages ago. Now Mr. Graham lets us cops use it for free pretty much whenever we want to. It's a great place to unwind." He shot her a glance. "Or hide out."

The yellow A-frame structure with the double oak doors looked simple and elegant from the front. From memory, he knew the back walls were heavy glass overlooking the lake.

Instead of parking in the front, he pulled around to the back and shut the engine off. "The nearest neighbor is about a quarter of a mile in any direction. Hunter's granddaddy wanted his privacy and plenty of room for his large family. There's an alarm that beeps anytime someone turns into the drive. You'll have plenty of advance warning should anyone be headed this way." He opened the door for her, then walked around to let the tailgate down. He gave a short whistle and the dogs bolted from the back of the truck.

"And if they don't use the drive?"

He closed the tailgate and said, "That's what the dogs are for." He gave her the once-over. "Seeing as how you're pretty much without a wardrobe, I think you'll find some clothes that will fit you in the master bedroom. Hunter said his cousin, Claire, has two wardrobes. She keeps one at home and leaves one here. Y'all are about the same size."

He led her into the house and cut the alarm off. Then showed her how to arm it. She practiced it a couple of times until he was satisfied. "Keep it on at all times, all right?"

"I will."

Three short beeps sounded and Colton smiled at her startled jerk. "That's Jonah."

Colton gave the man about sixty seconds to reach the end of the drive and park. He went to the door and opened it, welcoming his friend. "Thanks for coming."

"No problem." The man's dark almond eyes and olive skin showed off his Asian heritage. Well-toned muscles rippled beneath his shirt, and Colton knew Jonah was well equipped to handle anything that came his way. He looked at Jillian. "Glad to meet you."

"You too." She shook his hand. "Thanks for doing this. Hopefully this will be an easy and uneventful job for you."

"Just the way I like them." He handed her a phone. "It's

programmed and ready to go." He looked at Colton. "I texted you the number so you have it."

Colton checked his phone. "Got it. Thanks."

"No problem. I'll be checking the perimeter." Then he was gone, leaving her alone with Colton. She shoved the phone into the back pocket of her shorts and wandered to the kitchen, then into the den, touching the furniture, familiarizing herself with the place.

He let her do that for a couple of minutes, then said, "Come on, I'll give you the tour."

She followed him, her quiet demeanor worrying him. He threw open the door to one of the bedrooms and felt his phone vibrate. He checked the number and frowned.

"What is it?"

"My aunt is texting me, wants to know if I've heard from my cousin Carmen."

Wariness crossed her face. "I remember her. She's Frank's daughter. Are y'all that close?"

"Yes. And no. Carmen and I have an understanding." He tapped the keyboard of the phone and answered that he hadn't heard from Carmen. To Jillian he said, "She's had a lot of problems. As a teen, she was very rebellious, very anti-authority. She even ran away from home when she was fourteen. My aunt and uncle sent her to a boarding school for kids with emotional problems."

"Did it help?"

He shrugged. "Maybe some. She's in college and hasn't flunked out yet, so that's an improvement."

Jillian sighed and walked over to the closet. When she opened it, she just stood there.

He frowned. "Jillian?"

She turned to face him and his heart nearly broke in two at how lost she appeared. Lost and very, very scared. Old instincts, mixed with new, rose up. Colton hesitated for only a moment, then walked over to pull her into his arms, ignoring her soft gasp of surprise.

9

Jillian couldn't help it. She was scared. Scared and feeling very vulnerable right now. Only the fact that she still had her gun nestled comfortably in the small of her back kept her from giving in to the panic flooding her. Well, the gun and Colton's strong arms around her once again.

She snuggled into the crook of his neck and felt his pulse jump against her cheek. Some of the fear subsided. Comfort like she hadn't allowed herself to feel in so long tumbled through her.

Colton's arms . . .

She jerked away, stunned that she'd allowed herself to start falling for him again so easily. Again? Who was she kidding? She'd never gotten over him. His hand brushed her lower back. This time it was his turn to be surprised. "What's that?"

Her hand reached around to grasp the butt of the gun. With a smooth move, she pulled it from her waistband and held it pointing toward the floor. "Insurance."

"A gun?"

His shout ricocheted off the bedroom walls and she winced. "Yes, a gun."

"Where did you get that? Do you have a license for it? Those things are dangerous!" His protective blustering had her instantly on guard.

She widened her eyes and held the gun up. "Dangerous? For real?"

He snapped his mouth shut and glared at her. "Give it to me before you hurt someone."

Jillian narrowed her eyes and dropped the sarcasm. "Colton, I'm perfectly capable of handling this gun. I've done so for the last six years. And yes, I have a permit for a concealed carry. So stop worrying."

If she'd reached up and slapped him, she didn't think he'd be more stunned.

The outrage and surprise faded from his face. But his eyes grew sad. "Jillian . . . I don't know what to say. A gun? And you know how to use it." A statement this time, not a question.

"This has been my life since I left ten years ago, Colton," she whispered. But she couldn't stop the lone tear that slid down her cheek as she stuck the gun back into the comfortable spot between her lower back and the waistband of her jeans.

His left hand reached up to thumb the wetness away. "Aw, Jillian, what am I going to do with you?"

She drew in a shuddering breath as his hands grasped her upper arms and pulled her back against him.

Against his chest, she muttered, "You're going to help me put a killer behind bars."

He set her back from him and wiped her eyes one more time. "I've got to go. I'm going to find Uncle Frank and talk to him about all this and then I'm going to come back here and explain the mess-up."

Jillian jerked from the light grasp he had on her upper arms. "No. I'm serious about this, Colton. I don't want you talking to him yet. You do, and you could put yourself in danger too." She thought about that. "No, not 'too.' Again."

Anger flashed. "I'm going to prove you wrong." He headed for the bedroom door and she followed on his heels right down the steps, through the den area, into the kitchen, and out the front door of the house.

"Colton, no! Don't do this." She stormed after him, and when he opened the driver's door of his truck, she rounded him to slam it shut. "If you ever cared anything about me, don't do this."

He looked back at her and whatever he saw in her face must have gotten through to him. He sighed and leaned against the truck. "Think about it. You would do the exact same thing if our positions were reversed. Can't you see this from my point of view too?"

She stopped, snapped her mouth shut, and stared at him—and thought about it. Finally, her shoulders drooped and she sighed. "Yeah. I can. In a way. But it doesn't mean you should still do this. Give me the benefit of the doubt for a minute. What if I'm right and you're wrong?"

Colton's lips twisted into a frown as he studied her. He looked away and then back as he rubbed a hand over his hair. "Look, I need to talk to him. I'll just be subtle about how I phrase the questions. Will that work for you?"

"Subtle how?"

He thought for a moment as the dogs came to sit at his feet. Absently, he scratched their ears. "I'll figure something out when I get there. I texted him and he said for me to come out to his house. He's waiting on me."

"Colton . . ." She didn't bother to continue. He was determined.

She just prayed his determination didn't result in her death—or his.

———■———

The killer pressed the phone to his ear and watched Colton Brady pull out from the gravel drive. He was alone. A smile slid across his face as he thought about how vulnerable his prey would be now.

He'd seen the other man drive in, but he'd be easy enough to dispose of since the element of surprise was on his side. An ambush should be a piece of cake.

As Colton's taillights disappeared, the killer pulled a pair of black gloves from the glove compartment. He slid the suppressor on the end of the Mk22 pistol. Even though the area was isolated, no sense in taking a chance on anyone being in the wrong place at the wrong time hearing two gunshots.

He eyed the dogs bounding around the front yard.

Make that four.

The phone rang one more time, then Frank answered with an abrupt, "What?"

"She's got a bodyguard, but I'm getting ready to take care of the problem."

Silence echoed back at him. Then, "Where's Colton?"

"He just left."

"Where's Jillian?"

"He stashed her at Hunter's grandfather's lake house."

"Okay, so what are you going to do?"

"I've got a plan. I'll call you when I'm finished."

He hung up and picked up the black ski mask from the seat beside him and grimaced. Almost a hundred degrees outside and he was going to have to dress like it was thirty. Sweat popped out on his brow just thinking about it. Well, it didn't matter. It had to be done.

He'd just make sure Jillian suffered a little more for making him sweat.

10

Colton figured Jillian was right about one thing. He was definitely going to do his best to catch the person after her and put that person behind bars.

But it wasn't going to be his uncle.

Was it?

He couldn't stop the doubt from niggling at him as he drove back toward town. She was so sure, so insistent about what happened that night . . . and so obviously in danger.

He was about forty minutes away from his uncle's home. Driving on Richard Franklin Road, he headed toward I-26 while his brain processed everything he'd learned over the last twenty-four hours.

A question tickled the back of his mind and forced its way forward.

What was he going to do if Uncle Frank was involved? He'd have to do what he was trained to do. He would recuse himself and watch one of his friends arrest his uncle. The thought pierced deep. Or he could request permission to stay on the case . . .

And what about his other cases? Cases that needed his attention? *Deserved* his attention. He'd have to delegate, see if some of the other detectives would be willing to take over some of them.

Colton snatched his phone and made a few calls. When he was satisfied his most important cases were taken care of, he hung up and dialed Hunter. His friend and fellow detective answered on the second ring. "Hello?"

"Hey, you got anything from the fire?"

"No, but Serena's out for blood. It's a good thing her animals weren't there at the time."

Colton winced. He could only imagine Serena's grief if something had happened to her beloved pets. "What about the evidence from the tree?"

"Rick's in the lab right now working on it. He's been at it all night."

"Aw, poor thing." He knew his voice held only mock sympathy. They all put in long hours when a case was hot. But he was grateful for Rick's hard work.

Hunter laughed. "Yeah, he's milking this one for all he can get." A pause, then more seriously, "You know he's threatened to have the captain make us attend a mandatory seminar Rick's teaching on new technology in crime solving, don't you?"

"So that was the weird look on his face."

"What?"

"He had this little secret smile when he was at the airport working the crime scene. The more I think about it, he had that handy little fingerprint gadget and didn't even try to tell us how it worked."

"I know how it works."

"No, you know the result you get with it. You don't know every stinking detail about how to get that result."

"True."

"We have to think of some reason we can't be there." Colton was all for new technology and appreciated that it made his job easier, but there was no way he wanted to sit in a classroom and listen to Rick lecture. As much as he liked the man, Rick's sense of humor fled when he taught.

Hunter said, "After Rick finished with the tree and the playhouse, he worked with the arson investigator to get samples from Serena's house. He isolated three different substances off the piece of fabric that also matched residue in the house."

"Like what?"

"Sulfuric acid, sugar, and potassium chlorate."

"So what does that mean?"

"It makes for an interesting mixture. Put it all together and you get a bomb that ignites on impact. No fuse needed."

Colton let out a low whistle. "Like a homemade hand grenade? But how did he launch it from the neighbor's house into Serena's? There's no way he could have thrown it that far."

"There are a number of possibilities. We'll keep looking and see if we can figure out which one is the right one."

Colton pursed his lips as he thought. "All right. What about the guy who was killed at the airport?"

"Nothing on him yet. Rick's still processing everything. Guy didn't have any ID on him. Rick will run his prints through AFIS and see if anything turns up."

Rick would do a thorough job. Colton just wished he'd hurry it up. "I'm headed to see my uncle. I left Jillian stashed in a safe place for now."

"Where?"

"I'd rather not say over the phone."

"I understand. Just let me know if you need anything else."

"Will do."

Colton hung up the phone and tapped his fingers on the steering wheel. Ten more minutes and maybe he'd be able to get to the bottom of everything. At least he didn't have to worry about Jillian getting into trouble while he questioned his uncle.

———■———

Meg looked at the clock and groaned. She'd just gotten to school and already she wanted to be home and in the barn.

Or with her mother. She missed her and she didn't even have a phone number to call.

"Meg?"

Meg's head snapped up at the teacher's voice. "Ma'am?"

"Can you answer the question?"

"No, ma'am."

Mrs. Burcell's brows drew together in a frown. "Is everything all right, Meg?"

Meg glanced around at her snickering classmates and stiffened her spine. "Yes, ma'am. Everything is just fine."

"Class, that's enough," Mrs. Burcell said sharply. The class quieted somewhat. She said to Meg, "All right. Well, maybe you can try the next problem?"

She looked at the book, hating the fact she could feel the heat rising in her cheeks. "What number?"

"Seven."

Meg studied the problem. Easy peasy. "The answer is twelve."

Mrs. Burcell lifted a brow. "That's correct. You want to tell us the steps you took to get to that answer?"

So Meg explained the math problem while her mind went to wondering what her mother and Blake were up to.

And if she should be worried about the man she saw hanging around the parking lot at school.

After giving herself a tour of the house, Jillian decided to check out the clothes. The outfit she had on was the one she'd worn yesterday and desperately needed washing. She picked two outfits from Claire's closet and tried them on. They fit well enough. She kept on the last outfit and walked back into the kitchen where the computer on the desk snagged her attention. Longing hit her. She needed to see Meg's sweet face, hear her laughter. She needed to tell her daughter she loved her.

But did she dare?

She shivered and crossed her arms over her stomach.

No, she couldn't take any chances.

Meg would be wondering why she hadn't called. So would Blake. Blake Wyatt, who was only six years older than she, but he seemed older. Wiser. He'd always been that way. When she'd finally broken down and told him most of the truth about her past and that she was on the run, he'd insisted on teaching her how to defend herself.

As a former Army Ranger, he'd been more than qualified. He'd also wanted to investigate and find out who was after her, but Jillian refused to give him that information. He'd grudgingly accepted she wasn't going to talk and agreed to help her by training her and teaching her.

And Jillian needed to get word to him that she was fine. Well, as fine as could be expected at the moment.

An email would work.

She drew in a deep breath. She'd been so careful. She couldn't mess up now. But she couldn't afford for Blake to start looking for her either.

An idea formed. She walked into the kitchen and found the phone. She heard barking as she dialed Colton's number. The sound made the hair on the back of her neck stand up and she walked to the window to investigate. One of the animals sat at the base of a tree staring up, his tail thumping the ground. Jonah, making his rounds, saw her and gave her a wave. Jillian waved back and her nerves settled at Colton's, "What's up?"

"How safe is this computer?"

"I'm fine, thanks, how are you?"

"Colton, you just left."

He chuckled. "It's safe, why?"

"I want to send an email."

"To who?"

"A friend." Why was he being so nosy?

"Why are you being so secretive?"

She flinched. She didn't want to have secrets from him, but for now, she had no choice.

"Jillian?"

"I'm just being careful, Colton. How do you know the computer is safe?"

He drew in a deep breath. "Because I've used it for work. It has all kinds of security."

"Okay. Good." She paced to stand in front of the machine.

"Hey, Jilly?"

She gulped at the nickname. And wondered why it didn't flame her anger like it had earlier. "Yes?"

"Be careful. Stay inside and keep the alarm on. I'll be back soon."

"Right." She paused. "Colton, you're the one who needs to be careful. I know you're family, but his career's on the line and if you—"

"I'll be fine. I'll call you soon. Jonah just texted and he said all was clear, but just . . . keep the dogs close, okay?"

"Sure. Bye."

She hung up and whispered, "Please, God, let this be the right thing. Don't let him get hurt."

Jillian walked into the den and seated herself in the leather chair to face the flat screen monitor. Before she could change her mind, she pulled up the website Blake had shown her and started typing.

Blake, just a quick note to let you know I'm fine. Working on righting a wrong and facing my past. Give my love to the girl. Hugs, Jillian.

She pressed Send and sat back with a sigh. How she missed Meg's sweet snaggle-toothed face, her sweaty little-girl smell after she spent time in the barn with the horses. Jillian's empty arms ached to hold and hug her.

But all that would have to wait. She drew in another steadying breath. Her growling stomach distracted her and she decided to fix a bite to eat. The ham and cheese sandwich supplies Colton had sent along in the cooler filled her up but didn't provide her any relief from her spiraling thoughts.

Time slowed so much Jillian felt sure all the clocks in the house had to be broken. Colton had to be at his uncle's house by now. Had he confronted the man yet?

Restlessness smacked her and she stood to pace the room from the kitchen to the den and back. She needed to be doing something, researching, helping Colton face down his uncle. Something.

Anything except this crazy waiting.

She grunted. She sure didn't think much of Colton's Plan B.

11

Colton pulled into his uncle's driveway and parked at the top of the circle. Uncle Frank had done well for himself. He knew his mother took pride in her brother's wealth and position in the state. She enjoyed the benefits that came with being his sister. He couldn't help wondering how she would handle it if Frank's career came to an abrupt, scandalous end.

Colton shuddered at the thought. She wouldn't handle it well at all. As he looked around, he realized how much he'd taken for granted his family's affluence.

Until he'd met Jillian.

She'd been like no other girl in the high school. She'd drawn him like a moth to a flame and had been irresistible to him. Her sweetness, her lack of guile, everything about her. When she'd shown up in the youth group at the church, he'd been thrilled.

For Colton, the youth group had been a place where he could be real. Could express his newfound faith and grow in it. Regardless of what his parents believed.

He still prayed for them even though he didn't see them very much. The tension was just too high.

Shrugging off the thoughts of the family he loved, but had nothing in common with, Colton jogged up the brick steps and knocked on the door. Calling ahead had seemed like a good idea at the time, only now, the place looked deserted. He knocked again.

The door swung open.

"Ian."

Ian gave him a fatherly smile, showing dimples in each cheek. It made him look younger than his sixty-some years. "Colton, it's been awhile. Come on in."

Relieved to get out of the heat, Colton stepped inside, welcoming the delicious coolness as he shook hands with his uncle's . . . friend? Hired hand? Household help? Colton was never really sure how to think of Ian. But he liked the man. "I'm looking for Uncle Frank. I called and he said he'd be here all day."

A frown wrinkled Ian's forehead. "He got a phone call about fifteen minutes ago. About five minutes after that, he came storming out of his office yelling something about an emergency campaign meeting at the headquarters and he'd be back when he was done."

"He didn't stop to tell you I was coming?"

"No, I'm sorry."

Colton shrugged, hiding the sudden swell of anxiety. Did his uncle really have an emergency or was he avoiding Colton? His cell phone vibrated and he snatched it from his pocket.

Uncle Frank. "Hello?"

"Colton, boy, I forgot you were coming. I got a phone call and had to head over to headquarters." His regret came through loud and clear.

Colton relaxed. "It's all right, Uncle Frank. But I do need to talk to you soon."

"I don't know how long this is going to take. Why don't I give you a call tomorrow morning? Maybe we can meet for lunch."

"Sounds good."

Colton hung up the phone and guilt swarmed him for doubting the man. It had to be a misunderstanding. There was no way his uncle would kill anyone. Especially Governor Martin. Jillian must have seen something else.

But what? Shooting someone was pretty straightforward. Kind of hard to misinterpret that. So what had happened?

He stood in the foyer thinking.

Ian had left, probably to give him some privacy with his phone call.

Colton decided to take advantage of the moment and walked down the hall to his uncle's office.

The home had changed little since he'd been a kid. A few new pieces of furniture, new paint, and updated light fixtures. But other than that, he remembered the fun he'd had in this house chasing his younger cousins and fighting with his older ones. He was one of two children, but his mother had four sisters and a brother, his uncle Frank. Which meant holidays were full of family, laughter, and fun. At least until he'd defied his parents' wishes and told them he wasn't sure he wanted to go into the family law business.

At his uncle's desk, Colton picked up the picture of him with his family. It had been taken at the lake out on the boat. He had been about sixteen years old and his sister, Marie, had been twelve. Happier times. Good times. A picture of Uncle Frank, Aunt Elizabeth, and Carmen sat next to Colton's family. More pictures lined the credenza on the opposite wall. Frank was a family man. And as far as Colton was concerned, he had no reason to question that.

His attention swiveled to his uncle's gun collection, mounted proudly on the wall behind Frank's desk.

Minus the one he'd been cleaning that now lay on the desk. Jillian had said the man had used one of the antique guns. It would be impossible to tell now. Ten years and many cleanings later would have wiped away all traces of any wrongdoing. Or right doing for that matter. Any traces of anything.

He picked up the one that had been left on the desk. Frank had left in a hurry, discarding the gun and cloth in his haste to get to the meeting.

"Colton?"

He spun to find his Aunt Elizabeth and cousin Carmen standing in the doorway. "Hi." He put the weapon back on the desk. "I came to see Uncle Frank, but he had some emergency meeting." He smiled at his twenty-year-old cousin. "Hey, squirt."

Her dark eyes rimmed in black eyeliner met his. "Hey there." Even in the midst of her most rebellious stage she'd always seemed to appreciate him—even if she didn't listen to his advice.

He gave her a quick hug, then looked down at her. "Taking a break from summer school?" he asked.

She finally smiled and he was glad to see the dark shadows that usually inhabited her eyes were absent for once. "I was coming home on Friday, but there was some kind of power issue on campus and they canceled classes until Monday." She feigned a pout. "Really rotten luck, huh?"

Shocked she'd actually made a joke, he gave a quick laugh to cover his surprise.

He kissed the top of her head and she spun back to her mother. "I'm going to put our stuff away." With a wave to Colton, she strode out the door.

Elizabeth watched her go with an indulgent smile tinged with sadness, then looked back at Colton. She must have read his expression because she laughed. "I know. I spoil her."

"Yeah, you do. But she looks like she's doing well right now. Hope it continues."

"I do too." Elizabeth waved for him to follow her into the kitchen, opened the refrigerator, and pulled out a bottle of vitamin water. She handed it to him, then pulled a glass from the cabinet.

He smiled. "It wouldn't hurt you to drink out of the bottle, you know."

She lifted a brow and gave him a haughty look. "Me? Drink out of a bottle? How long have you known me, darling?"

"Long enough."

She turned serious and studied him. "What's on your mind, Colton?"

She'd always been able to read him pretty well. He took another sip of the water. Maybe she was the one to talk to instead of Frank. "Was Uncle Frank friends with Governor Martin?"

His aunt froze for a moment. "Harrison Martin." A sigh slipped between her lips. "Well, I haven't heard that name in a long time."

"Were they friends?" he asked again.

"Yes. I suppose they were. They worked together quite a bit. Golfed together on occasion." She lifted a shoulder in a delicate shrug. "I'd say they were friends."

"How did the governor die again?"

"A car wreck." Sadness etched lines into her forehead. "He lost control on Culver Park Road and crashed into a tree. Tragic."

Colton nodded as he rubbed the water bottle between his palms. "Is Uncle Frank all right?"

"All right?" She tilted her head. "Well, yes, as far as I know. Why?"

He shook his head. He knew this was something he needed to discuss with his uncle in private. "Just haven't seen him for a while—except on TV—and thought I'd come by and have a chat."

Her eyes narrowed. "What are you not telling me?"

Colton suppressed a grimace. He never should have opened his mouth. He sighed and walked to the closet where she kept the recycle bin. He tossed the empty bottle in and turned back. "Honestly, I'm not sure what I'm not telling you, Aunt Elizabeth, but I need to talk to Uncle Frank. Will you tell him to call me as soon as he gets home? Doesn't matter how late it is. I need to talk to him tonight."

Jillian walked into the den to look out. Glass windows lined the wall, providing her a view of the backyard and the lake beyond it. The beautiful sunny day with temperatures in the midnineties made her want to take a dip in the lake.

One of the dogs zipped past the window and disappeared into the trees at the edge of the property. His twin followed closely behind. Their barks reached her ears and she paused, nerves on edge. She wondered if she'd ever be able to relax again.

When the dogs didn't reappear, Jillian turned from the window and picked up the remote to the large flat screen television mounted on the wall. Then she tossed it back on the coffee table.

"Argh! I need to be doing something!" The words echoed back at her, mocking her inability to do anything or know what was going on with Colton and his uncle. No one knew she was here, right? Why not go for a walk with the dogs? Or take a swim in the lake?

Or call her dad?

She still didn't know why the man hadn't called her back, although she could probably guess. Pain darted through her. She'd stayed away, not calling, not writing, nothing. She supposed she understood his silence. Maybe after all of this was over, they could at least talk and she could explain everything. And introduce him to Meg.

She dialed his number, and just like the last couple of times, it went to voice mail. She left another message and hung up, sadness pressing in on her. She missed her parents. Her mother especially.

Her dad had always been too busy traveling and working for her to feel very close to him. She knew he loved her, though. She never doubted that. Now she wanted to talk to him, see him. Give him a hug and tell him she was sorry she'd stayed silent for ten years.

A shiver slid up her spine. She was tired of being alone—and lonely. Of course she had Meg and Blake, but . . . she wanted more.

She went to the door and whistled for the dogs, wondering if that would work for her like it had for Colton. If she couldn't hang out with friends or family, she'd take the company of the two friendly animals.

The dogs came from the woods, tongues lolling. One, she thought it was Ernie, yelped and stumbled to the ground. Concerned, she started out the door to go to him. Bert had stopped to see what was wrong with his buddy, then a second later, gave a matching cry, spread his legs as though trying to keep his balance, then fell next to Ernie.

Realization and horror hit her. Someone had shot the dogs. With a suppressor because she hadn't heard a thing. Where was Jonah?

Whirling back into the house, she slammed the door, locked it, and leaned against it.

Sorrow for the dogs and worry for the man who was supposed to be protecting her turned her insides to lead. Then a mixture of cold dread and sheer terror slid up her spine.

Someone knew she was here.

12

Jillian reached for the cell phone in her back pocket. And came up empty. "Think. Think." Where had she left it? On the bed in the pocket of the other pair of shorts.

She raced to the kitchen, grabbed the cordless handset, and put it to her ear.

The silence mocked her.

"Okay. No dial tone. You need a plan." The dogs had been shot. But no shots had sounded. If she hadn't been watching out the door, she never would have known anything had happened. Jonah was supposed to be on guard, but had shown no sign that he knew what had happened to the dogs. Or that she was in trouble.

She needed to get upstairs and get the cell phone, but if whoever was after her came inside while she was upstairs, she'd be trapped. She preferred to stay downstairs and watch the entrances while she figured out how she was going to get away.

Her heartbeat picked up and her breaths came closer together. But her mind clicked as she forced the panic away. "Remember," she whispered. "Remember what he taught you. You can take care of yourself, he made sure of that." Still, she'd never had to face down someone who truly wanted to hurt her.

To kill her.

And she didn't want to start now.

She pulled the Glock 19 from her waistband and held it steady, comfortably, in her right hand. If she had to, she'd shoot. But if she could get away, she'd do that instead. She had no desire to shoot someone and have to answer a bunch of questions from the authorities, have the media involved, be held for questioning at the police station where he could get to her . . .

A shudder ripped through her. No way. Running, escaping, was her only option.

But which way to go?

She needed to know where he was.

So she waited, gun ready.

The minutes ticked by.

What was he doing?

Her nerves screamed at her to *do* something.

She checked the windows at the back again. No, he wouldn't expose himself that way. He'd come through the front.

Wouldn't he?

Jillian glanced back at the large wall of windows. Then again, he could be playing sniper. She had to find a way out other than the back door.

The garage area?

A window? An extra door?

She bit her lip and silently screamed at herself for her lapse. Her carelessness. One of the first things she'd been taught to do when entering a new place was to find an escape route. At least one. Two if she could.

All of Blake's teaching, the hours she'd spent learning, and already she'd failed one of the first lessons.

Jillian drew in a deep breath. *Steady, be steady. It won't happen again.*

If she lived through today it wouldn't. Right now, she had to survive. She had no doubt the person outside had no intention of letting her live.

But she had to.

Meg's sweet face flashed before her eyes. *Oh please, Lord, let me live . . .*

Fingers wrapped around the weapon, she closed her eyes, forced herself to calm—and to listen. Just listen.

She turned slowly, silently, in a complete circle.

And still heard nothing.

Time passed but seemed to stand still.

On quiet feet, Jillian walked to the door that led to the garage, wishing she had the cell phone. Colton had said the nearest neighbor was about a quarter of a mile away. She could make that on foot easily and do it fast too. She just had to make sure she wasn't followed.

Or ambushed on her way out of the house.

Where is he? What is he doing? What is he waiting for?

Her fingers curved around the knob that would lead her to the garage.

Before she opened the door, she took a good look around.

Nothing that she could see from her position at the side of the door. Slowly, she twisted the knob. The door opened in one smooth movement and, tense, expectant, she stepped into the muggy heat trapped in the enclosed space. The garage door was down, but the flick of her finger on the button would raise it.

And make noise the intruder would hear. No, she couldn't open it until the last minute. Her eyes took in the details of the garage. The attic steps had been partially pulled down. Interesting. Why? No time to dwell on that. She kept looking.

No cars.

But there was a motorcycle.

Where were the keys?

Heart pounding, Jillian checked the ignition.

Empty.

Were they hanging up somewhere? Or had the owner taken the key with him? Or her?

Her blood hummed through her veins as she listened again. Where was he? Would he try to get in the house or just wait for her to come out?

Indecision warred inside her.

Look for the keys to the bike? Or find a place to hide?

"Wait a minute," she whispered.

Jillian whirled to look back into the kitchen. There. By the phone. Hanging on a row of hooks. A few single keys and a group of keys on a chain. She stepped back inside the house and bolted for the keys.

A creaking sound from above made her breath catch in her throat.

Soft footfalls, almost nonexistent, reached her ears. He was in the house.

How? She'd set the alarm. She risked a glance at the keypad by the kitchen door. It blinked green.

Sheer terror shot through her. Frank had known she was here all along. The intruder knew the code. A code he'd gotten from Frank Hoffman.

Or had Colton set her up?

Fury with herself zinged up her spine. She'd been insane to trust him. To let her past feelings for him scramble her brain.

Another part of her shouted he wouldn't do that.

She wasn't sure which part to believe.

She reached out with shaking fingers and took all of the keys from the hook.

Another creak. He was searching the upstairs? Or headed her way? How had he gotten in up there without setting the alarm off?

Jillian pictured the winding stairs from the deck off the double doors upstairs and knew how he'd gotten in. She just didn't understand why the alarm hadn't gone off.

Jillian's gaze bounced between the front door, the garage door, and the stairs. If she went for the front door and he appeared at the top of the stairs, he would have a perfect view to pick her off just like he'd done with the dogs. She headed back toward the still-open garage door, eyes on the staircase.

The footsteps came closer. Hit the top step.

Breaths coming in fast pants, Jillian slipped through the garage door and shut it behind her. She had very little time now to figure out what to do.

She jammed a key into the ignition of the motorcycle.

Wrong one.

Tossing it to the floor, she tried the next, then the next. She glanced up and froze as a shadow passed by the window of the kitchen door.

It wouldn't be long before he figured out where she was. He could now see the entire downstairs. And the fact that she wasn't there.

Breath hitching, she knew she had to hide.

Now.

But where?

Colton checked the time on the dash clock again. 12:45. It had been almost thirty-five minutes since he'd left his uncle's house with no answers, and he'd been away from Jillian long enough to make him nervous.

He chided his jumpiness. She was fine. No one knew she was there.

The pep talk didn't help.

He couldn't help it, he just didn't want to leave her too long. No telling what kind of trouble she could come up with on her own. He punched the speed-dial number for the lake house.

And listened to the phone ring.

He frowned, hung up, and tried again. Once more, the voice mail picked up. He tried her cell phone. Still nothing.

Why didn't she answer?

"Come on, Jillian. What are you doing that you can't answer the phone?"

———■———

Jillian waited, nearly strangling with the need to gasp. She pulled in a slow, silent breath. Be still. Be quiet.

And wait.

The intruder opened the door and stepped into the garage. He just stood there, the door open, eyes glittering in the holes of the ski mask. Green eyes, she noted. She had a clear view of him from her position in the attic.

Soon, he would look up.

Oh God, please don't let this get me killed.

The gun pressed against her lower back. A comforting weight. A weight that gave her courage. Maybe it was a false courage, but it was too late to change the plan now. If she had to shoot him, she would. But she didn't want to. She needed him alive and able to talk.

Although, deciding to take him on by herself was probably the dumbest thing she'd ever done.

But she'd had no choice. No way to run, no plan of escape. No rescue in sight.

Breathing another prayer, she waited.

His eyes finally lifted. She wondered if he could see her hunched in the dark of the attic, the stairs gripped in one hand, the other ready to reach for her weapon.

"Well, well, Jillian Carter," he rasped. "It seems this is my lucky day."

She remained silent.

He stepped closer. "You know you can't stay holed up there forever. There's no other way out. Now," his voice hardened, "why don't you make this easy on both of us and just come down?"

"Why do you want me dead?" She knew why, but she needed to keep him talking. And moving.

He took one more step.

Come on, she thought, *two more steps.*

"I don't. But my boss does."

"Frank Hoffman," she spat.

"Names don't really matter at this point, do they?" He lifted his gun. She still didn't think he could see her very well in the dark, but if he started shooting, he probably wouldn't miss.

"Names matter. I've already told my story to people who believe me. If I wind up dead, the investigation will still continue."

He paused, then took another step. "That's a shame then. It looks like my job won't end with you after all. I suppose you've talked to Serena and Alexia."

Jillian shuddered at the emptiness staring back at her. She refused to acknowledge his last statement. "If you want me, then come get me."

A low growl of frustration sounded in his throat. "Fine. Have it your way."

He stepped forward and she shoved the stairs with a mighty push. They rumbled on the track and slid like a greased pig through a child's hands at the county fair. The ski mask hid his expression, but she saw his eyes widen in shock as the bottom step clipped him on the forehead.

He went down with a thud, his gun skittering across the concrete floor, coming to a stop under the front wheel of the motorcycle.

Without stopping to think, Jillian scrambled down the steps, heart thudding, blood humming, adrenaline rushing so hard, it almost made her dizzy.

At the bottom of the attic stairs, she jumped over the prone body and backed away from him, putting distance between them. She had the brief thought to stop and pull his mask off, but saw his arm move, heard him groan a curse.

She had to move fast. At the garage door, she hit the button and heard the mechanical door start to crank open. She turned to see the man clasping his head, struggling to his feet.

Hurry! Her mind screamed the word.

Shoving the last key into the ignition, she turned it and cranked the machine.

He came at her.

She lifted one foot and slammed it into his stomach.

He gave a cry and stumbled back, going to his knees, clasping his head.

Jillian gunned the motor and backed out of the garage with a screech of tires.

Her intruder managed to move fast, get his gun, and lift it to take aim.

Colton hung up the phone and slapped a hand against the wheel. Why wouldn't she answer?

Had she gone outside? The lure of the water might have been too tempting to her. She'd always been a swimmer.

But he'd told her to stay inside. The Jillian he'd known as a teenager would have done as he'd said. This ten-years-later Jillian?

A bad feeling started to grow in his gut and he pressed the gas pedal a little harder as he hit the number one more time.

She still didn't pick up.

His jaw hardened. This day just was not going the way he'd planned. Just a minute more and he'd be at the drive. He pressed the gas and started to pray.

13

The motorcycle came out of nowhere. Colton jerked the wheel to the right and the truck bounced along the edge of the drive, gravel sputtering as his tires spun. Gaining control and getting back onto the drive, fear settled in his stomach as he realized the crazy driver was Jillian.

What was she doing?

He braked and did a three-point turn, gunning the gas to catch up to her. As he came to the end of the drive, he saw her parked at the end, standing there waiting for him. Colton slammed on the brakes once again and the truck jerked to a stop.

Jillian reached for the passenger door even as he leaned over to throw it open for her. "What are you doing? Are you crazy?"

"No! You are!"

"What?"

"Coming back to make sure he finished the job?" She swung a fist at him.

He ducked and grabbed it as it missed him by millimeters. "Jillian! Stop it! What's gotten into you?"

"He's there!"

"Who?"

"The guy who's trying to kill me. And he knew the code to the alarm!" Her breaths came in pants and the fear in her eyes hadn't lessened. "He let himself in as easy as if I'd just left the door open."

Colton tried to piece together what she was saying. "You think I had something to do with that?"

"Who else? After all, this lake house idea was your Plan B, remember? Well, I'm going back to Plan A!"

"Stop it!"

But she continued. "I'm better off taking care of myself rather than relying on a traitor."

Fury spurted. He snagged her arm. "Calm down. I didn't have anything to do with that. Where's Jonah?"

She jerked away from him. "I don't know. I haven't seen him." She bit her lip. "I'm worried about him."

Concern filled him. "All right. Stay here and let me take care of this."

She gripped his arm, her face softening a fraction. "I need to warn you, I think he killed the dogs."

He blanched. "Killed the—" Sorrow lanced through him and he swallowed hard.

Colton grabbed his cell phone and punched speed-dial number two as he whipped the truck back toward the house. When Hunter answered, Colton spit out their location. "I need backup at the lake house now! Someone attacked Jillian and she said he's still there."

"I'll have Columbia PD get out there. I'm on the way."

Colton felt conflicted. He wanted to get to the house and see if he could catch the guy, but he didn't want to take Jillian back into the danger she'd just escaped from. Danger she thought he'd brought down on her. More sorrow hit him as he realized it would take time for her to trust him when she thought his uncle was a killer. He'd have to prove himself to her.

"What are you waiting for?" she asked.

"Backup."

Before he could make his way toward the house, movement in

front of the truck grasped his attention. Colton braked again, reached for his weapon, and blinked when he saw Ernie appear from the tree line. The dog walked a few steps, then sat down, rolled onto his side, tongue lolling, panting hard.

Jillian gasped and opened her door. She ran toward the dog and knelt beside him, running her fingers over his coat. Colton followed, his mind churning, eyes watchful. "I thought you said he shot the dogs."

"He did. I don't understand . . ." She stopped and pulled back. Blood covered her fingers.

Colton examined the wound himself and pulled a small dart from Ernie's side. "Tranquilizers."

Hope blossomed on her face. "Then he's going to be okay?"

"Yes. Get back in the truck and stay down. I don't want you out in the open until we find this guy." Colton murmured soft words to his canine buddy as he picked him up and put him in the back of the truck.

Two county cruisers pulled into the drive and came toward them, lights flashing, but sirens silent. The first car came up beside him. Colton had given Hunter a description of his truck to pass on to the officers. Colton flashed his badge and said, "Follow me."

He and Jillian climbed back into the truck and headed the last few yards down the drive. Colton stopped and looked at Jillian. "Stay here, lock the doors, and keep your head down."

He didn't give her a chance to argue with him. He got out of the truck, pulled his gun, and walked toward the open garage.

He heard the officers bringing up the rear. Turning, he said to the closest one, "Check the perimeter, will you?"

"Sure." The officer took off and Colton and the second cop, whose name tag read T. Vincent, cleared the garage. Colton led the way to the door that would open into the kitchen. It was cracked. He pushed it open with his foot, gun ready.

Everything looked just as he'd left it only a few hours ago. They checked the pantry, behind the furniture, anywhere someone could hide. "Clear," he finally called. He could see Bert through the den window still and motionless in the backyard near the trees. Concern tugged him, but the dog would have to wait. And where was Jonah? The man hadn't answered his cell.

The officer headed for the stairs with Colton right behind him.

It didn't take long to clear the second level. Colton descended the stairs and walked out the front door to find the first officer carrying Bert toward the truck.

Colton's concern blossomed. "Thanks."

"I think he's all right. Just still woozy. He's got a dart in his side."

"Yeah." Colton took the dog from the officer and placed him beside Ernie in the back of the truck. Ernie whined and pawed at his companion. Bert lifted his head, then dropped it. Colton would get them to the vet as soon as he had everything wrapped up here.

Jillian opened the door and climbed out. "He got away, didn't he?"

"Yeah. He's gone. Probably had a car parked somewhere close by—"

"And Jonah?"

"We're searching the wooded area and the—"

"Hey, Colton!" He turned at Hunter's shout. Hunter stood from his kneeling position next to a tree. "It's Jonah. He's alive but unconscious. I've called for an ambulance."

Colton rushed down the sloping hill to the tree line. Jillian followed him. Hunter held up a dart that matched the ones from the dogs. Relief filled him. His friend would be all right.

Colton placed his hands on his hips and looked around. "It's pretty remote out here, but it's summer and there are people around. Let's get officers questioning everyone."

Jillian frowned and muttered, "I should have shot him."

He jerked and looked at her in surprise. "What?"

"I could have, after I hurt him. But I didn't. I should have."

Officers nearby exchanged glances and raised eyebrows. Colton looked at them and shook his head. To Jillian, he said, "You said he was hurt. How bad?"

"I almost had him knocked out cold. He's got a head injury. I hope he has a massive concussion." She drew in a breath. "I had to act fast. The attic stairs were down in the garage. I saw a can of oil, grabbed it and greased the metal brackets pretty good as I climbed up. Then I pulled the steps up and waited. He saw me, walked toward me . . ." She stopped and shuddered.

Colton felt his insides tense as he imagined the scene she described.

"And when he got to the right spot, I gave the stairs a shove and they flew down like I'd shot them out of a cannon." She blinked and Colton saw the fear in her eyes as she remembered. But she shrugged. "He went down hard. But not hard enough, unfortunately. If he'd been unconscious, I would have figured out a way to tie him up and call for help."

Colton closed his eyes, grateful Jillian was still alive. If the intruder had gotten his hands on her . . .

He couldn't go there. He walked over to stand in front of the garage. While part of the drive was gravel, the area directly in front of the garage was concrete. Hands on his hips, he simply surveyed the area. He didn't know what he was looking for, but he'd know it when he saw it.

"What's going on?"

Colton turned at Katie's voice and saw her standing with the officers. For the next few minutes, he filled them in.

Katie walked to the edge of the garage and crouched. "Hey, you got a crime scene kit?" She pointed to the concrete. "I think this is blood."

—■—

Jillian stood by the truck, watching as the detectives collected what little evidence had been left behind. A crime scene unit had been dispatched, but hadn't arrived yet.

She'd been printed so they could compare her prints to any they found. She'd overheard Colton talking to Hunter—they'd caught a break. The place had been professionally cleaned by a local service after the last time it had been used. All they had to do was rule out the cleaning crew's prints, hers, and Colton's, and see if the intruder had left any behind. But if she remembered correctly, he'd been wearing gloves.

Jillian walked back to the truck to check on the dogs and climbed through the small door into the cool area. They lay on their sides, eyes open, ears pricked toward the sounds going on around them. Sweat ran down the back of her neck and she was glad Colton had the back of the truck covered with a canopy. He'd left the vehicle running and the air conditioner blew full blast, cooling the area where the dogs lay.

"It's all right, boys, you're going to be fine," she murmured as she ran a hand down Ernie's side. He lifted his head to lick her hand, then lay back down and closed his eyes.

Gravel crunched and she saw Rick pulling in the driveway. He gave her a wave and kept going.

"Jillian?"

She turned to see Colton standing at the end of the truck bed, right behind her. He helped her back out and she nodded toward the house. "They find anything?"

"Some, not much."

"I heard someone say something about a blood sample."

He nodded. "Rick'll run it through the database and see if there's a match for anyone. It was dry, so we're not sure how long it's been there. As hot as it is today, it would have dried almost instantly." He placed his hands on his hips and squinted down at her. "Now the problem remains. Who knew you were here? How did they find out, and what are we going to do with you now?"

"Good question." She frowned as she stared down at the dogs.

"What is it?" he asked.

"You didn't have anything to do with it, did you?"

He slipped a hand under her chin and looked square in her eyes. "No, Jillian. I thought you'd be safe. I'd never do anything to hurt you."

She swallowed at the truth she saw there and nodded. "Okay. I believe you."

Relief glinted in his gaze. The gaze that dropped to her lips. Her heart shuddered as his head lowered. A gentle kiss caressed her lips. Then his head lifted and it was over. Much too soon, if you asked her.

"Thank you," he said.

14

The ride to the vet had been a silent one. Dr. Wainsworth had promised to check the dogs and keep them overnight. He'd be in touch soon.

"Thanks." Colton paused. "Do you mind boarding them until I get back to you?"

"Working a case?"

"Yeah."

Jillian watched the exchange. Obviously not the first time Colton had left them with the doctor.

As they pulled into the parking lot of the police station, Colton's tension radiated from him. Jillian kept quiet, grateful for the opportunity to just think for a minute. Colton had taken every precaution to stash her away safely and still she'd been found. Chills raced up and down her spine. Or was it all just to look good? Had he told his uncle she was there? Immediately, she pushed those thoughts away. Again. He wouldn't do that to her.

Would he?

His phone rang and he left the car running while he answered. "Yes sir." She listened and raised a brow when his jaw tightened. He let out a sigh and grimaced but nodded. "Yes sir. I'm not sure that's necessary, but we'll do whatever you want." He listened and finally hung up with a low grunt.

"What is it?"

"I'm going to kill Rick Shelton."

She smothered a smile at his disgust. "What's he done?"

"Convinced the captain that there are some of us who need to attend his seminar on the latest crime-solving technology."

"What's wrong with that? Seems like you would have to do that kind of thing in your line of work."

"Yeah. We do. But not with Rick."

"Why not?"

"It's hard to explain, but Rick . . . you see, Rick is . . ." He waved a hand. "Rick's a great guy, but when it comes to teaching, he's better than a sleeping pill."

"Ah, I get it."

"Yeah." They climbed out of the car.

Colton took her arm as they stepped into the station and gently propelled her toward his office. He didn't stop to speak to his fellow officers. Instead he seated her in his chair, said, "Stay here for a minute," and disappeared from view.

Jillian leaned back and stared at the ceiling. She'd just noticed the fresh paint smell mingled with the scent of coffee. Coffee. She stood. That might help.

She spied the coffeemaker on a rolling cart in the corner and made a beeline for it. Her mind churned as her hands went through the motions necessary to produce a pot of coffee. She needed a place to stay. A place where no one would think to look for her. But where? She also needed to talk to Serena. The first step in proving what happened ten years ago would be to prove how the governor died.

Because she knew it wasn't a car wreck.

Jillian walked over to the phone on the desk, picked it up, and dialed.

Serena answered.

"I'm so sorry, Serena."

"I am too. But you and Colton are alive—I can't even worry about the house right now."

"But your things," Jillian whispered, grief and guilt cutting a fresh path through her once again.

"Hey, they're just things. The animals were safe, I have copies of every important paper and picture in a safe deposit box. Trust me, it's okay."

Jillian didn't feel a whole lot better. "I wanted to stick around and apologize last night, but Colton rushed me out of there so fast . . . and I wasn't really thinking straight . . . and . . ."

"Jill, hush, it's okay."

"But your house," Jillian wailed as tears floated to the surface for the umpteenth time.

Serena sighed. "I have insurance. Now," her voice took on that no-nonsense tone she'd learned at an early age, "tell me what I can do to help you. Do you want to stay with Mom and Dad and Camille? They'd love to have you and they have a great security system."

"And put them in danger? No way!" She pushed a file to the side and sat in the chair behind the desk. "Besides, you had a great security system, and that didn't stop them from blowing your house up." She didn't give Serena a chance to answer. "No, I'll figure something out. I can always go to a homeless shelter."

Serena drew in a sharp breath. "Jill . . ."

"Bad joke, sorry. I had enough of those the first few months after I left that night." Quiet echoed back at her. "Serena, I need to ask you something."

"Sure."

"How well do you know Colton now?"

"Pretty well. We spent a lot of time together when he helped track my serial killer. Why?"

Jillian sighed and wondered if she should voice her thoughts.

Serena asked, "Jill? What's going through that mind of yours?"

"I'm questioning whether I can trust Colton. I mean . . . it's his uncle I'm accusing. I just . . . I mean I do trust him. I think." At least she did earlier when he'd declared he'd never do anything to hurt her.

"You can trust him," Serena insisted. "I have no doubts about that."

Her reassurances helped. "It's hard. I had to learn to be suspicious of everyone, to trust no one, and now . . . ," she bit her lip at the irony, "and now—how can I trust the nephew of the man who's trying to have me killed? It doesn't really make sense."

"I suppose when you look at it that way, it does seem a little crazy, but I promise, if I had any doubts about Colton, I'd warn you. I don't. He's a good man and he's missed you terribly." She paused. "You never told me what you did after you left. How you survived. How you took care of Meg."

Jillian winced. "I know. It just didn't seem important. Even though I used a pay phone when I called, I was never 100 percent sure someone wouldn't figure out a way to find me through it."

"I'm sorry for everything you've been through. I can't imagine it. I wish—"

"Don't. It's okay. Or it will be as soon as I can prove Frank Hoffman killed Governor Martin."

"And how do you plan to do that?"

"I want you—and me—to talk to the ME who did the autopsy on the governor."

"That was ten years ago."

"I know. Can you find out who handled it?"

"Hold on a sec." Clicking keys filtered through the phone line and Jillian waited. She tapped her foot, shook her leg. Blew a breath through pursed lips.

Serena finally came back on the line. "Jillian?"

"Yeah?"

"His name was Gerald Benjamin. And . . . this is crazy, but . . . he's dead."

They both went silent as they processed that bit of information. Jillian asked, "You think that was a coincidence?"

"I don't know what to think." Her friend paused. "So, now what?"

"New plan."

"You and your plans. What?"

"We're going to dig up the ME's body—and you're going to do another autopsy."

———■———

"You're going to what?" Colton couldn't help the raised voice or the blurted question. He'd walked in just in time to hear Jillian talk about digging up a dead body. "That's illegal, you know."

She finished her call and hung up. When she turned to face him, she notched her chin a bit higher in the air. "I'm not going to do anything illegal. You're going to get a court order for it."

"Based on what?"

"An eyewitness testimony that the governor was shot and his car accident was a cover-up."

Colton digested her words. The smell of fresh coffee distracted him for a moment. He darted for the cart to pour himself a cup while shooting daggers at this woman who'd managed to turn his world upside down *again*. His brows shot north as he took a sip. "Hey, this is good."

A ghost of a smile graced her lips. "If there's one thing I know, it's how to make a good pot of coffee." She turned serious again. "So anyway, you just need to get the court order, get the body to Serena, meet her at the lab, and wait for her to do the autopsy."

"You really think it's going to be that easy?"

"No." She studied him. "But with your help, we can get it done."

110

"I don't have any reason other than your say-so. I can't just take that to a judge. I need something more."

"Like what?"

"Like proof."

She groaned and wilted, dropping her head to his desk. "That's why I need his body exhumed. The proof is in his body. Serena just told me the ME who did the original autopsy, Gerald Benjamin, died about three weeks later. That's not a coincidence, Colton." She slapped a hand on the desk, her cheeks red, eyes spitting determination.

"How did he die?" he asked. He could look, but he knew she knew.

She stuck her thumbnail between her teeth and stared at him. Dropping her hand, she said, "Anaphylactic shock from multiple bee stings while he was fishing. Alone."

He sighed, exasperation building. "And you're seeing a murder there? That kind of stuff happens, Jillian."

He dropped into his chair and pulled up a website. Clicking, he logged in.

"It's not a coincidence!" She stood and jabbed a finger into his chest, pushing him back into the chair. "I know what I saw. Governor Martin was shot by your uncle. Martin did not die in a car wreck and Gerald Benjamin may have died of anaphylactic shock, but it was because someone knew he was allergic to bees and made sure he ran across a bunch of them."

"But why would Benjamin agree to file a false cause of death? That's grounds for losing his license, not to mention jail time. He would be ruined if it was discovered."

Two more clicks with his mouse.

She paced to the door, then back to the desk. "I don't know why. Maybe he was being blackmailed. Maybe he owed a favor. Maybe he was promised money. I don't know. What are the usual reasons someone does something like that? I just know that he probably did and he died for it."

Colton sipped the coffee. Slowly the red faded from her cheeks and he could see her brain working.

She snagged his gaze with hers. "The car wreck investigation for the governor. Can you get me the file from that?"

"What for?"

"They would have taken pictures, written a report. I want to see the pictures and read the report."

He didn't answer her right away. Instead he looked at her, saw her absolute belief that she was right. It worried him. Made him start to doubt his uncle. "I can do that."

Relief flickered in her pretty brown eyes. "Good. When?"

"Right after I make this bid."

"What bid?"

"A bid for tickets for the World Series in October."

"Those things are super hard to get. How can you just hit a few buttons and have tickets?"

"They're up for bid on an online auction for charity." He glanced at her. "I'm going to be the highest bidder."

"I didn't realize you were such a big baseball fan."

"I'm not. I mean I like the game, but I need these for a bribe." She blinked and he clicked.

"Okay. Good luck." She fell silent for a moment. "So?"

"So what?"

"The car wreck investigation files?"

"Right." Colton let out a sigh and pushed the mouse away. "If you really think the ME's death is somehow connected to the death of the governor, then that might be a good enough reason for the judge to give a court order for an exhumation."

"Then get his file too. Everything."

"It's a closed case. An accidental death."

"The file is still in storage."

Did he really want to do this? He didn't see that he had a choice. He either had to prove his uncle innocent and Jillian wrong—or put the man in jail for murder. Actually, he'd have to recuse himself from this crazy investigation and watch a fellow officer arrest his uncle. Some choice. But as of now, nothing had been connected to his uncle other than Jillian's say-so. And the man couldn't be arrested on that.

Jillian asked, "If we find evidence, would you go to the judge and get a court order?"

He gave a slow nod. "Yeah. It might take some convincing, but," he rubbed a hand across his eyes, "but I could probably do it."

She stilled. "And would you?"

Colton felt tension run along his jawline. "If only to prove you wrong."

She grimaced. "I'm sorry, Colton, but I'm not wrong."

"Then let's see if we can prove it." He pulled his phone from his pocket, punched in a number and hit speaker. Serena answered on the third ring. "Hey, Serena, looks like I have a favor to ask of you too."

"Sure, Colton, what do you need?"

He told her. Silence met his request. "Serena?"

"You said the deaths were ruled accidental. But you don't think they were. So, you think just like Jillian? The two deaths are related?" she asked.

"Let's just say we're going to find out one way or the other and we need your help to do it."

"All right." She paused. "These aren't cold cases. They're closed cases. They're public record."

"The reports are. The pictures are a different matter. The police investigation files are no problem. But the pictures from the ME's office might be a little hard to get ahold of. I'm going to get a court order from a judge. He's a friend of mine, and while he won't do anything unethical, he trusts me and will listen to me. If he thinks I have something worthwhile, he'll be willing to give me a little more latitude than some of the other judges I know."

"I can send everything to my work email account and access it from a secure computer. You have one of those?"

"I do."

"How soon can you get the court order to me?"

"Give me thirty minutes." He saw Jillian give him a satisfied nod. "All right. When do you want to start going over it?"

"What time can you be at my house?"

15

Hunter stepped inside and clapped Colton on the shoulder. "Alexia sends her regrets. She's working."

"No problem. Tell her we missed her."

"Where's Jillian?"

"Right here."

Hunter walked over to her and handed her a bag. "Alexia said you'd probably need this stuff. Some clothes, a toothbrush, and whatever she deemed necessary."

Jillian blinked back tears and accepted the gift with a watery thanks.

Then Dominic entered, carrying a green bag by the handles, followed by Serena, Katie, and a nice-looking man Jillian had never seen before.

"I brought pizza supplies," Serena announced with a grin. She turned to Jillian. "And I went shopping. I brought you a couple of shirts. I would have volunteered my shorts, but they'd probably look like pants on you."

Jillian laughed as she eyed her friend's five-foot-nine frame. "No doubt, but thanks for the T-shirts. I was afraid I'd have to go shopping too—and that might not be the safest thing to do right now."

Dominic took the bag into the kitchen, saying over his shoulder, "Anyone else experiencing a bit of déjà vu?"

Jillian lifted a brow at Colton and he smiled. "Last month we got together to search through files, and Serena made us her homemade pizza. It's been that long since we've all gotten together." He frowned. "That's a shame, if you ask me."

"Definitely," Hunter agreed.

Serena waved them toward the den. "Why don't you get started while I put these pizzas together."

"Need some help?" Katie asked.

Serena looked surprised. "Sure."

Katie said, "This is Grayson. He's my brother's best friend and a cop in Florida. When I told Grayson what we were doing, he insisted on coming along."

Grayson shot the group a sheepish smile. "Can't resist a good investigation."

Colton laughed. "I don't know a cop who can. This is a closed case, nothing confidential here, so welcome to the group."

Shoulders relaxing, Grayson made his way into the den and found a seat on one end of Colton's brown leather L-shaped couch. Although a large piece of furniture, it fit the room and log cabin atmosphere. Wood beams graced the ceiling. Across from the couch, an oversized fireplace had the potential to heat the entire downstairs.

"This reminds me of a hunting lodge," Grayson said to Jillian.

She laughed and agreed. "It appears rustic and yet it's not." She swept a hand around the room. "All the comforts you could ask for."

"Tasteful. Classy."

"Yeah."

Colton came into the room, head bent over his phone.

Hunter followed. "You're seriously going to spend that much money on tickets?"

"It's for a good cause."

"Which one?" Hunter snickered. "The real charity or the Colton charity case?"

Colton looked up and lasered Hunter with a glare. "Just so you know, he's added your name to the list."

Hunter paled. "He didn't."

"He did."

Hunter gulped. "I'll go halves."

"What list?" Jillian asked.

Dominic looked confused. "What are you up to?"

Hunter said, "Rick's decided that we don't respect crime solving technology like we should and has suggested to our captain that we attend one of his seminars on the subject."

Dominic winced. "One of those all-day things?"

"One of those *weekend* things," Colton said with a shudder. "He mentioned last year that he'd never been to the World Series and it was his dream to get there one day." He waved the phone. "I'm bidding on tickets."

Jillian lifted a brow. "And you think bribing him is going to get you out of going?"

Hunter gave a vigorous nod. "Oh yeah."

Colton finally set his phone aside and picked up several files. "All right, let's get busy. These are the police files. Serena's going to pull up the ME reports in just a few minutes. So, everyone have a seat and let me tell you what's going on."

Colton took a moment to settle his own thoughts, then said, "Just thought I'd fill you in on how Jonah's doing. The hospital is keeping him for observation, but it looks like he'll make a full recovery."

"How'd our killer get the drop on him?" Dominic asked.

"Jonah said he thought he saw some movement down by the trees where Hunter found him. Said he started walking that way and that's the last thing he remembers."

Hunter shook his head and Dominic blew out a breath. "He's lucky it was a tranquilizer gun."

"Amen," Colton said. He picked up a file. "All right. You already know some of it. Let me just rehash and we'll go from there. Ten years ago, Jillian says she saw my uncle Frank shoot Governor Harrison Martin." Nods greeted his sentence. "That's what she really believes and there's no question she saw something—and someone wants her dead for it." More nods. "Martin's death was reported as accidental. Three weeks later, the ME who issued the report also died."

Murmurs and raised eyebrows echoed around the room and Jillian twisted with impatience. She wanted to grab the files from Colton's hands and dig in. She forced herself to still, to wait. Serena came in and sat at the computer. Katie followed and sat next to Grayson.

Colton went on. "The ME's death was *also* ruled accidental. He died from multiple bee stings. Anaphylactic shock. Probably would have only taken one or two stings to cause him some trouble, but he was stung over fifty times."

Hunter winced and Dominic grimaced. "That would have killed him pretty fast."

"Almost instantly," Katie agreed.

"Poor man." Serena's gaze softened with compassion.

"Back to the governor. An autopsy was done because his wife demanded it. She said he hated Culver Park Road and wouldn't have been on it; their nephew died on that road his senior year. She said that Martin went out of his way to avoid the road, and the fact that he was on it was a huge red flag for her."

"But no one listened to the grief-stricken wife, eh?" Grayson asked.

Colton tapped the file folder. "Not really. It's noted in the report, but that's about it."

"But she got the autopsy," Katie said.

"She paid for it herself."

"And the ME didn't find anything suspicious," Hunter stated.

Colton shook his head. "Not according to his report."

"We need to talk to Mrs. Martin."

Dominic nodded. "Put her on the list."

Jillian watched Serena's fingers fly over the keyboard. Images flickered, then settled as she started to read.

Grayson rubbed his hands together. "So, we're looking for something off in the reports that indicates there was something more than fate at work?"

Colton eyed the detective. "Something like that."

Jillian wondered why Katie had brought the man—then looked around and realized everyone was "coupled" off. Dominic and Serena, she and Colton, and Hunter and Alexia. Although Alexia hadn't been able to make it, Katie probably hadn't known that when she invited Grayson to come along.

Interesting. She wouldn't have thought the woman would have been bothered by that kind of thing. At least not the Katie she remembered from high school. She supposed everyone had their own insecurities whether they liked to admit it or not.

She also thought it funny that she'd coupled herself with Colton almost without thinking about it. Definitely interesting. And a little scary.

Colton shifted, his expression troubled. "Not that I expect it to happen, but just let me say now if any proof comes to light that shows my uncle guilty of any wrongdoing, I'll recuse myself from the investigation. Right now, there's no evidence of his involvement in *anything* other than what Jillian is saying. My captain was intrigued enough with the deaths of these two men and a possible connection—not to mention the attempts on Jillian's life—that he's given me the green light to see what I can find out. He's also given me a deadline. We have seventy-two hours." He spread the files on the table. "It's not a lot. I thought we could take turns reading it, see if anything jumps out at you." He looked at Serena whose gaze hadn't left the computer screen. "Serena?"

She jumped and turned, brow raised. "Yes?"

"You found anything yet?"

"I'm looking at the governor's autopsy report. Nothing stands out to me yet. It's pretty routine."

"Okay, sorry. I won't bother you again. Just holler if you learn something."

Serena sniffed and lifted her nose. "When have you ever known me to 'holler'?" She turned back to the computer.

Her friend's haughty pronouncement made Jillian grin. Dominic, too, had a smile on his face. Eyes filled with love, he simply stared at the back of Serena's head. A pang of longing shot through Jillian as she dared let her gaze swing back to Colton. He used to have that look in his eyes when he looked at her. She allowed herself to wonder. *What would it take to get it back?*

She sighed. She doubted proving his uncle guilty of murder would inspire the look. Or telling him he had a daughter, a secret she'd kept for the past ten years.

Jillian hardened her resolve. She had to do this. And if she lost Colton forever in the process, then she would have to find a way to live with it.

Ignoring the pain slicing through her, she closed her eyes and offered up a prayer for help and discernment.

And a desperate plea for her daughter's continued safety.

7:45 PM

Frank studied the note as dread welled up. It had been a couple of weeks since the last one, and he'd dared to hope he'd scared Jillian into silence.

And now this.

TELL WHAT YOU DID . . . OR I WILL.

120

"Does that mean you haven't?" he muttered as he tossed the letter into his desk drawer and picked up his phone. Colton had texted him. At the moment Frank wished he hadn't given in to his daughter's urging that he be technologically savvy. But she'd seemed so excited about actually teaching him something, he'd listened and enjoyed the rare moment of camaraderie with her.

He read Colton's message again. NEED 2 TALK TO U. CALL ME ASAP.

The back door slammed and Frank sighed as he glanced at his watch. Carmen and Elizabeth. They'd been to some special mother/daughter dinner at the church Elizabeth had insisted Carmen go to. No one had been more surprised than he when his daughter had shown up on their doorstep saying she was home for the week. Something about a power failure on campus. Classes and dorms had been closed. Frank actually called the school to find out if her story was true. After being lied to for so many years, he couldn't help his suspicious nature when it came to Carmen and her stories. Even more surprising was the fact that she actually went to the dinner with Elizabeth.

Carmen's voice reached him. Chattering on the phone with one of her college friends, it sounded like. At least going to college seemed to soften some of her hard edges. She wasn't quite so sullen and angry. Maybe she was finally working through whatever it was that turned her from his sweet girl into a sullen creature he couldn't relate to.

Elizabeth's footsteps sounded on the hardwoods, clicking her way toward him. Frank forced his facial muscles to relax. He'd left the door open as he always did lately. No sense in having her wonder if he was hiding something. She was always suspicious. His shoulders tensed as her steps slowed.

"Frank? Are you here?"

"Yes, Elizabeth, I'm here."

She appeared in the doorway, exasperation on her face. "Are you still working?"

"No. Not really. Just . . . thinking."

"About what?" Exasperation turned to wariness.

"Nothing much. Just the campaign and how I feel like I'm always walking on a tightrope."

"That's politics, darling. Haven't you figured that out yet?"

He sighed. Why did he even bother? "Yes." He kept his tone neutral. "I've figured it out. I'm going to give Colton a call and see what he wants. He texted me."

Elizabeth hesitated, a small set of lines appearing on her forehead. "You're frowning. What is it?"

"Colton was here today."

"I know. I was supposed to meet him, but had to run out at the last minute. I forgot to call and tell him."

"He was acting rather strange."

It was Frank's turn to pause for a split second. Then he asked, "Why do you say that?"

"He asked if you were friends with Harrison Martin."

Frank felt his insides grow cold. He struggled to keep his face neutral. Forcing a lightness he didn't feel, he said, "Harrison? Why on earth would he be asking about a man who's been dead for ten years?"

"I have no idea. He just did. You're getting ready to call him, ask him."

"Yes, yes, I'll do that."

She nodded, still studying him.

He shifted. "Was there something else?"

"Colton also asked if you were all right."

A chill slithered through him. "Meaning?"

She shrugged. "Again, I don't know, but I thought the whole visit very odd."

So did Frank. He held up the handset of the cordless phone. "I'll call him."

"I'm going to read in the sunroom for a while." And then she was gone.

Frank wilted into the chair where he seemed to spend the majority of his time. What was he going to do?

He punched in the first six numbers of Colton's cell number, then stopped. What if Jillian had told him what she saw that night? His stomach twisted tighter. What was he going to say? What if Colton asked him outright if he killed the governor?

He'd deny it of course. And Colton would believe him. Wouldn't he?

He looked at his hands, then the guns on the wall behind him.

One way or another Jillian had to be silenced. If she went public with her accusations, it would kill his career. And if she died after she talked, he would definitely look guilty. If she died now, he could do damage control. Couldn't he?

Of course he could. He had no choice.

She had to die before she said anything.

And he had to have an airtight alibi when it happened.

Frank punched a number into his phone. And it wasn't Colton's.

16

Jillian finished off her last bit of pizza as she watched her friends work together. Serena's six large pizzas were gone, every last bite consumed in record time. The clock pushed toward ten, and she had nowhere to sleep tonight. She supposed she'd better think about that.

"I've got something. I think." Serena's voice broke into the silence.

Jillian sat straight up, a surge of adrenaline sweeping away her fatigue.

Colton stepped across the room to stand beside Serena. Jillian took up residence on the other side.

"What is it?" she asked.

"I didn't see anything that jumped out at me on the governor's autopsy report so I moved to the ME's file. These pictures aren't pretty," Serena warned with a concerned look.

Jillian moved closer. "I can handle it. Just show us, please."

"Okay. I've read through the report here. There wasn't an autopsy, but this is an official death record. The pictures are from the site where the body was found."

"Who found the body?"

"His fishing buddy, Conrad Pike."

Colton shifted and Jillian got a whiff of his subtle, yet spicy cologne. Memories of Colton in high school wanted to kick in, but Jillian pushed them away with a hard swallow and forced herself to focus.

Colton said, "So he wasn't there when Gerald got stung?"

"No."

"Is his statement in there?"

"Yes." Serena frowned. "A brief one. I don't think you'll find it very helpful. You'll probably want to go talk to the source and get it from him. But this is interesting, something that doesn't fit."

Jillian felt her heart thump a little faster. Had she been right?

Serena was pointing to a picture she'd pulled up on the screen. "See this right here? This is a picture of what he looked like by the time the photographer got there. He's bloated, swollen, and discolored. The poison in his system really did a number on this poor man. All of that looks exactly like it should for someone to die the way he did."

"But?" Jillian leaned in, the sight of the man making her stomach turn. What a horrible way to die.

"But," Serena glanced at her, then Colton, "this right here—" she used the end of a ballpoint pen to point to the dead man's wrist— "this is weird. I've worked on victims like this guy before and I've never seen this except on victims who've had their wrists tied up."

Colton leaned closer. "I don't see anything."

"Look closer."

Jillian finally saw it. A faint raised line encircled his lower wrist. Colton drew in a deep breath.

Serena zoomed out, then back in on the other wrist.

"The wrist marks match. There's no way that's an accident," Colton said.

Serena nodded. "I would say so."

Jillian's throat tightened. "But why?" she whispered. "If he went along with him and falsified the autopsy report, why kill him?"

125

"Because he was a liability," Hunter answered from behind her. Katie, Grayson, Dominic, and Hunter had gathered behind Serena so they could see.

Katie nodded. "If what you say is true."

"It's true." Jillian walked over to the couch and slumped onto it. She was so tired. She just wanted this to be over with. "Is it enough to exhume the governor's body?"

Colton pursed his lips and rubbed the back of his neck. He looked as tired as she felt. "Let me take it to the judge in the morning." He looked at Serena. "You're sure." Jillian noticed the two words weren't a question.

"I'm 99 percent sure those are rope burns."

"And yet his death was declared an accident," Colton murmured.

Serena shrugged. "I spent forty-five minutes sitting here, working on the pictures, zooming in and out, to be sure. This man's in very bad shape. It would be easy to miss if you weren't looking for something other than an accidental death. I was looking for something, anything. The ME who got this one wouldn't have thought anything was wrong. I might have come to the same conclusion. The rope burns do kind of blend in with the stings, the discoloration, everything." She looked at the picture one more time. "Yeah, it would be an easy thing to miss."

"Anything on his ankles?"

She shook her head. "I looked. But he did have a contusion on the back of his head. The ME attributed that to Gerald panicking and trying to get away from the bees. He tripped and fell on a thick tree branch, which might have rendered him unconscious."

Colton exchanged a glance with Hunter. Katie raised a brow and said, "Or the branch rendered him unconscious before the bees were sicced on him."

Jillian shuddered. "Really?"

"I say we talk to Gerald's wife and see what she has to say," Katie said.

126

"What about Conrad Pike's statement?"

Serena switched screens to read. She said, "Mr. Pike stated that they were to meet at the lake to go fishing. It's a rather isolated area but they'd been going there for years. Mr. Pike said he got an email from Gerald saying he was going to be late and could they reschedule for two hours after the original time. Pike responded that was fine. Two hours later, he showed up and found his friend on the ground. Dead." She scrolled down a little farther, then stopped and shrugged. "That's basically it. His death was ruled an accident and his body released to the funeral home."

"Sounds to me like you need to have a little talk with a few people," Grayson said.

Katie nodded. "I think we need to talk to Pike and also Gerald's wife. And Harrison Martin's wife."

Serena yawned and rubbed her eyes. "Y'all figure that out. I'm headed to my parents' for a good night's sleep. I've got to work tomorrow."

Jillian felt another familiar pang of guilt—and gratitude. She stood and wrapped her friend in a hug. "Thanks for doing this. I'm sorry we kept you so late."

Serena returned the hug with a fierce squeeze. "You're worth the lost sleep."

Dominic wrapped an arm around his fiancée's shoulders and led her toward the door. Looking back, his gaze met Jillian's. "We'll figure this out."

She nodded, appreciating—and marveling at—these people, willing to jump right in and help her. Even if one of them didn't totally believe her. At least he hadn't dismissed her outright and left her to fend for herself.

But she hadn't really thought Colton would do that. It wasn't his style.

Dominic and Serena were gone. Hunter hung back behind Katie and Grayson as they said their goodbyes. Grayson looked at Jillian.

"Don't you think it would be safer for you to simply go to the media about this?"

She frowned. "No. Not really."

"Why not?"

"Because I don't have proof. If I say anything now, it's my word against his." She lifted a brow. "And who do you think they're going to believe?"

"But wouldn't it be protection even without the proof? If you go public with what you say you saw ten years ago, then he'd be stupid to keep going after you. If anything happened to you, his guilt would be sealed."

"And I would still be dead." She shook her head. "I'm an investigative reporter. I don't throw out accusations I can't back up. The proof is there, I just have to find it."

Colton said, "And there's no reason to ruin a man's career over something that's not—" He broke off and Jillian felt hurt sweep through her. He still didn't fully believe her. She shoved the hurt aside as he finished with, "—something that could be a misunderstanding. No, we need to wait to go public."

Jillian felt her anger rise and tamped it back. In time, he would see. They all would. She grabbed her bag and stopped. "Can someone call me a cab?"

———■———

Colton gave a short laugh. "A cab. Right." He sobered and looked at Hunter, who hadn't had a chance to answer Jillian. "I'll take her. Why don't you follow behind and keep an eye out?"

Hunter nodded and pulled his keys from his pocket.

To Jillian, Colton said, "I'll take you to a hotel and arrange for the security to keep you safe." He considered telling Jillian she could just stay with him. He stopped himself. Probably not a good idea, being alone with her. And besides, whoever was after Jillian was aware Colton was helping her. The incident at the lake house still puzzled him—scared him. He thought he'd been careful to watch and make sure no one followed. He'd taken a circuitous route and had seen nothing.

His lips tightened. Obviously he hadn't been careful enough.

And it had almost cost Jillian her life.

Well, it wouldn't happen again.

They climbed into his truck and Colton watched Katie and Grayson's taillights disappear as she turned onto the highway.

Jillian gave a sigh and set the bag from Alexia between her feet. "Where are we going? I don't have any way to pay for a hotel room. I—"

He placed a finger on her lips and she went silent, eyes wide. He said, "I've got it taken care of, okay?"

Under the dome light of the truck, a wariness he didn't like flitted across her features. Then she sighed. "I guess I don't have much choice, do I?"

Frustration welled up inside him. "Why is it so hard for you to accept help?"

"I'm accepting help," she protested. "Everyone at your house tonight was there to help. And I'm grateful for it."

"Then it must just be me." He cranked the truck and felt his gut twist when she didn't protest *that* statement. He pulled his phone and sent a text to Hunter. When he got his reply, he pulled out of the drive, one eye alternating between the rearview mirror and the side mirrors, the other on the road.

They rode in silence for about ten minutes until Colton's phone rang. "You have a tail."

Colton narrowed his eyes, looking for it. "I don't see it. Just lights."

"Busy highway on a dark night. He's subtle, but he's there."

"Keep an eye on him. I'm going to take the next exit."

Jillian's troubled gaze drilled him as he kept Hunter on the line. He said to Jillian, "We might have a problem."

"Someone's following us?"

"Yes."

She nodded, her brow furrowed. "I'm not surprised. They need to get rid of me as fast as possible."

Colton whipped the truck off the highway at the next exit. Jillian watched the lights of a gas station grow closer, then whip past. Her heart picked up speed as the blood rushed in her veins.

"He still on me?" Colton asked Hunter.

"He's still there. I'm calling for backup."

The phone now on speaker, Jillian heard every word.

"Has he made you?" Colton followed the two-lane road and Jillian wondered where he thought he was heading. There was nothing along this lonely stretch of road except farms and trees and the occasional trailer park.

"No, don't think so. He's focused on you. I'm closing in to get the plate."

Colton slowed. "About two miles up ahead is the bridge. Right beyond is that old mill with the big parking lot. I'm going to turn in and swing around. Have backup meet us there. We'll trap him."

"10-4."

Colton's phone went silent and Jillian's pulse pounded. Was this the same guy from the lake house? And would that plan work? They rode in silence until Colton tapped his brakes. He said, "Okay, we're going to get away from this guy and then we're going to go on the offensive."

"What do you mean?"

The shattered back windshield cut off his response even as Hunter's warning yell came through the phone.

Jillian gave a short scream as Colton reached out to shove her head down below window level. The truck jerked to the right and she heard him yell, "Stay down!" As another bullet slammed into the passenger window behind her, Jillian grabbed the gun from the back of her waistband and heard Hunter's voice come through the speaker of the phone, now resting in the cup holder. She felt shaky and sick. Felt like her heart would beat straight from her chest.

"Don't!" Colton ordered. "Hunter's taking care of it." He spun the wheel to the left and rounded a corner. Jillian lost her grip on her weapon and grunted as it fell to the floorboard while the right side of her head snapped into the window. Pain shot through her forehead. Ignoring it, she leaned over and felt for the gun.

"Where is he?" Colton hollered.

"Right behind you. I've got his plate and backup is on the way. I'm going to try and run him off the road. Stay to the left. He's shooting from the driver's side through the open passenger window."

Colton pulled to the left. Jillian hung on and watched the side mirror from her awkward position of half on the seat, half on the floor. She could see headlights behind the other car. Hunter. Her breaths came in short pants. She sent up prayers as her fingers finally curled around the weapon.

A sudden burst of gunfire erupted behind them. Jillian tensed and ducked, expecting to feel shattered glass rain down over her. Instead, Colton swerved again. Urgency shadowed his voice. "Hunter! Hunter, you there?"

No answer.

Jillian dared a look in the mirror and saw only one set of headlights closing in fast. Fear made her blood hum. "Where is he? Where's Hunter?"

"I don't know. Hang on. Here he comes again."

"Where's your backup?"

"On the way," he gritted. "Hunter! Talk to me!"

Hunter remained silent and Jillian whispered a fervent prayer for him. Jillian's breath strangled in her throat as she clutched the gun, praying she could use it if she had to. Being a crack shot at targets on a range was a far cry from aiming at a living, breathing person with an eternal soul. But she wouldn't die without a fight, she had too much to live for.

It felt like an hour had passed since the first bullet hit the truck. In reality, the dash clock said only three minutes had elapsed. They now approached the bridge. "Almost there. Just another mile or so." He sped faster, hit the start of the bridge, and glanced in the rearview mirror. She saw his eyes widen even as he ordered, "Brace yourself."

Jillian felt the impact and heard the half scream, half yelp that escaped from her throat. The hard slam from the attacking car hurled them to the edge of the bridge and into the guardrail. Metal screeched on metal as Colton struggled for control of the vehicle. The end of the bridge came into view. Another vicious ramming from behind spun the truck off the bridge, straight toward a small embankment that led to a grassy field.

"Jillian! Hold on!"

Colton's cry registered as the truck slammed into the ground. Shards of pain raced through her right shoulder even as the air bag deployed and kept her from going too far. Her head snapped forward, then back. The sudden silence made her flinch.

The truck was upright, thank God. *We're alive. Thank you, Jesus, thank you.* Or were they? Smoke billowed from the engine and a new panic hit her. Was the truck on fire?

"Colton." Her voice came out in a squeak. She squinted against the smoke from the air bag. Dust covered her, coating the inside of her nose. She reached for the passenger door and breathed a sigh of relief when it opened without trouble. "Come on, Colton. Let's get out."

He didn't answer. The interior of the truck resembled a foggy morning on a mountain, the fine mist made it hard to see, but she finally was able to get her seatbelt off and move closer to him.

Colton lay slumped against the driver's window, unmoving.

"Colton!" she gasped. She placed a hand on his chest and pushed him gently back. His head lolled against the steering wheel, his face deathly pale. "Oh no. Don't you dare do this to me!" Desperate, Jillian's eyes went to the cup holder. His phone was gone, tumbling who knew where upon impact. *Oh dear, Lord, please help . . .*

Where had their attacker gone? She didn't remember the sound of a car driving off. Was he near? Watching to see if he'd killed them? She slid back toward the open passenger door. Ignoring the pain racing through her, she had one goal. To get help.

A crunch sounded to her right.

To Colton, she said, "Help's coming. Hang on."

She whirled to see a dark shape standing in the open door. Friend or enemy? She gulped. "I need your phone. Colton's hurt. Maybe dead."

"Good," the figure grunted as he lifted a hand. Jillian sucked in a deep breath as the barrel of the weapon centered on her forehead.

17

With a cry, Jillian threw her right arm up in a form block just the way she and Blake had practiced. The side of her forearm caught her attacker above the wrist, knocking the gun away and up as his finger pulled the trigger. The bullet pierced the roof of the car.

Jillian grabbed his arm and shoved it as hard as she could above her, using the edge of the car window as leverage. Pushing, straining, she held on as he reached in with his left hand to grab her by the hair.

She cried out again and new pain clamped down and radiated through her head. But she felt the gun bounce off her thigh as he lost his grip. Curses flew from his lips as he gave another yank on the hunk of hair. Jillian tumbled from the vehicle and fell to the ground.

He hauled her to her feet, his breath coming in pants, his curses assaulting her ears.

Pain radiated through Colton's head. He thought he heard Jillian calling his name. Nausea swirled in the pit of his stomach. Awareness returned with a suddenness that made him jerk.

Then wretch.

"Jillian." He meant the word to be a yell, but it came out a weak whisper. *Oh God, keep her safe.* He moved and shuddered as the pain rolled over him again. Ignoring it, he reached for the door and gave it a shove. It protested with a screech that made his stomach threaten again.

Sounds reached him.

Harsh breaths, a grunt. The sound of a punch?

"Jillian!" His shout ricocheted inside his head and blackness swirled across his vision.

His gun. Where was it?

Backup would be waiting at the old mill. They wouldn't know where he was. He and Jillian were on their own. And what had happened to Hunter?

The man who'd pulled her from the car dragged her a few more steps before her legs gave out. Her head throbbed from the impact with the window and his grip on her hair.

"Come on," he muttered, letting go of his hold on her hair, forcing her back to her feet, his clasp on her upper arm bruising and cruel. She could see his car at the top of the embankment and knew if he managed to get her inside, she was dead.

Jillian faked another stumble and went down to her knees, then to her left hip. Her move pulled him off balance and she gained a moment of freedom as his grip loosened and her right arm slipped free.

Just like Blake taught her, she brought her leg around and jammed her heel into her attacker's knee.

He screamed and went down beside her, his hands grasping, reaching. Scuttling like a crab, Jillian backed away, her fingers searching blindly for a weapon on the grassy slope. She had to get away, get help for Colton.

And she had to live for Meg.

Her head throbbed, her whole body felt like one big bruise.

The man hobbled after her, his curses ringing in the air. Frantic, she tossed her gaze one way, then the next. She could see Colton's truck resting nose down against the bottom of the embankment.

Movement caught her attention as she scrambled to her feet to limp-run back toward the vehicle. She had no idea what she would do when she got there, but she knew two guns were somewhere in the truck. Having a weapon was her only hope of surviving this. She looked back to gauge his progress.

He came toward her, his speed hampered by his knee. The mask obscured his features but nothing could hide the pain and fury burning in those eyes.

Above her, sirens sounded in the distance and her attacker froze, indecision evident in his stance. A split second later, he started toward her, eyes narrowed against the pain of his knee, his intent clear.

A shot rang out and he dropped to the grass.

Jillian turned to see Colton leaning against the truck, weapon held in a shaky grip. Relief flooded through her as the sirens drew closer. Then fear tripled her heartbeat as Colton slid down to sit on the ground, the gun still held on the man who now began to crawl up the embankment.

Colton aimed. Fired. And missed.

The man scrambled out of sight and a few seconds later she heard the roar of an engine and the screech of rubber on asphalt.

Jillian raced to Colton's side and dropped down beside him. "Colton, are you okay?"

"There's four of you," he muttered.

She looked at the blood running down the left side of his head. "You probably have a concussion." The sirens drew closer.

Colton closed his eyes, opened them, and squinted. "Stop moving."

"I'm not." She glanced up the hill and knew she and Colton were invisible from the road. "I'm going to flag down whoever belongs to those sirens."

"I'll come with you. He might still be up there."

"He's not. Now stay put." Without waiting for him to answer, she ignored her screaming muscles and began the climb back up the hill. Thank goodness it wasn't too steep or she'd never make it.

At the top, she leaned over and placed her hands on her knees as she waited for a sudden bout of nausea to pass. A fatigue like she'd never felt before nearly took her to her knees.

Gritting her teeth, she fought it off. The sirens were nearly upon her.

Standing, wincing at the pain shooting through her, she lifted her arms to flag down the approaching cruisers.

Jillian endured the poking and prodding at the hospital while answering as many questions as the doctor allowed before banning the authorities from her bedside. She knew she would be all right, but Colton had a head injury and that worried her, as did not knowing what had happened to Hunter.

Serena peeked around the edge of the curtain and Jillian burst into tears. She didn't know how her friend knew she was at the hospital, but she didn't care.

Serena didn't say a word, she simply walked over and wrapped her arms around Jillian's shoulders. "I'm so sorry this is happening to you." She waited as the tears slowed. When Jillian gave a weary sigh and rested her head against her friend, Serena whispered, "How's Meg? Have you been able to talk to her?"

Jillian shook her head. "I don't dare. I'm almost afraid to even think about her."

"I'd offer to contact her for you, but I think whoever's after you is still watching me."

That brought Jillian's head up. Her eyes searched her friend's. "Why do you say that?"

"Just a feeling."

"Yeah. I know that feeling." She frowned. "Is Dominic sticking close?"

"Like glue."

"Good."

And then their conversation ended as the curtain parted and a young lady about Jillian and Serena's age stepped inside. The doctor who'd done the earlier poking and prodding. Dr. Franklin, if Jillian remembered correctly. Dr. Franklin held a chart and wore a smile. To Serena, she said, "Do you mind if I have a moment with the patient?"

Serena started to leave and Jillian caught her hand. She said, "She can stay."

Dr. Franklin nodded. "All right. Well, your MRI was clear and the X-rays showed nothing broken. You're just bruised up pretty good. Good thing you had your seatbelt on."

"How's Colton Brady?" she asked. She had to know.

Dr. Franklin frowned. "I'm not sure. I don't remember seeing that name."

"He had a head injury, probably a concussion."

Still nothing registered in the doctor's eyes, although her brows dipped in concern. "He must have been seen by one of the other doctors."

"Could you find out?"

"I'm fine, Jillian." Colton's voice came from the other side of the curtain. "May I come in?"

Her heart leapt with relief. "Yes."

The curtain swung aside and his large frame filled the yawning space. Tears threatened again. "Are you sure you're all right?" she asked. The bandage on the side of his head didn't bode well.

But the smile that curved his lips soothed her worry. For him. She asked, "How's Hunter?"

"Alexia's with him now. The bullet missed him. He crashed his car, he's in a lot of pain, but he'll live."

Jillian's anger toward Frank Hoffman rose up within her. More than ever she wanted to see that man in prison. She clamped her lips tight and sent up a silent prayer of thanks for Hunter's life. That they were all alive. The comforting weight of Serena's hand in hers and Colton's presence brought thankful tears to her eyes. Blinking them back, she looked at Colton. "What's the plan now?"

He shook his head. "You like your plans, don't you? Okay, how about this? Plan A is to make sure you're safe. That's the priority. Once that's been established, we've got the plate of the car and his gun. We'll find him."

TUESDAY

18

Colton escorted her into the hotel suite in downtown Columbia and shut the door, wincing as it clicked behind him. The sound reverberated through his aching head.

He got on the phone with Katie. "Were we followed?"

"No, not that I could tell. You took the long, winding route, backtracked, and double-checked. I'm carsick, but you're good," she grumbled.

"Glad to hear it. Take a Dramamine."

"Your sympathy overwhelms me."

He felt a grin tug at the corners of his mouth as he hung up and told Jillian, "We weren't followed."

"Wonderful." She looked relieved, then worried again. "And they're sure Hunter's going to be all right?"

"Absolutely. The bullet just missed him, but startled him enough he jerked the wheel and ran off the road. His phone slid up under the seat and he couldn't get to it. But he was able to radio our route to the guys waiting at the mill."

"But the shooter got away," she muttered.

"Yeah, but at least we're alive to regret that fact."

"I've already thought about that." She touched the white bandage on his head. "Are you sure you don't have a concussion?"

"Nope."

She frowned. "But you were unconscious."

"But I don't have a concussion or at least if I did, it was mild enough that I don't have any aftereffects. One of the benefits of having a really hard head, I suppose." He was happy to see her lips quirk upward. "Doc said it was okay. I promise, it's really not that bad. Trust me, I've felt worse." He glanced around with satisfaction. He'd picked one of the nicest hotels in town. One with a two-bedroom suite—and a private hot tub in each room. His aching muscles begged him to hurry up and find the way to his. "Think this will work for you?"

She gave him a weary smile. "It's lovely. Much nicer than I needed, but thanks." Then she frowned and bit her lip. "I don't even know how I'm going to pay you back. I have no credit cards, debit cards, cash. Nothing."

"I'm not worried about that, Jillian." He held up a hand to stop the rush of words he could see coming. "I know *you* are, but I'm not, I promise." She snapped her lips closed and he said, "We'll talk later after this is over." He studied her for a moment, then stepped toward her. He settled his hands on her shoulders and was shocked at the tension he could feel running through her. "Do you ever relax?"

Jillian lifted a brow at him. "Not when I've just eluded an attempted-kidnapping-slash-murder and know that the guy could decide to strike again at any given moment." She shook her head and grimaced. "I've been looking over my shoulder and hiding for the last ten years. I wouldn't know how to stop."

He tightened his grip into a gentle massaging motion. He didn't want to hurt her, but her shoulders were bricks. She flinched when he pressed a little too hard on her right shoulder. "Seatbelt?" he asked.

"Yes."

"Want me to stop?"

"Not yet."

His fingers moved to the base of her neck and lingered as he worked the muscles. Her forehead dropped to his chest and he closed his eyes at the memories and renewed feelings for her. *God, help me. Show me the truth. Give me the strength to do what I've got to do.*

Jillian shifted and Colton opened his eyes to look down at her. The longing there nearly brought him to his knees. Her lips trembled and he lowered his head to capture them beneath his. She froze, then gave a soft sigh and kissed him back. And that was all it took. Old love mixed with new exploded through him and he knew, God willing, they would be together somehow. He wouldn't survive losing her again.

Slowly, reluctantly, he lifted his head. She opened her eyes and took him back ten years. That look she had now was the same one she'd given him when he'd told her he loved her and wanted to marry her.

Then she blinked and it was gone.

Regret, sorrow for losing what might have been, flowed through him.

But he thought she might have loosened up a fraction before she moved away with a nervous clasp of her hands. He almost smiled. *Don't get cocky, man,* he warned himself. He was surprised to find his enmity toward her had disappeared and that he was no longer angry or bitter about her leaving. He even understood it now. He didn't necessarily like it, but he understood it.

He fingered the straight dark brown hair and gave it a tug. "I miss your curls." A strangled sound escaped her throat and he rested his forehead against hers. "I just want to help you, Jillian. Let the past be the past." He paused, then said, "This may not be the time to bring this up, but . . ."

"What?" Curiosity darkened her eyes. The dark smudges underneath her lashes told him she needed to make her way to her room and fall into bed. But after that kiss he couldn't resist asking, "Do you think we can move forward from this point? Maybe see if we can build on what we used to have?" She froze, eyes widening like a deer in the headlights. His heart hit bottom and he gave a humorless laugh. Maybe he'd moved too soon. Maybe he'd misread her. Maybe the kiss hadn't meant as much to her as it did to him. "What? The idea's that distasteful?"

Jillian's eyes closed again and she shook her head as a red flush tinted her cheeks. "No," she whispered, "not distasteful at all. Just—impossible."

Ouch. That hurt. "Why?"

Tears coated her lashes. She opened her eyes and his heart nearly broke at the grief, the anger, the sheer helplessness he saw there. "Jillian?"

"It's just not possible right now, Colton. Trust me on that, okay? There are things you don't—" She bit her lip and looked at the ceiling as though trying to get a grip on her emotions.

He leapt on the two words that offered him hope. "Right now?"

She brought her hands to her face and swiped at the tears. "Yeah. Right now. Maybe we can talk again after all this is over." A pause. "Assuming I'm still alive to talk about it."

Colton reached for her in a sudden move that had them both wincing, but he didn't let go. Instead, he pulled her close, wrapping his arms around her and resting his chin on her head. "Don't start thinking like that. You'll be fine. We'll figure this out. Hopefully tomorrow will add to the answers we got today."

She didn't say anything, but she didn't pull away from him either.

Instead, he felt some of the tension start to finally leave her. His heart twisted and his blood hummed. Holding her close brought a rush of memories he was better off not thinking about. With an effort, he gave her a gentle shove toward the bedroom on the left. "Go get some sleep."

He waited until he heard the click of the lock before he allowed himself to give in to the weariness invading him. He also breathed a short prayer that whoever was after Jillian would have to take time to think of another plan before he struck again.

Because Colton needed time to recover and come up with a plan of his own.

A plan that would keep Jillian safe while proving his uncle's innocence—or guilt.

19

Morning arrived before Jillian was ready. The memory of Colton's words and their kiss simmered at the forefront of her mind. Oh how she'd wanted to promise him they could explore a future together, but she couldn't. Not until he knew about Meg. And not until she knew that he wouldn't consider Meg a mistake. The thought tightened her stomach into a knot.

Burying her face in the pillow, she did her best to ignore her protesting muscles, bruised shoulder, aching head, and spinning thoughts and return to sleep. However, the smell of bacon, eggs, and cinnamon tempted her enough to push back the covers, swing her legs over the side of the bed, and make her way to the shower.

Ten minutes later, Jillian dressed in a pair of denim capris and a pink T-shirt provided by Alexia. She rubbed the towel over her damp hair, then braided it. Her shoulders protested the movement and by the time she was done, she was ready for some ibuprofen.

A knock on the door startled her. Heart thumping, she told herself it was just Colton, but she couldn't help her initial reaction. Jillian opened the door to find Colton, freshly shaven and smelling good. She swallowed hard. "Hey."

"Morning." His eyes glittered and she could see the memory

of last night simmering in their depths. Nervous, she waited for him to say something.

Instead, he swept a hand behind him toward a cart laden with silver-covered dishes. "Room service."

"With a smile," Hunter called as he stepped in from the balcony.

Relief swept through her as she pushed aside her crazy reaction and entered the living area. To Hunter, she said, "You're really all right."

He nodded. "Yep. Had a raging headache all night from cracking my head on the window, but it's better this morning."

"I'm sorry," she whispered, the guilt flaring. Maybe she should have left well enough alone and just stayed in California.

Hunter's brows dipped. "It's not your fault, Jillian. This is what we do."

She nodded and bit her lip, not fully convinced. She couldn't help kicking herself for being so emotional. This is what *she* did as an investigative reporter. Only usually her life wasn't the one on the line. Or the lives of those she cared about.

"We're working on a plan of action for today," Colton said. "You want to join us?"

"Of course."

"Grab some food and have a seat. Dominic's on his way."

Jillian uncovered the food and fixed herself a plate. She took a seat at the table and began to eat. For the first time in a while, she realized she was actually hungry. "So, what's the plan?" she asked between bites.

Colton snagged a piece of bacon. "We're going to do some interviews today." He looked at his phone and frowned. "And I'm going to get ahold of my uncle."

She shot him a look but kept her mouth shut. He knew where she stood when it came to Frank Hoffman. His lips tightened, but he didn't say anything about it either.

He swallowed a sip of coffee, then said, "The plate was traced to a vehicle reported stolen about two hours before the attack on us."

"Of course it was. What about the gun?"

"Ballistics has it. I'm still waiting for the report on that. My guess is it's a street gun, purchased for this very purpose."

"To kill me?"

"Yeah. It'll be untraceable, but kept for evidence when we catch the guy. Might have some prints on it."

A knock on the door had Hunter and Colton reaching for their weapons.

Each took up residence on either side of the door. "Who is it?" Colton asked.

"Dominic."

Colton relaxed. He unlocked the door and stepped to the side. Dominic slipped inside and threw her a smile. "Morning."

"Morning," she said.

Dominic looked at Colton. "I talked to Rick about twenty minutes ago. He said he'd been trying to call you."

"I've been a little busy. What's up?"

Everyone found a seat and Jillian leaned back against the soft cushioned chair to listen. Dominic said, "He had his night team work on the lake house evidence—go over your truck."

Colton's right brow lifted. "And?"

"First thing, he ran the DNA on that blood sample from the driveway. Said the person wasn't in the system so until you have a suspect, we don't have anything to compare it to."

"Right. What else?"

"There were some fingerprints and we're still working on identifying them and matching them up. That may take awhile. We've ruled out you and Jillian and most of the cleaning crew, but we've got a few more to go through."

"Doesn't matter," Colton sighed. "He had gloves on."

"Figures. Could have told me that little detail before we started working the prints."

"Sorry. It's been a long couple of days."

"Yeah, well, this is going to make it longer."

Great. "What?"

"You had a tracker mounted right behind your license plate."

Colton went white and stilled, muttered something under his breath. Then ran a hand through his hair. "So, that's how he found Jillian at the lake house."

"And found you last night."

"When would he have put it on?" Colton asked. Jillian didn't think he was asking the group, but rather thinking out loud.

"The fire," she said. The thought came to her from nowhere, but she figured she was right.

He looked up at her and gave a slow nod. "I parked down the street out of the way. We got out and walked back to the scene." Disgust filled his face. "I can't believe I didn't check for something like that."

Hunter slapped him on the back. "No need to beat yourself up. You had no reason to believe he'd use you to get to Jillian at that point. Shake it off." He looked around. "But we need to move. He may have followed you to the hotel at one point."

"Fine." Colton looked at Jillian. "Go pack and let's check out."

Dominic pulled out his phone, stood, and moved toward the door to quietly take a call.

"Okay, so at least we know we need to be sure to check for bugs and GPS trackers from now on." Colton checked his phone, then looked at Hunter. "Did you get ahold of the dead medical examiner's wife? Mrs. Benjamin?"

"Sure did. She's expecting us in thirty minutes."

"Great."

"He what?" Dominic's explosive question grabbed their attention. Jillian saw the man's face pale as he moved toward a chair. He sank onto it and closed his eyes. He reached up and rubbed them as he listened. Finally he said, "I'll be there in a few minutes."

He hung up and the silence in the room made Jillian's ears hurt.

Dominic looked up and saw them staring at him. "Sorry. That

151

was Alexia. My dad's had a massive heart attack. They don't expect him to live much longer."

"Oh no!" Jillian cried. "I'm so sorry."

"Yeah." He looked torn as he stood and walked toward the door. "I'm going to go to the hospital. At least for a little while."

Colton jumped up and gave Dominic a man hug. "Get over there now. We've got this covered."

Serena had told her a little bit on the phone the last time she'd called. The man had been a lousy father and abandoned his family at one point, only to land in jail a few years ago. Upon his release, he'd made his way to town last month only to be diagnosed with Alzheimer's.

"Yeah, thanks. I'll be in touch." Dominic left.

Jillian watched as Hunter and Colton discussed plans to visit Gerald Benjamin's widow. Plans that didn't sound like they included her. "I'm going with you guys, right?"

Hunter looked up, the protest on his lips formed but not voiced. She glared at him and he backed down with a deferential wave at Colton.

"Jillian, you—"

She stood and planted her hands on her hips, and Colton sighed.

"Actually, you'll have to. We can't take a chance that the person tracked you here. Yeah. You're going, but you keep silent and do your best to fade into the background, okay?"

———※———

Colton's phone rang as he pulled to the curb. "Dominic?"

"Yeah, hey. I'm headed into the hospital, but I got a call on some information I'd requested and you need this before you talk to the widow."

"What's that?"

"Background on Benjamin."

"You found something?"

"Something big. He had a large deposit made into his account two days after the governor's car wreck was ruled an accident."

"Whoa." Colton blew out a breath. "Where did it come from?"

"A local bank. It was from the account of a Mr. Raymond Vance."

"How large a deposit?"

"Fifty grand."

"Any large sums going out?"

"Yeah. Fifty grand. To the hospital I'm getting ready to walk into."

The money went to the hospital? Colton frowned. "What was the money used for? Did he have some big medical need?"

"I'm not sure, but I'll do my best to find out while I'm here."

"Hey, you focus on your dad. I'll ask Mrs. Benjamin about the money."

Dominic agreed and hung up.

Colton stepped up to the door of the two-story house set in the middle-class neighborhood and rapped his knuckles against the freshly painted wood. Hunter and Jillian stood behind him. He had conflicting thoughts about bringing her along, but the truth of the matter was, he had no idea where he could leave her and not worry about her.

Within seconds, he could hear footsteps approaching.

The door opened and Mrs. Annabelle Benjamin questioned them with her eyes. "Detective?" Dressed in a black velour warm-up suit, she looked composed and classy.

"Yes, ma'am." Colton held up his badge. "I'm Detective Colton Brady. This is Detective Hunter Graham and Jillian Carter. Could we speak to you for a moment?"

"Of course, come in." They stepped into the foyer and waited for her to shut the door. She turned right into the formal living area and motioned for them to have a seat. "Now the detective I spoke with on the phone was rather vague, just said it was about Gerald's death. Could you be a little more specific?"

Colton leaned in. "We're investigating a case and it's led us to your husband's death."

"That was ten years ago."

"Yes, ma'am." He took a deep breath. "Is there anything you can think of about his death that struck you as . . . odd?"

Her lips tightened and she glanced back and forth between Colton and Hunter. Finally her gaze landed on Jillian who'd been sitting quietly, apparently doing her best to obey Colton's orders for silence and fading.

"Odd?" Her hands twisted together as she sat in the red-and-gray wingback chair. "Why do you ask? Ten years after the fact?"

Colton rubbed his chin. "We've recently come across some evidence related to another case that suggests his death may not have been an . . . accident."

She narrowed her eyes as she leaned in with nostrils flaring. "I've said that until I was blue in the face. Why listen to me now?"

"Ma'am, we weren't working that case back then and I'm sorry no one seemed to listen. Could you just go through it all with us? We're listening now, I promise."

Some of her defensive anger left her. "All right. Why not?" She stood and paced to the mantel to look up at the portrait hanging on the wall above. The man in the painting sat in a red leather chair behind a desk. He wore a lab coat, and the stethoscope around his neck looked like it belonged there. He had styled salt-and-pepper hair and blue eyes that sparkled with gentle humor. "He was a good man with a tender, godly heart. We have three children, all grown now, married and with children of their own." Sadness tightened the area around her eyes. "They'll never know him or benefit from his wisdom."

Colton thought he saw a sheen of tears in Jillian's eyes before she looked down at the floor. Hunter, although not without sympathy, shifted as though he wanted to hurry the woman along, but Colton shook his head in silent communication to let her talk.

Mrs. Benjamin continued. "That's what eats at me. That his grandchildren will never know him. He was only forty-nine when he died." She took a deep breath and turned to face them. "Yes, he was allergic to bees. But he always carried his epi-pen. Why was it still in the cooler? The minute he felt the first sting, he would have gone for the pen. And yet the cooler sat by the chair, untouched." She shrugged. "When I brought that up to the police, they didn't seem concerned. I went to the captain. He said it could be that Gerald wasn't near enough to get to the cooler. But I looked at the pictures of the scene. He was right in front of the chair, the cooler not more than three feet behind him. And where did the bees come from? That was Gerald's favorite spot. He always kept the area sprayed so he didn't have to worry about being stung. He loved the outdoors, but took precautions. And yet, a swarm of bees made their way to that particular area on that particular day." She shook her head. "I don't believe it."

"We didn't know he had the area sprayed," Colton said. "Did anyone else?"

"Just Conrad and Miranda."

"The Pikes?"

"Yes. Conrad was his fishing buddy. They were supposed to meet that morning at 9:00, but Conrad got an email from Gerald asking him to wait a couple of hours before coming because Gerald had a last-minute autopsy to do."

"Did he?" Hunter asked.

"Not that I knew about. When I questioned the hospital, they said there was one on the books, but Gerald never showed up."

"Then why would he send Mr. Pike the email if he didn't plan on doing the autopsy?" Jillian asked.

Colton shot her a look that he hoped conveyed his need for her to be quiet. But the question was a good one. He looked to Mrs. Benjamin and waited for her answer.

She said, "I've asked that very same question. I checked his email and there was definitely one sent to Conrad, but it didn't come from Gerald's computer." She sniffed. "I had a friend of ours who is a computer expert look into it and he said the email had been routed through so many IP addresses, it would take him days to figure it out. I told him to find out and would pay him for his trouble. He wouldn't take my money but managed to discover that the email was sent from a local internet café, Cooper's Corner, over on Green Street."

"That's on the University of South Carolina campus. There's no way to even trace that today, much less ten years ago," Colton said. Hunter nodded.

"Exactly." Mrs. Benjamin drew in a deep breath. "My husband would not go to an internet café to send an email when he could do it from home. The officers I spoke to suggested he was there for reasons he didn't want me to know about. Then I . . . received something in the mail that suggested I might not want to continue my questions. At that point, I dropped it and decided to pray about it." She offered a slight smile. "I wonder if you're my answer."

20

Jillian felt quite sure they were the answer. This woman had been praying ten years for justice. So had Jillian. Only Jillian knew the time had come to act on those prayers. *God, please allow me to survive this and bring justice to the men who deserve it.*

"He has people working for him," she said softly.

"What?" Mrs. Benjamin looked at her, seeming to really take a good look at her for the first time. Jillian ignored Colton's exasperated look and said, "Whoever killed your husband isn't working alone. He has friends in high places."

"You're not one of the detectives, are you?"

"No. I . . . saw something ten years ago. It's one of the things that's led us to you. I can't tell you what I saw yet, but trust me, your husband was murdered because of something he knew."

Grief flickered in the woman's eyes. "I couldn't figure out why someone would want him dead, but a few weeks before he died, he was jittery and constantly looking over his shoulder. He wanted me to leave and go visit my mother, or stay with one of the children, but I had a daughter recovering from an operation and didn't have time for that. And all of my questioning and prying wouldn't loosen his tongue." She swallowed hard. "I caught him praying in his study, his head bent—he was weeping and begging God for forgiveness."

"For what?" Hunter asked.

"I don't know." She shook her head. "It was such a private moment between him and God, I simply turned and walked to my bedroom, knelt by the bed, and added my prayers to his." Tears leapt into her eyes. "I don't know if you understand this, but even though I didn't know what Gerald was praying for, God knew. And he would hear my prayers too."

"Did Gerald ever tell you?"

"No." The woman lifted a hand to swipe a stray tear. Her forehead crinkled as she thought. "But he did say he'd made a decision. He said he'd done something he couldn't live with and now he had to make it right."

Colton said, "Did anything significant happen in the weeks before your husband's death? Something he would have needed a lot of money for?"

The frown stayed in place. She stared at Colton. "Why would you ask that?"

"Fifty thousand dollars was deposited into your husband's checking account on June 10th. On June 11th, that same amount was paid out to Baptist Hospital."

The woman went so pale that Colton rose, ready to catch her should she fall from the chair. She steadied herself and he lowered back into his seat. "Tracy's surgery."

"What?"

"My daughter had a kidney transplant." She rubbed her lips and closed her eyes. "We were swimming in debt, the house was mortgaged to the hilt. Tracy was dying and needed a kidney. She'd had a car accident as a teen and had to have her left kidney removed." She shrugged. "We were concerned, but she had another good kidney and people live productive, healthy lives with one kidney. Only now, her good kidney was barely functioning. Dialysis was working for her, but she'd let her insurance lapse and we didn't know it. She came to us and told us she needed fifty thousand dollars before the hospital would even consider putting her on the list for a transplant. I was devastated. We didn't have that kind of money, not with all of our debt. We were barely hanging on to the house. We started selling things off, asked neighbors to help collect donations." She gave a little self-conscious laugh. "On the outside, we looked like we had it all. A wealthy doctor's family. But on the inside . . ." She sighed. "On the inside, we were spinning our wheels to keep up the appearance. Only by this time, I didn't care." She snorted. "Appearances. What did that matter when my daughter's life was at stake?"

Mrs. Benjamin stood, walked over to the desk, and picked up the picture of a young woman dressed in a hospital gown. "Miraculously, my husband found the money. He borrowed it from my parents. I'll never know where they found the money—and they're not saying—but they gave it to us." She looked up. "And Tracy got her kidney. On June 14th. And my husband was a different man from that point on. Happy and depressed at the same time. Angry one minute, then apologetic the next. I asked and asked him what was wrong. And he wouldn't tell me. He started losing weight, spending time in his study praying and crying." She spread her hands in a helpless gesture that made Jillian want to hug her. "Then he died—and I was left with even more questions."

Colton said, "Well, maybe we can find some of those answers for you. Are you still in touch with Conrad Pike and his wife?"

Mrs. Benjamin smiled as she placed her daughter's photo back in its spot on the desk. "Yes. Every once in a while we'll have dinner, but it's not the same."

"Have you discussed your husband's death with them?"

"Of course. They also agree something wasn't right, but we just never got anywhere with the authorities."

"What are your parents' names?"

"Ray and Sheila Vance. Why?"

Before Colton could answer, Jillian asked, "What did you get in the mail that made you decide to quit asking questions?"

Mrs. Benjamin stared at them for a moment, then went to the desk in the corner of the room. She opened the bottom drawer and withdrew a manila envelope. "This."

With a raised brow, Colton took the envelope from her and opened it. Jillian scooted forward to peer over his shoulder.

Colton reached in and pulled out a photo. Jillian gasped and looked up at the woman who stood with her hands clasped in front of her. "Is that your daughter?"

"Yes. My other daughter, Amelia, with her husband and my grandson. She'd just had the baby about two months before that came."

Jillian shuddered. "So that's why you stopped asking questions and started praying."

"Exactly." The sweet picture of the family was marred by the big red bull's-eye drawn around it with the words, "Stop being nosy or they're next." Jillian read the words aloud.

"I put the envelope in the drawer and never said another word about anything. Until now."

Jillian looked at Colton, then Hunter. "So what do we do now?"

"Get this to Rick." Colton slid the picture back in the envelope. "I don't know that he can find anything off of here but we'll try." He looked at Hunter. "Will you get me an evidence bag from the car?"

"Sure." Hunter left and Colton looked at Mrs. Benjamin. "Thank you for talking to us."

"I want justice done." She tightened her lips and lifted her chin. "It's what Gerald would have wanted too." She frowned. "I just hope I haven't placed my daughter's family in danger."

"We'll keep it quiet."

She nodded and escorted them to the door where they met Hunter coming back from the car. Colton slid the envelope in the evidence bag and sealed it.

Mrs. Benjamin shut the door behind them and Colton looked at Jillian and Hunter. "Looks like we have a busy day ahead of us. Let's grab some lunch and then go see what the Pikes have to say." They made their way to the vehicle and Colton pulled his phone out. "Katie, I need you to make a visit to a Mr. and Mrs. Vance." He spouted the address Jillian figured he'd looked up even as he was interviewing Mrs. Benjamin. "Find out where that fifty grand came from that they gave to their daughter on June 10th, 2002."

He hung up and looked at Jillian. "Let's get some food. I'm starved."

21

Hunter climbed into his vehicle and pulled away from the curb. Colton settled in the driver's seat of his rental truck and cranked the engine, ready to follow Hunter's exit. Jillian sat beside him, staring out the window. The look in her eyes said she was thinking about what Gerald's widow had revealed.

He couldn't deny something weird was going on—or that someone was after Jillian. And his gut said his uncle was involved somehow. He simply couldn't deny the evidence that seemed to be unfolding with every question they asked and answer they got. He glanced at his phone. Still no call from Uncle Frank.

Jaw set, he punched in the man's number—and listened to it ring until it went to voice mail.

Pulling away from the curb, he shot a look over his shoulder and caught sight of a gray sedan sitting two houses down against the curb. It hadn't been there when they'd pulled up.

"What is it?"

Jillian's question jerked his attention to her then back to the rearview mirror. "Hunker down. There's a car parked on the curb behind us."

Fear shot across Jillian's features, but her jaw tightened and her hand sneaked around to her lower back where she kept her weapon. The gun had been rescued from the wreckage of his truck and returned to her. He wasn't sure that was such a great idea.

Colton got back on the phone, one eye still on the mirror as he pressed the gas to head down the street. The gray sedan followed. "I've got a tail. Gray sedan. Wait until I get out of the neighborhood, then let's play oreo. I want to know who's back there."

"Got it."

"Oreo?" Jillian asked.

"You'll see."

He sensed Jillian tense as he got closer to exiting the subdivision. The gray car was still behind him. To Hunter, he said, "He's not even trying to hide. Might just be a neighbor."

"Guess we'll find out."

Colton stopped at the stop sign, then pulled out into the street. He went fifty yards with the sedan still on his tail, then slammed on his brakes. The car behind him did the same but was nearly bumper to bumper with Colton. Hunter pulled up fast, trapping the vehicle between him and Colton. Colton opened the door to get out of his car. He told Jillian, "Stay down, will you?"

"Be careful."

The gray sedan's driver door opened and a tall man stepped out, hands held in plain sight. "Is there a problem?"

"Blake?" Jillian's screech nearly punctured Colton's eardrum. Before he could stop her, she was out of the car and racing for the hulk of a man who'd turned to face them.

When Jillian launched herself into the man's arms, something twisted inside Colton. Something dark and—green.

He was jealous. He took his time getting out of the vehicle since she didn't appear to be in any danger from the one she'd called Blake.

Blake. Who still had his arms around Jillian. "I take it you know this guy?"

Jillian spun out of the man's embrace to look back at Colton. "Yes. This is Blake Wyatt. Blake, Colton Brady and Hunter Graham."

Colton cast glances up and down the road. He saw nothing, but that didn't mean anything. "Can you get back in the truck? I don't like you exposed out here in the open."

"Sure." Jillian backed toward the vehicle without taking her eyes off Blake.

Colton wished he could read what she was trying to communicate. Whatever it was, Blake seemed to understand, because he gave her a slow nod, then shifted his eyes to Colton with an unreadable look.

Colton turned to Hunter. "I've got a new hotel arranged." He gave him the address. "Rendezvous there?"

"Yeah." Hunter speared Blake Wyatt with a look. "You follow me, I'll follow them. Clear?"

Blake's eyes narrowed. "Crystal."

Jillian figured she'd be grilled like a steak on the way to the hotel, but Colton kept his lips sealed and his jaw tight enough to shatter.

She swallowed hard and shook her head. When she'd realized it was Blake, she'd been terrified something had happened to Meg, but his first words were that Meg was fine.

Her pulse pounded in her ears. Why hadn't Colton said anything? Why did he look so angry? "You okay?"

"I'm great."

Which was a big no. "What's wrong?"

He lifted a brow and glanced at her then back at the road. "You're kidding, right?"

"No. Why are you so . . . angry and closed up?"

"Who's Blake Wyatt?" he clipped.

She lifted a brow and said just as short, "A friend."

A snort slipped from him. "A friend? Come on, Jilly, I saw the way he looked at you."

Jillian felt her hackles rise. "He looked at me like a brother looks at a sister, or a friend looks at another friend. There's nothing romantic about our feelings for one another."

For a moment he didn't say anything. Then he asked, "How do you know him?"

She sighed and glanced out the window. "He saved my life."

"How?"

"After I left home that night, I took bus after bus. I didn't stop to sleep or eat or . . ." She winced at the memories. "By the time I got to California, I was about to collapse." She waved a hand as though there were too many reasons to list. And there were. "I ended up in a homeless shelter, and one night when I went to take a shower, a man was there, waiting." She gulped and blinked at the awful memory. "He told me not to scream and he wouldn't kill me. I screamed anyway—and fought like a madwoman." She'd had a baby to protect. Colton's baby. A short laugh slipped out. "I think it shocked him and bought me enough time for someone to come to the rescue."

"Blake." His voice was subdued. She looked at his face and saw the tension in his jawline.

"Yes. Blake. He was out in the lobby, trying to talk his brother into coming home with him. When he heard the commotion, he beat security to the bathroom."

"You seem to have a lot of trouble with bathrooms."

The memory of the incident at the airport made her shudder. "Well, one every ten years isn't terrible. That first incident was a lot scarier." At least this time she'd been on her guard and known a few things about defending herself.

"So Blake rescued you and ten years later you're still friends with nothing romantic between you?"

His disbelief hurt—and roused her temper. "His wife wouldn't have appreciated it," she snapped.

Colton's eyes closed for a split second before he opened them

165

to watch the road. Then he shot her a sidelong glance. "His wife, huh?"

"Yep. His wife. A woman who ended up being one of the best friends I've ever had." Sara, who'd taken her in and accepted her. Who'd loved her like a sister and taken care of Meg when Jillian couldn't. Sara, who'd been diagnosed with ovarian cancer too late. Sara, who'd died in Blake's arms on a wintery night in December three years ago. Jillian crossed her arms across her chest and clamped her jaw tight as she stared straight ahead. The hotel came into view and Colton wheeled into the parking lot.

He pulled into the nearest spot and spoke into his phone. "Any tails?" After a short pause, he nodded and said, "Headed to check in, then up to the room. Meet you there."

Jillian grabbed the handle and shoved the door open.

Colton's hand clamped down on her left wrist and she turned to glare at him.

"I'm sorry."

His quiet apology slid under her anger, cooling her ire and easing some of the tension in her shoulders. "Don't judge me, please." *Not yet anyway*, she added in her thoughts. He had a right to be furious with her, but not about Blake.

He released her wrist and sighed. "Okay." But still his eyes bored into her. "I have a feeling there's so much you're not telling me." His phone buzzed and he broke eye contact to ask, "What have you got on Wyatt?"

Jillian tensed. He was checking out Blake? More listening. "Right. Okay. Thanks." He paused, then glanced at the entrance to the building. "Still clear?"

She waited, got a short nod from him, and slipped from the car.

Once inside the lobby of the hotel, she stepped to the elevator. Colton joined her. "Wyatt checks out clean."

"I never thought he wouldn't."

As Colton went to check in, Jillian scanned the lobby, her eyes taking in every detail, noticing each person who even glanced at her. Her blood hummed and her adrenaline surged.

The lobby doors swooshed open as Hunter and Blake entered. Colton waved them over as his phone rang. He snagged it. Pressing it to his ear, he once again did a lot of listening as they rode to their floor.

The elevator dinged and Hunter stepped out first. Colton put his phone away and Blake held her back until Hunter gave the all clear.

Jillian shook her head at all the drama. She accepted that it was necessary, but she wanted her life back.

Once they reached the room, she looked around. It was practically a twin to the one they'd just left. She turned to the guys. "I need a few minutes." She went straight into one of the bedrooms and shut the door. Her heart thudded, pounding out a familiar rhythm of fear and anxiety as she set her small bag on the bed. What was she going to do? Blake was here. He'd obviously remembered that Colton was the name of Meg's father. What if he slipped up and said something before she had a chance?

She slumped on the bed and dropped her head into her hands.

She had to tell Colton about Meg. Jumping to her feet, she faced the mirror and took a good hard look at herself. "You can do this. You knew this day was coming. It's time for the truth to come out." The words bounced off the mirror. "Truth. That's what you're here for, remember?"

"Jillian? You okay?" Colton's words floated through the wooden door.

"Yeah, I'll be out in a second."

"I've got some information to talk about and I don't want to repeat it."

"Coming."

Right. Okay. The pep talk helped. Prayer would do more. She bowed her head and went still for a full minute, petitioning the

One she'd come to trust. The One who could protect. Elohim. Almighty God.

Jillian opened the door and came face-to-face with Blake, his fist lifted to knock. "Are you all right?"

"I'm fine." Jillian lifted a brow. "Is she fine?"

"Yes."

Relief stooped her shoulders for a brief moment. Then she stood straight and slipped around him, putting the problem his presence presented on the back burner for the moment. She looked at Colton as she took a seat on the couch. "What information do you have?"

"Dominic just called. We have the identity of the man who attacked you in the airport bathroom."

1:45 PM

Frank crumpled the note that had arrived an hour ago. He'd barely made it to the mailbox before Elizabeth.

"I'm perfectly capable of getting the mail, dear," she'd stated with exasperation tinting her voice. He wouldn't have been a bit surprised if she'd rolled her eyes.

"I know that." Without bothering to try to come up with an elaborate excuse, he shoved a few pieces of junk mail at her. "I'm expecting a check from a contributor."

Forcing a smile, he motioned for her to go ahead of him into the house. With another puzzled, slightly irritated look over her shoulder, she shook her head and walked into the foyer. Frank shut the door behind him and turned left to head to his office.

"Frank?"

He stopped and turned. "Yes?"

"Have you talked to Colton yet?"

"No, why?"

She gave a delicate shrug. "I was just wondering what he wanted. That's all."

"I'll give him a quick call." Anything to get away from her prying eyes. He thought about the papers hidden away in his safe. Maybe it was time—

No. Not yet. After the election.

"What do you have there?" she asked, pointing toward his hands.

Frank's fingers curled around the mail. "What do you mean?"

"You're gripping it like it's gold and someone's going to take it away from you."

His anger flared at her mocking smile. "Don't be silly, Elizabeth. I'll be in my office."

Without another word, he turned on his heel and strode down the hall to his haven. He shut the door just as his phone vibrated.

He snatched it from his pocket. "Hello?"

"She's got a protection detail to rival the president's," the voice rumbled in his ear.

"What now?"

"I'm having trouble getting close to her. She's got protection all over her. You'd think the woman was someone important."

Silence echoed back at him. Then his partner said, "I saw something interesting this afternoon. Something that might be her weak link."

"What's that?"

"I was trying to get close but was maintaining a distance while they were at Gerald's house."

"Gerald's house?" Frank felt a coronary coming on.

"Don't worry, she can't tell them anything." As Frank was about to protest, the man went on, "Anyway, someone else was tailing her. Her watchdogs clamped down on him."

"Someone else? Who?"

"I don't know who he is, but Jillian was happy to see him, gave him a big old hug. Like she hadn't seen him in a while."

"We need to know who he is."

"I'm working on it."

"What else?"

"I'm guessing if they talked to Mrs. Benjamin, Conrad Pike and his wife are somewhere on their list to talk to."

Frank scoffed, but it lacked confidence. "They don't know anything."

"I'll keep you posted."

Frank hung up and tucked the phone back into his pocket with a frown. Too many people were too close to Jillian. He couldn't kill them all.

His eyes landed on the newspaper he'd just read this morning and an idea started to take shape.

He opened his fist and laid the crumpled note on his desk. Using two hands that weren't quite steady, he smoothed the bumps and ridges until he could read, "THE CLOCK IS TICKING. SOON THEY WILL KNOW WHAT I KNOW."

Yes, it was always good to have a Plan B.

22

"Nicholas Tremaine," Jillian repeated. "Who's that?"

"Dominic's digging into it while he's at the hospital with his father. What we now know is the man was former Navy. He wasn't in the AFIS fingerprint system. Dominic had the idea to check the military database and found him. We're looking into his unit and will see if any connections turn up," Colton said. "Except for one incident, the man had a stellar record, but was something of a rogue. His last psych eval showed some red flags, and when told he would have to go through mandatory counseling, he finished his term and opted to get out. Honorably, but with that kind of screwup . . ." He shook his head. "You don't get over that."

"What kind of red flags?"

"A mission that went south. He was a sniper. He hit the wrong target."

"What?" Blake snorted. "That's Navy for you."

Colton lifted a brow. "Hunter said you're Army."

"Yep."

"Special Forces."

"Yep."

Even if Hunter hadn't passed on the information, Colton would have guessed it. Blake had a tenseness, a special watchfulness and constant awareness of what was going on around him that shouted military. He looked at Jillian. Kind of like her. Only she wasn't military. Was Blake the one who'd taught her how to use a gun? Defend herself? Look for the extraordinary in the ordinary, like disturbed birds suddenly taking flight?

Probably.

He told Blake, "Well, to give the man his due, he was given the name by his superiors. They just had the wrong name."

Blake winced, a flicker of compassion showing in his hard blue eyes. Maybe the man wasn't all bad. He shook his head. "Guess I can see how that could mess a dude up."

"What's his relationship with your uncle?" Jillian asked, her voice soft, yet firm.

Colton stiffened. "No relationship. Why?"

"Did you ask?"

No. He hadn't. He hadn't even thought about it. Keeping his gaze on hers, he pressed Dominic's speed-dial number. When he answered, Colton said, "One more thing. See if you can find out if there's a connection between Tremaine and my uncle."

"I thought about that. Was going to do that anyway, but now I don't have to sneak it."

Ouch. "Right. Thanks."

"Just kidding. I knew you'd ask for it." Approval tinged his friend's voice, but it still rankled Colton that Jillian had to remind him to check that. Maybe he needed to start wrapping his mind around the possibility that his uncle might have something to hide. Like murder. And remove himself from the investigation. "Yeah."

He hung up and Jillian bit her lip and dropped her gaze. She murmured, "Thanks."

"Sure." Colton sighed.

As soon as he hung up, his phone buzzed again. He watched Jillian stand and walk to the window. She stood to the side, moving the curtain a fraction in order to look out.

Caution.

As Colton answered the phone, his stomach clenched when Blake strode over to stand next to Jillian.

"Yo! Brady, you there?"

Rick. "I'm here." Colton turned his back on the pair so he would be able to concentrate. "What is it?"

"Bad day?"

Colton hadn't meant to sound so sharp. "Something like that, sorry."

"Maybe this will help make things a little better." A pause, a shuffle of papers, then, "That scrap of material you pulled from the tree is pretty interesting."

"Why's that?"

"Because it had paint on it."

That was interesting? "Paint?"

"Yeah, the kind used on boats."

That stopped him. Colton asked, "So we're looking for someone who's been painting his boat, or someone who visited a boat being painted, or—"

"Okay," Rick interrupted. "It could be anyone, but it's probably a good place to start."

Colton's fingers tightened around the phone. His uncle owned a boat. Had it been freshly painted? He blew out a frustrated breath. "We've got to find this guy, Rick. He's not going to stop until she's dead."

He could almost see the man nodding. "I know. I'll keep you posted on anything else I can come up with."

"Thanks."

"Oh, and Colton?"

"Yeah?" He turned back toward the window again.

"I had a nice chat with your captain."

Colton narrowed his eyes on Jillian and Blake. The two were in deep conversation, heads bent toward one another. "So I hear."

With Blake Wyatt in the hotel room, the air felt thick, like he was trying to breathe through a pillow.

"I just think it's important that law enforcement stay up to date on the latest technology available to them."

"I understand that. And can appreciate you looking out for us like that."

A pause. "What are you up to?"

Colton grinned. "What do you mean?"

"You're up to something." He could almost see Rick's furrowed brow as he paced the floor of the lab. "You guys need this. You're not going to get out of it."

"Wouldn't even try."

Silence echoed through the phone line. Then Rick muttered, "I gotta go. I'm watching my back, though."

"Rick, Rick." Colton clicked his tongue. "So paranoid."

"Where do you think I learned it from?" he snapped.

The phone clicked off and Colton laughed out loud. Then looked over to see Jillian and Blake still talking.

He did his best to control the little green monster inside, but didn't have much success. Jillian had told him the man was married. But to some men, a wedding ring didn't mean squat. Colton decided he'd keep a close eye on Blake, figure out what his game was—and his position in Jillian's life.

However, the mutinous expression on her face at the moment didn't bode well for the man on the receiving end.

Colton couldn't help the dart of satisfaction that shot through him.

"Coming out here was a dumb move," Jillian hissed. "This was not part of the plan. What about Meg?"

Blake narrowed his eyes. "Meg's fine. She's safe."

"She *was* safe. They're watching every move I make. I guarantee they saw me and my brainless greeting of you out there in the middle of the street." She shook her head and shut her eyes as a tremor rippled through her. How could she have been so thought-less? So careless? Why hadn't she stayed in the car and pretended she didn't know the man?

Hindsight was twenty-twenty, as they say.

Only now, she had to consider that whoever was after her could find out who Blake was, where he lived, and everything else.

Including Meg's location.

Then again, she could be worried for nothing. If no one had been watching . . .

But she couldn't hinge her hopes on that. They'd already man-aged to find Julie Carson, an alias she'd adopted as soon as she'd crossed the California border. She still didn't know what tipped them off.

"Everything okay?"

Jillian whirled to see Colton standing too close for her comfort. She moved aside to get control of her heart rate. Part of it had to do with Colton's nearness. The other part, the majority of it, had to do with the fact that one of her best friends could have put her daughter in danger. She forced a smile. "It's been a rough couple of days, Colton. It's scary how this person after me seems to know my every move and doesn't care who gets in his way when he's coming after me." She shrugged. "Other than that, I'm good." Colton frowned at her and she grimaced. No need to take her bad mood out on the man who was doing his best to help her. "Sorry."

His expression softened. "It's all right. I'm a little snappy my-self today." He looked at Blake and his eyes cooled. "How long are you here for?"

Blake lifted a brow. "For as long as Jillian needs me."

Colton grunted and turned to Hunter, who had his phone pressed to his ear. When Hunter waved Colton over to share in the conver-sation, Jillian grabbed Blake's forearm. "You have to move Meg. If she's at the farm, it's not safe. You can be tracked to it."

His brow furrowed, eyes narrowed, Blake said, "You didn't tell me everything, did you?"

Jillian didn't break eye contact with him. She kept her voice even. "No. I didn't."

Blake ran a hand down his face and paced to the window, then back. "You said you saw a murder and that person was after you and you had to get out of town to keep you and Meg safe. You never mentioned how powerful these people were."

"I know," she whispered with a glance at Hunter and Colton.

"You really think they'd go all the way to California to get her just to use her against you?"

"With everything in me, I believe it." She raked back some loose hair and tears filled her eyes. She blinked them back. "It's been days since I've talked to her." Longing for her child swelled to the point she thought her heart would rupture. "Days, Blake. I miss her so much, it's like a piece of my heart has been cut out."

An expression she'd only seen in him once before flitted through his eyes. Fear. Not for himself, but for the little girl he'd helped raise and loved as his own. He finally got it. He gave a short nod. "I'll take care of it."

WEDNESDAY

23

"His name is Blake Wyatt."

"What else?" Frank pulled out into the traffic stream and headed for the capitol building.

"He's from Somis, California. Has a huge equestrian ranch out there."

"Is that where Jillian was living?"

"From what I can tell."

"Do some more background on this Wyatt character. I want to know what his connection to Jillian is."

"I've already got a friend working on that."

"And what have you found out?"

"There's a kid living at the ranch, a girl about ten years old. She's there along with Blake's mother."

"Blake's kid?"

"No, that's the funny part. Blake's wife died about three years ago. They never had children."

Frank rubbed his chin. "And this matters how?"

"I think the girl belongs to Jillian."

Frank came to attention. "Well, that puts a different light on things, doesn't it?"

"Definitely."

"When are you going to grab her?"

A pause, then, "I've already been in touch with your PI. He's on the way to the ranch as we speak."

Finally. A way to get to Jillian.

"What about Jillian's father?"

"I checked. He's out of town right now at some kind of marketing conference and won't be home for another three days . . ."

"So we need the girl."

"That was my thought."

"Let me know when you have her."

Frank turned into the parking lot and shut off the car. He climbed out into the heat and felt an instant sweat break over his forehead. He forced a smile to his lips and pulled in a deep breath of the humid air.

As he walked into the building, he nodded and shook hands with those who greeted him, never revealing the turmoil rumbling inside him.

After all, appearances were everything in his position.

He entered his office, took his seat, and unfolded the paper a page had left on his desk. Frank smiled. Whoever had come up with the idea of pages on the floor—college students looking to get a foot in the door of politics—had been a very smart man. At the press of a button, he had someone at his beck and call for as long as he sat in this seat.

Then Jillian's terrified, accusing stare from ten years ago intruded. Frank's memory of that night was so fuzzy, but he clearly remembered the argument with the governor, grabbing the gun off the wall, and shooting the man. He remembered Jillian and her running from him.

But not much after that.

He drew in a deep breath. *Why* couldn't he remember any more than that? *Why* was everything so vague, like it was a dream he was trying to remember instead of something he'd lived through?

Frank looked at the paper. The idea that had bubbled to the surface earlier morphed into an outright plan. He picked up the phone and dialed the number. When his contact came on the line, he said carefully, "You know, there is a high school reunion next Saturday."

"Yeah?"

"Several of our young people will be attending."

A pause. "I see. Should be a night to remember."

"Indeed."

Frank hung up. He straightened his tie and glanced at the clock. What did Colton know? What did he believe?

He breathed out a deep sigh.

Maybe it was time to stop avoiding his nephew and find out.

Colton set his feet on the coffee table and leaned back. The sun had risen once again. He couldn't keep up with the days passing. It seemed like he never had enough hours to do all he needed to do before his body begged for rest. If he didn't have to sleep, he could do so much more.

Knowing Jillian was safe with Blake, Colton had gone into the office this morning and worked on his other cases. Or rather did his best to delegate the ones he hadn't been able to a couple of days ago.

But now he sat in the living area of the hotel suite sipping a cup of dark coffee and thinking. The Pikes weren't answering, Jillian had been as jumpy as a junkie in a room full of cops, and Colton was tired of analyzing his feelings for the girl he'd never forgotten. She'd finally slipped into her bedroom, saying she needed some time alone.

That was fine with Colton. He needed some time himself. Time to wrap his mind around the fact that his uncle might possibly be a killer.

It was incomprehensible. Uncle Frank had been a big influence in Colton's life, supporting him when his parents didn't, letting him crash in a spare bedroom when the tension at home had become too thick to deal with. A murderer?

Yet Colton knew even good guys could turn bad.

But Uncle Frank?

He didn't want to believe it, but he had to know.

Colton glanced at the clock on the wall. 2:15. He flicked a look toward the closed bedroom door. Blake had disappeared into the other bedroom thirty minutes ago when his phone rang. Last night, Blake Wyatt had insisted on staying and helping keep watch over Jillian. Colton had chosen to let the man have the room while he took the couch. The couch that was smack dab in between Blake's room and Jillian's.

Jaw tight, Colton punched in his uncle's number one more time. The cell phone clicked immediately over to voice mail. He tried the home number.

To his surprise, his uncle answered on the second ring. "Colton, how are you, son?"

"Full of questions. How are you?"

An awkward silence descended for a moment before Frank gave a short laugh. "Well, not full of answers if that's what you're hoping to hear."

"I need to talk to you about something and I need to do it face-to-face." He glanced at the clock. "Are you available for a cup of coffee around 3:00?"

"Hold on a second, let me check my calendar." Frank loved his iPhone, but Colton knew he used a small binder where he wrote down all of his appointments. "Sorry, son. I've got a 3:00 meeting that's going to take me straight through to about 4:30. Then after that I have a doctor's appointment."

"What about supper?"

"Nope, I have that fundraiser dinner tonight from around 6:30 till 9:00 or so."

Colton grimaced. "Come on, Uncle Frank, you've never made me work this hard to get some time with you."

A light sigh filtered through the line. He heard a crinkling sound like his uncle had turned a page in the calendar. "How about I call you? I'll try to clear some time for tomorrow."

"Uncle Frank . . ."

"It's the best I can do, son."

He'd give the man one more chance. "All right. But call me before the fundraiser."

"Sure, sure. See you soon."

Colton heard the click and hung up his own phone. Weariness tugged at him. Uncle Frank's avoidance wasn't earning the man any kind of trust points as far as Colton was concerned.

Determination hardened inside him. He was going to talk to his uncle tonight. If the man didn't call him back before the fundraiser, he'd track him down.

The next few hours passed in a blur of room service and phone calls. Rick reported nothing new. Colton kept an eye on the clock while he read over a case file he had to be in court to testify on. Jillian's restlessness came through loud and clear.

When she wasn't pacing, she was typing on a laptop Blake had managed to provide.

"No internet or email," Colton had warned.

"I know."

"It's secure," Blake assured him, but Colton wasn't taking any chances.

And for the next four hours, she typed, putting every detail she could remember about that night into the document.

Every once in a while, she'd stand and stretch. She'd walk to the window, hold herself to the side, and crack the curtain.

The slight bulge under the back of her shirt said she didn't feel secure enough to leave the gun in her room. He frowned.

And glanced at the clock again.

"He still hasn't called, has he?"

183

Colton looked up to see Jillian staring at him. He sighed. "No."

"So what are you going to do?"

"Find him." Colton dialed his uncle's cell phone.

No answer.

He tried the house.

When his aunt answered, he grimaced. "Hi, Aunt Elizabeth. Is Uncle Frank around?"

"No, he's already left for the fundraiser. I didn't go with him because I'm not feeling well."

Colton's brow lifted. His aunt? Not feeling well? "Since when did that stop you from attending a fundraiser?"

Her short, humorless laugh filtered through the line. "Since my head decided it wanted to explode earlier. I'm better now, though." She paused. "And Frank still hasn't called you?"

"No, ma'am."

"How odd."

Odd. Yeah. That was one way of looking at it. He changed the subject. "Has Uncle Frank recently had his boat painted?"

"The boat? Why are you asking about the boat?"

"I just need to know, Aunt Elizabeth."

"Well, no, he hasn't had it painted. Not that I know of, anyway. I mean, he hasn't said anything to me about it."

Colton breathed a relieved sigh. "Okay, good."

"Then again, that doesn't really mean anything these days."

Something in her tone snagged his attention. "Everything all right between you two?"

She gave a breathless laugh. "Of course, silly. He's just so busy with the campaign and work that we haven't had a whole lot of time to spend talking. Hopefully after the election, we'll have a few minutes to breathe. And talk."

He rubbed a hand over his chin. "Where's the fundraiser?"

"At the Embassy Suites on Stoneridge."

"Are my parents there?"

184

"No, not this one. They had something else on the calendar tonight. I think it was one of your mother's charity dinners."

"All right. Thanks."

"You really should talk to them more, Colton."

Her gentle chiding made him wince. "I know."

She must have decided to let him off the hook because she said, "Well, he'll be finished around 9:00 and Ian will pick him up and bring him home. You want me to tell him to call you when he gets in?"

"I'm not too far from there. I think I'll go see if he'll let me give him a ride home. We could get a good talk in during that time." And the man wouldn't be able to brush him off or come up with a reason he couldn't spend a few minutes with Colton.

"All right. I'll let Ian know you're going to pick him up."

Colton smiled. "Thanks."

He hung up and walked over to rap on Jillian's door.

After a second, he heard rustling, then her beautiful face appeared in front of him. She'd taken a shower and had a towel wrapped around her head. "Are you all right?"

"Yes." She grimaced. "I thought a shower might help me relax enough to get some rest, but it's not working so well for me right now."

He nodded. "I'm going to see if I can catch my uncle. He's just a few blocks over at the Embassy Suites finishing up a fundraiser. I'm going to see if he'll let me give him a ride home so we can talk."

She frowned and her face tightened. "I want to go."

"No." Colton shook his head and held up a hand. "No way. Let me talk to him first."

"He'll deny it." Her jaw jutted.

Of course he would. Especially if he was innocent. Which Colton found himself doubting as the hours passed and each new piece of information came to light. "How do you feel about being left with Blake?" Colton didn't like it one bit, but he needed to confront

185

his uncle. Now. And Blake certainly had the skills to protect her if something happened. Which it wouldn't. *Please, God.*

She shrugged. "I'm fine with it. But it doesn't matter because I'm going with you."

"Jillian, that's a really bad idea. I won't be gone long."

She bit her lip. "I want him to look me in the eye and deny it."

"Not yet. I need to do this alone."

She opened her mouth to protest and Colton braced himself for an argument. Then she pressed her lips together and nodded. "Fine."

"Really?"

"Go. Before I change my mind."

"I need to tell Blake—"

"I'll take care of Blake."

Colton gave a short nod and left without another word.

24

Jillian locked the suite's door behind Colton, giving an absent twist to the dead bolt.

"Everything all right?"

She turned to see Blake standing in the doorway of the second bedroom. She'd convinced Colton to let the man stay, that he'd be a help in the investigation and not a hindrance. Colton hadn't like it, she could tell, but he'd given in when she hadn't budged on her stance. She gave Blake the once-over, studying him, staring at him. He shifted and frowned. "What is it?"

"Colton's jealous of you." She said it with wonder.

"Oh. That. Yeah, I noticed." He smirked.

Jillian shot him a reproving glance. "Stop it."

"Can't help it."

"You're the brother I never had, Blake. There's never been any romantic feelings between us. Why can't Colton see that?"

Blake sighed and turned serious. "Because he's a man in love and you've been out of his life for the last ten years. I've been *in* your life and it's got to make him nervous."

Rattled, she jerked her head up and the towel wobbled, almost falling off. "He can't still love me. I'm not the same person I was when I left here ten years ago."

"Maybe not in some ways, but in all the ways that matter to him, you are."

"He's going to hate me when I tell him about Meg," she whispered.

"Yeah, he's going to be mad about that."

Jillian grimaced, but Blake was honest to a fault.

"But," Blake continued, "he'll get over it. He's seen the danger you're in firsthand. He'll understand why you did what you did."

"He's going to confront his uncle about everything."

Blake frowned. "What? Now?"

"Yes." She bit her lip. "Blake, Frank Hoffman is bad news. He's evil wrapped up in a pretty package. He's killed one man that I know of. Probably had a hand in killing a couple more." She paced to the window, then back. "What if Colton confronts his uncle and Frank has him killed?"

"Hoffman's politicking. I doubt he'll do anything right there at the hotel."

"But what if he does? Frank's never seemed like a very stable man. What if Colton confronting him sends him over the edge?"

"I think you're grasping at straws."

"Maybe. But what if I'm not?"

His phone buzzed. Blake looked at the text and paled.

"What?" she asked. "Is it your mother? . . . Meg?"

Blake cleared his throat and shook his head. "No." He turned the phone around so she could read the message. WE HAVE LITTLE MEG AND HER FATHER'S NEXT. TO SHOW YOU WE'RE SERIOUS, HE DIES TONIGHT.

Her knees gave out and she sank to the floor.

She felt Blake's hands on her forearms. "How do they know? Where did they get your number?" she cried when she finally found her breath.

She looked at her friend and saw agony written on his now-ashen features. "Me," he whispered. "Just like you feared, they traced her through me."

"Then they have your address. That's how they knew where Meg was," she whispered.

He swallowed hard and picked up his phone. One button speed-dialed his mother. Jillian waited, so tense she thought she might simply snap in two. Finally he spoke. "Mom, pick up if you're there. Meg's in danger. You know where to go. Go now."

He hung up and dialed her cell phone and left the same message.

"But how do they know Meg's mine?" she cried.

Blake held her shoulders. "Be strong. It could be a trap. They might not know—they might be guessing."

"Might be," Jillian whispered.

"Because of me." He ran a hand over his face. "They've got serious connections to trace me."

"Oh Blake . . ."

"I didn't know I needed to come under cover, Jillian. I'm sorry. If I'd known more—" He broke off and paced. "You didn't tell me . . ."

"I know. I know I didn't tell you. You're right. It's not all your fault. I'm sorry," she said. "I should have trusted you with the whole truth. After everything you did for me and Meg, I—"

He stopped his agitated pacing and placed a finger over her lips. "It's okay. Or at least it will be."

"But how?" she cried.

"I've got contacts. Let me call them. Try to keep it together until we find out something for sure."

She shuddered and gave a short nod. "Yes. Of course. You're right again." She swiped a hand down her face and ordered herself to calm down. To think. "I've got to warn Colton," Jillian murmured. "He's in danger and he doesn't even know about Meg." She looked at Blake. "Call him, please. Then try your mother again."

"What are you going to say? You haven't told him about Meg yet. How will you explain the letter?"

"I don't know, but that doesn't matter right now if he's in danger. Call him."

Blake dialed the number. After a minute, he shook his head. "No answer."

"If he's talking to his uncle, he won't." She bit her lip. "Can you send him a text?"

"Sure." Blake typed, then tapped the screen and began scrolling. "I'll call Hunter and Katie and tell them I have reason to believe Colton's in danger."

Jillian made a decision. Before Blake had a chance to look up from the number he was dialing, she spun on her heel and headed into the bedroom to get her shoes and phone.

And lose the towel around her head.

It was time to shed what was left of Julie Carson and find Jillian Carter once again. The new Jillian Carter. The one who'd learned to stand up for herself and dig in for the long fight to get at the truth of whatever she'd been investigating.

They'd threatened her daughter. "We need to find out if Meg is really in danger or if they're just trying to scare us. Try your mom again."

"I got Hunter. He's on his way over to the hotel. Katie didn't answer, but Hunter's about twenty minutes away."

Jillian shivered. "Colton may not have twenty minutes." She grabbed her tennis shoes and walked out to the living area.

"Wait a minute," Blake said. "I'm guessing Colton probably told you to stay here."

"He did," she said as she brushed past him to sit on the couch and slip her shoes on her feet. "But if he's heading into trouble, I owe it to him to go there with him. I've wasted ten years hiding. This is why I came back. I can't just sit here and wait for things to happen. I *need* to *make* them happen." She lasered him with a look. "I *need* to know if Meg's in danger." Her inability to see that Meg was safe ripped her insides to shreds. "I also *need* to make sure Colton is safe." She stood and combed her fingers through her hair, shaking it, hoping it fell like it was supposed to. "And in order to do that, maybe it's time to face the man that started all of this."

Blake's brows rose as he reached out to snag a lock of her hair. Hair she hadn't bothered to straighten, but allowed to curl naturally. He held it so she could see it. "Where did you get the stuff to change your hair back to your natural color?"

"Alexia sent it with the clothes." She motioned to his phone. "Your mother, Blake, please!" She had to really stuff the terror down in order to function. Doing something proactive helped.

Blake tried his mother's number again while Jillian paced. "Still no answer." He shoved his hands into the front pockets of his jeans and leaned back on his heels. His ferocious frown simply made her straighten her shoulders and lock her eyes on his. Letting out a low growl, Blake snapped, "You do remember that this is the man who wants you dead."

"I know. I think that letter was a pretty good confirmation of that. I came back to find the truth. Frank Hoffman knows it." She narrowed her eyes. "And if Meg's in danger, he'll know it."

"We don't know someone has her." Blake ran a hand over his close-cropped head.

"We don't know someone doesn't!" Her throat clogged with tears at the thought of her baby in someone else's hands. Someone who wouldn't hesitate to harm her in order to get at her mother.

"We could arrange a meeting, you know. A safe, secure meeting."

Jillian swallowed her tears and hardened her resolve as she looked into her friend's eyes. "There's no such thing. I'm not going to be safe until the truth is exposed. And neither is Meg. I want to catch Hoffman by surprise. If we give him advance notice, he'll bring his hired guns and have time to practice his lies. Or he'll simply refuse, since agreeing to meet would practically be an admission of guilt." She held her ground. "No one knows where I am so they won't be watching for me to leave. No one knows where I'm going, so no one will be waiting for me to get there. I think this is way more safe than setting something up that could be sabotaged or booby-trapped. Don't you see?"

"I don't like it. But you do make a pretty good point. Maybe." Blake shook his head and rubbed his square chin. Then he dialed his mother's number again. "Fine. If you're determined to go, I'm going with you."

9:20 PM

Colton stood outside the hotel, leaning against one of the majestic columns as he watched people come and go. Twenty minutes passed, but it didn't faze him. He flashed his badge at two officers assigned to security. They nodded and focused their attention back on the surrounding area.

Everywhere he turned, a new scent greeted him. He loved this city even when it was hot and humid and threatened to suck the last breath from his lungs. Smells from the nearby interstate mingled with ones that drifted out of the hotel with each swoosh of the electric door.

Right now, though, he really wanted to *see* his uncle's face when he told him Jillian's story. From his vantage point, he could see inside the hotel. People in glittering evening dress swarmed in front of the doors, causing them to open and close in a rhythmic motion. Thankfully, Colton was close enough to get a blast of refreshing cool air every once in a while.

Finally, the man he wanted to see appeared in the entrance followed by two black-suited males Colton took to be his security for the evening's event. As his uncle stepped through the doors, well-wishers slapped him on the back and shook his hand.

Colton simply waited, placing himself where Frank couldn't miss him.

His uncle finally looked up and their eyes connected as Colton's phone vibrated. Frank's eyes flared with surprise, then narrowed

192

as his face tightened with displeasure a fraction of a second before it smoothed into his politician friendliness.

Colton's stomach dropped. His uncle had never reacted that way to seeing him. Colton offered a small smile and waited for the man to approach him. Frank's expression morphed into the usual hearty grin that Colton associated with him. "Colton, good to see you, son. What are you doing here?"

If Colton hadn't been watching for any sign that his uncle was hiding something, he never would have seen the uneasiness, the microtightening around the corners of his mouth. The frown behind the smile.

Colton reached out and gave the man their typical greeting, a slight man hug with one firm slap on the back. He said, "You're a hard man to track down these days."

"I've got an election coming up." He clapped Colton on the shoulder. "But I've always got time for my favorite nephew."

"Hey, Frank, you got a minute before you leave?"

Colton and his uncle turned as one to see a well-dressed man in his late forties accompanied by a tall slender man, who looked like he might have been a basketball player at some point in his youth. Colton recognized the shorter man who'd spoken as Elliott Darwin, his uncle's campaign manager and best friend for the past thirty years. They'd met in college and had been tight ever since. Elliott was like another uncle to Colton. When Elliott spied him, a big grin crossed his face. "Colton! Hey, man, good to see you."

Colton accepted the firm handshake with a smile of his own. Even though he had a bone to pick with his uncle, he was truly glad to see Elliott.

"You too, El. I just stopped by to talk to Uncle Frank a few minutes."

Elliott lowered his voice and bent his graying head. "Hey, you mind if I make an introduction first?"

"No, go ahead."

His uncle shot him an apologetic look behind Elliott's back.

"Thanks." Elliott gave him another smile and turned back to the man who'd walked out of the hotel with him. As Elliott made the introductions, frustration bit at Colton although he did his best to hide it. This may have been a really bad idea. He'd not taken into consideration all of the people who'd want to linger and talk with Senator Frank Hoffman.

Colton listened in as the three men chatted. Elliott said, "This is Dennis Bray, an attorney here in town and very interested in supporting your campaign."

Colton shifted in the heat and felt a trickle of sweat run down the middle of his back. People moved around him, talking and laughing as they left the hotel. A few called out their goodbyes to the senator, who waved a friendly hand of acknowledgment even as he continued his conversation with Elliott and his new supporter.

Colton glanced down the sidewalk, then across the street. His eyes slammed into the pair heading his way. He blinked. And blinked again. She wouldn't have, would she?

All the air squeezed from his lungs and for a moment he felt light-headed. She did.

Jillian had dyed her hair back to its natural color. She'd skipped the straightener and her blond curls bounced around her shoulders with each step she took.

What did she think she was doing? She looked exactly as Colton remembered from high school. Her blue eyes caught his. Blue. Not brown. Jillian's eyes.

"Sir, are you all right?"

At first, Colton wondered why Elliott was calling him sir. He was speaking to Colton's uncle. While best friends, in public Elliott gave Frank every form of respect he could. Said it showed people that Frank was a man to respect, a man to follow, a man to trust.

A man who now looked like he was ready to faint dead away as he stared at the approaching duo.

Jillian's face had bleached to a pale white color as she honed in on his uncle. "How dare you!"

Uncle Frank stumbled back and Colton reached to catch him.

"Sir? Are you all right?" Elliott turned to a hotel employee who'd followed the group outside. "Can we get him a glass of water?"

An interesting—and condemning—reaction to Jillian's appearance. Colton felt dread gnaw on his insides.

Jillian stopped midstep and stared back. Her mouth opened. Her eyes snapped to his and her mouth slammed shut.

Those around Frank murmured. No doubt he realized the curious attention he was garnering. Colton watched his uncle take a deep breath and turn back to the tall man Elliott had introduced as though he hadn't been shaken by the woman who now stood in front of Colton.

Blake's gaze darted left, then right. Colton felt the muscles at the back of his neck go all twitchy. His jawline burned and he realized he had it clenched tight against the anger churning through him.

Anger at the certainty Jillian had told him the truth.

Anger at the fact she'd dared to show up like this.

Anger mixed with the fear that she'd just exposed herself.

Colton snagged her arm while Blake hovered in a protective stance. "You have absolutely lost your mind."

"That's along the lines of what Blake said." She jerked her arm and turned to face his uncle. "What did *he* say?"

"Nothing yet," Colton hissed as he edged her toward an area that looked like it might offer some cover from prying eyes and listening ears. Was she followed? He looked at Blake, who stood with his back to them, his muscles bunched as though ready to spring into action. Colton could also see the man's weapon in his shoulder holsters barely hidden by the long-sleeved button-down shirt he'd thrown over the white T-shirt. With his jeans and army boots, he looked decidedly out of place. And didn't care a bit.

Colton almost liked the guy at the moment.

He let his gaze swing back to his uncle, who had his back to him and Jillian. But the lines of tension in the man's neck spoke volumes.

Jillian squirmed. "I need to talk to him. In private. And I need for you to arrange that."

"There are better ways to go about getting what you want in this case."

She stared at him. Reached a hand up to touch his face. "You're okay."

"What?"

"I had to make sure you were okay."

He took Jillian's hand and pulled her around close against him, her back to his chest, and maneuvered her so that she was within his uncle's line of sight, yet protected by the large column he lined up with his spine. She glanced up at him, but didn't comment. His uncle looked up and did something Colton had never seen him do before. He stumbled over his words.

Colton was convinced.

And terribly afraid for the woman in front of him.

"Why wouldn't I be okay?"

She licked her lips. "Just call it a gut feeling."

"It's not me we need to be worried about."

Crack.

Jillian cried out and spun away from him. Her bright red blood splattered against his cheek.

25

Jillian fought the waves of pain and the desire to sink to the concrete beneath her feet. If she did, she'd be trampled by the sudden rush of the panicked crowd. She thought she heard Colton call her name.

A hand grabbed her good arm. "Are you all right?" Colton pulled her against him as another shot rang out.

"Yes," she gasped as screams seemed to come from every direction.

Blake caught her eye, saw Colton had her, and grabbed a terrified, frozen teenage girl from in front of the hotel doors and shoved her back through them. Jillian lost sight of Blake as Colton pulled her by the hand. People continued to scatter like ants. More terrified cries echoed around her as she ignored the fire in her arm and tried to keep up with Colton as he pushed his way through the crush of people.

An elbow knocked into her ribs and she gasped and turned, her hand slipping from Colton's grasp. She bounced off the side of the building, then tripped over someone's foot. Just as she went to her knees, another crack echoed and a bullet slammed into the concrete millimeters above her head. Particles stung her cheeks. The woman on her left screamed and ducked as she scurried to get to the parking lot to hide behind a car.

"Stay down!" Jillian glanced around. People still scrambled for cover. Okay, she got it. She was the target. She had to get away from the crowd before someone took a bullet meant for her. Where was Colton? Or Blake?

"Jillian!"

She heard her name but couldn't see through the crush of the bodies desperate to get out of the line of fire.

And she had no time to try to find them. She had to move, to get away from the people she'd put in danger.

Keeping low, forcing her terror aside and hoping she was hidden for the moment, she continued to ignore the increased throbbing in her left arm. Jillian stumbled, pushed, and shoved her way through the crowd that was finally thinning as people poured into any open door that would get them away from the front of the hotel and parking lot where the shots had come from.

Jillian made it to the side of the building and around the corner, dragging in deep breaths as she forced her brain to work, to come up with a plan. Stoneridge Drive lay in front of her, intersecting with Greystone Boulevard to her left. Across the street were sheltering trees. Hide behind a car? Or get to the trees?

Even though she'd made it around to the side of the building, she knew she couldn't stop now. Her mind clicked as she pictured where the bullets had hit against the building. The shooter had been in the parking lot.

A drive-by?

No way to tell until all this was over. People pressed past her. Some made it to their cars and sped away from the scene. Guilt ate at her as she scanned the area for a place to hide—and watch. She'd thought that by acting on impulse, no one would know where she was. No one would be able to follow her. No one would be able to make another attempt on her life this soon.

And now she'd brought danger to everyone within bullet range.

No time to think about it now.

Sirens sounded in the distance.

Where had Colton gone? She hadn't deliberately separated herself from him or Blake, but maybe it would be better if she wasn't anywhere near them right now.

She'd been stupid. Stupid. Stupid. Stupid. After being careful for so long, she'd really pulled a humdinger of stupid coming out to confront the senator like this.

But she'd had to warn Colton. Tell him he might be a target. And now someone was shooting at them. Had her coming here inspired the shots? Or had the person been here waiting on Colton?

But Colton hadn't planned on being here and neither had she. So how had someone known?

Harsh breaths pulled at her as she pushed fear aside to focus on staying alive. She ducked behind the nearest vehicle and grimaced as pain shot up her wounded arm. She rested against the back tire as she used her good arm to dig into her shorts pocket for the cell phone Colton had given her. She punched in his number and held the device to her ear.

Now what? *Think, Jillian. Think.*

The side mirror shattered behind her.

"Get down! Everybody stay down!" Colton swallowed hard as he tightened his grip on his weapon. The shooter had changed locations. The shot had sounded from around the side of the building. At least he thought so. Some of the screams were as loud as the shots.

Or were there two shooters? Two locations, two shooters?

Or had he moved?

His phone vibrated again and he snatched it.

Jillian's number. It had rung once, then shut off. He swept the scene one more time.

He'd seen Blake get the girl to safety, but Colton had lost his grip on Jillian when someone had slammed into her. Just as he'd reached out to help her, he'd been knocked from behind. By the time he'd gotten his balance, she was gone.

And now, from his crouched perch behind the white column, he still couldn't see her. She'd been hurt. That first bullet had hit her. He felt sure it was just a graze, but wished he could have kept her near him.

Colton saw Blake slink around the side of the hotel and slam up against the column opposite his own. "Where's Jillian?"

"I don't know. I lost my grip on her." It galled him to admit it.

Blake shot him a dark look, then asked, "You spot the shooter?"

The shooter. "No. But the bullets are coming from the parking lot. At least they were. I think I heard another one come from the side of the building." He nodded his head toward the left. Thankfully, the parking lot now resembled a ghost town. "That way. It's been quiet for the last few seconds."

"One or two shooters?"

"I can't tell, which is why I'm still right here." He watched and waited, praying Jillian was hunkered down hiding. "Where is he? Or is it 'they'?" he muttered, not expecting an answer. Blake held his weapon ready and Colton said, "You're deputized right now."

"Thanks." Blake nodded like he expected that.

"Don't make me regret it," Colton said. He would be responsible for the man.

Blake kept his attention on the parking lot as he said, "Security's good, they know what they're doing. They've got the hotel locked down. I told them to let me out first, then lock every entrance and exit. They were two steps ahead of me."

That meant the shooter couldn't get in. But if Jillian was still outside, that meant she couldn't either. His gut wound itself tighter, if that was even possible. "How far away is backup?"

"Should be here any minute."

"That's about a minute too long," Colton grunted.

Blake motioned he was going around, trying to see if the shooter was still in the same place he was when he first started shooting.

Another gunshot sounded from the side of the building to Colton's left. They exchanged a look. Colton asked, "You willing to risk it?" Risk there being a second shooter and as soon as they showed themselves, he'd pick one of them off. Blake nodded and together they popped from the protection of the columns and headed toward the sound of the latest gunshot.

26

When the bullet shattered the mirror, Jillian jerked and lost her grip on the phone. It skittered under the van. She dropped to her knees and gave a frantic look for the device, but she couldn't spot it. Footsteps sounded. She jumped up, and with terror pounding a hard beat through her veins, she raced across the parking lot, waiting for a bullet to find its mark this time.

Where was the shooter now? Behind her? She looked back. Nothing. Had he circled around to get in front of her? Was she racing straight toward him? Her heart pounded and she could almost taste her fear as it flooded every pore. She raced to the next vehicle, then the next, expecting to feel the bite of a bullet pierce her back as she made her way around the side of the hotel.

Oh God, please.

"Jillian!"

Colton's yell stopped her, freezing her blood in her veins as she dropped behind the nearest car. She almost answered, then bit her tongue as she slipped behind the nearest tree. She couldn't answer and give away her spot. The shooter was still there. Even with the sirens growing closer, she knew he was still there.

She pulled her weapon from the back of her shorts.

Movement from the parking lot grabbed her attention. A man in a black suit moved like he knew where he was going. Should she follow him? She took note of the baseball cap pulled low and hesitated.

"Jillian!"

The black suit paused and spun and she caught sight of the weapon in his right hand.

The shooter.

While he was looking away from her, distracted by Colton's voice, Jillian darted from car to car until she came full circle in front of the hotel. She shivered even as sweat ran down her face. What was Colton doing yelling her name like that?

Trying to divert the killer's attention back to him, Jillian figured. In fact, the more she thought about it, the more she knew it with a certainty that made her want to live to hug the man—and smack him. Once again he was trying to protect her. Colton had no idea where she was, but by pretending he did, he was hoping to scare off the shooter.

The sirens were nearly on top of her, but that didn't seem to faze the man who was determined to kill her.

———

Colton's tennis shoes slapped against the parking lot asphalt. "Where'd they go?"

"I have no idea." Blake hunkered behind a car and pointed. "Gunshots came from over there."

"Come on." Colton shook his head. "Lots of hiding places. Good for Jillian. Bad for us as far as finding this guy." They headed in the direction the shots had come from, keeping low and trying to use the trees for cover. No sense in standing out in the open and inviting a bullet in the brain if they didn't have to.

"Guy?" Blake asked as they ran. "So you're back to thinking it's just one shooter?"

"For now. Until I'm proven to be wrong."

The Ranger rubbed a hand over his eyes. "How many shots is that?"

"Six or seven. I lost count. You go that way, I'll take the—" His phone rang and he snatched it as he stepped behind a tree on Wildlife Boulevard, praying to see Jillian's new number on the screen.

Hope plummeted when he didn't recognize the number. But he pressed the answer button and held the phone to his ear. "Brady here."

"Colton, it's Jillian."

Her breathless, scared voice sent his pulse skittering. But relief filled him. She was alive. "Where are you?"

"With an officer. I'm safe for now."

27

Blue lights pulled into the parking area. Jillian stuffed her gun into the back of her waistband and pulled her shirt down over it. No sense in adding anything more to the chaos.

And then Colton was there with Blake right behind him. Colton kept his badge in plain sight as he made his way over to her. Officers swarmed the area and she watched them methodically and professionally begin to do what they were trained to do.

Colton hollered, "Clear the area." He pointed out eight officers. "Clear the perimeter as best you can but don't put yourselves in danger. This perp doesn't care who's in his line of fire."

And then his focus was on her.

Jillian didn't protest when Colton closed the distance to pull her into his arms. She could lean on his strength for a few moments. But only a few. And she couldn't get used to it. Not until she told him about Meg. But for now . . .

He asked, "How's your arm?"

"It hurts."

"Let me take a look at it." He started to push her back and she protested by wrapping both arms around his waist. "If I was hurt that bad, I wouldn't be able to do this."

He relaxed and let her stay there.

When she decided she wouldn't fall apart, she released her hold on him and looked around. "I'm an idiot," she whispered. "I'm sorry."

His hand cupped her chin. "We'll talk about it later. Fortunately no one was hit. Bumps and bruises from the panicked rush to get away, but that's it."

Jillian bit her lip and raised her good hand to rake it through her curls. "How did he know?"

"What do you mean?"

"The shooter. How did he know? My coming here was completely impulse. No planning, no agenda, not even a phone call to say I'm on my way. I simply walked out of our hotel and over to the Embassy Suites. How was he here waiting for me?"

Colton frowned. "He couldn't have been."

Blake nodded. "And I made sure no one followed us." His eyes hardened. "Trust me. I would have known if we had a tail. We were clean all the way from our hotel to this one."

She had no doubt Blake was right. If someone had been following them, Blake would have taken care of it right then. Jillian felt a clenching in her gut. "Then that means he was already at the hotel."

"Exactly," Colton said. "And that means we need to know who was at the hotel when you got here."

"We don't need to know about *every* person," Jillian said. She let her gaze linger on his. "We only need to know about those who have any connection to your uncle."

Colton's eyes narrowed, then he closed them and dropped his head. "You're right." He snapped his head back up and snagged his phone. "I'm going to make some calls."

Jillian wondered if the night would ever end. Exhaustion swamped her. Colton had Hunter and Katie and every other available detective working through the night checking with witnesses, comparing stories, and doing their best to help the crime scene unit gather every last shred of evidence that the shooter may have left behind.

She tried to get to Blake, to ask him if he'd heard from his mother, but she'd been corralled by a paramedic who'd patched up her arm and recommended she see her doctor about an antibiotic. Jillian made a mental note to ask Serena about that.

Colton paced in front of the ambulance, his phone pressed to his ear. When he finally stopped and turned to her, she'd just about fallen asleep on the gurney in the midst of prayers for Meg's safety.

She blinked up at him. "What is it?"

He nodded at the Embassy Suites. "I'm going inside to watch video of the parking lot and the hotel. See if we can pick up anything."

"I'm coming."

"Blake can take you back to our hotel. You look like you're about done in."

"I am. But that's never stopped me before."

Colton simply shook his head. "Right." He took her hand. "Come on and sit here a few minutes. I need to finish talking to these guys and I can't have you falling over."

Jillian followed him to a cruiser and climbed in the back. She leaned her head against the headrest and closed her eyes. Her thoughts swirled, but at the front was the fact that she could have been killed—again—tonight.

What would Meg do without her?

Blake slid into the seat beside her and she jerked. His hand patted hers, and before he could speak, she asked, "Anything from your mother?"

"Yeah. She texted me. They'd been at the movies when we called. They're at a friend's house and everything is fine."

Jillian gave a relieved cry and wilted. "Oh thank you, God."

Blake asked, "You all right?"

"I've been better."

"How's the arm?"

"Stinging."

"Not in the mood to talk?"

"Not so much."

He went quiet for about two seconds, then said, "I didn't know things were this crazy, Jillian, or I'd never have come out here. I didn't know I was putting Meg in danger."

Jillian's eyes flew open and her gaze whipped over to Colton who had the phone to his ear once again. "I know."

"You have to tell him. About the text tonight too."

"When?" she cried, swinging back around to shoot him a dark look. "In between being shot at, run off the road, or being blown to smithereens? Just when should I sit down and tell him?"

Blake didn't even flinch, just held her gaze with a steady look. She blinked back her surge of anger and frustration. It wasn't Blake's fault. Not completely anyway.

"They know about her. How do we keep her safe now?" Longing to talk to her daughter and hold her swept over her, nearly splitting her in two with the pain of the forced separation.

"I'll call my mother and tell her what's going on. I'll tell her to take Meg to Tony's and keep her there until I call her back. I've also got a former unit buddy watching them. If he sees anything that sets off his alarms, he'll have her on a plane out of there."

Jillian sighed and nodded. Her baby, her sweet innocent child who'd been protected and sheltered her entire life, was now the target of killers who wanted her mother.

It wasn't fair.

But God hadn't promised life would be fair, just that he would walk with her. It was a hard thing to accept sometimes, but . . .

"Everything all right?" Colton leaned in the open window.

Now that the immediate danger had passed, the media had descended with all of its ruthless commotion.

"Yes." She rubbed a hand over her eyes. "As all right as possible."

He nodded and started to slide into the front seat when Blake said, "You mind riding back here? I get carsick."

"We're not going anywhere," Colton said. "Just moving up to the front door."

Blake smiled. "I know, but it might take a few minutes to get through that mess."

The officer slipped behind the wheel as Blake got out and walked around to the front passenger side. Blake and Colton exchanged some male look that Jillian couldn't interpret, but she had a feeling it was what made Colton's tension ease slightly.

Colton clapped Blake on the shoulder. "Thanks." He walked around the cruiser and slid into the backseat.

Law enforcement held the media back, but barely, it seemed. Jillian was grateful for the protection of the squad car. And Colton's presence beside her.

He slid all the way over into the middle and wrapped an arm around her shoulders. She didn't try to question it, she simply leaned into him and let the officer fight the madness as they inched toward the front door.

She stayed silent while her brain whirled and her arm throbbed.

Finally, the officer motioned that it was safe to get out.

As they climbed out of the car, Blake hovered in a protective stance on her right. Colton covered her left. Jillian wasn't terribly worried. The shooter had done his damage for the night.

And escaped to try again another day.

"Nothing very helpful," Colton muttered as he stared at the screen. They'd spent the last two hours watching the hotel security footage. Arriving back at the hotel, Colton and the others had found the media waiting behind the tape to catch anyone coming or going. Dodging them had taken no small amount of skill, but they'd managed.

His uncle and his crew had been shuttled off to safety somewhere by the local police. CNN played a running loop of the reports with speculation that Frank Hoffman had been the target. Everything in Colton wanted to track down his uncle and question him until he got some answers. But first he had a job to do here.

On the flat screen in front of him, the security footage played. They had good cameras and great angles. Unfortunately the gunman had kept his head low, never looking up. The baseball cap did a good job of hiding his features.

"Watch it backward. Trace him back," Colton suggested.

Head of security for the hotel, Janice Dobson, complied immediately. The footage reversed and Colton pointed. "There. He's behind the car."

Hunter and Katie had arrived shortly after the viewing began. Hunter said, "He's got on a suit."

"He was someone in attendance with the fundraiser," Colton said. "Have we got the guest list?"

Katie nodded. "I've got it. Sent it over for background checks on everyone."

The bad feeling in the pit of his stomach hadn't left since his uncle's reaction to seeing Colton right before the shooting started. He knew it wasn't Frank pulling the trigger. But evidence suggested he was bankrolling the man who was.

"A nice suit and a baseball cap. Guy even has a tie on."

"Get a shot of that tie. Maybe someone will recognize it."

Katie snorted. "It's a solid-colored tie. You know how many black suits and solid-colored ties are at those kinds of events?"

Colton shot her a dark look, but couldn't deny she was right.

He looked back at the black-and-white security footage. They had a good view of the shooting, saw the whole thing unfold. They just couldn't pinpoint the shooter's face. The ball cap and hunched posture disguised him pretty well.

"We'll need the best shot you can get of him. Then we'll go room to room asking anyone if they recognize him," Colton said. He looked at Katie. "You want to see if anyone recognizes that tie?"

She smirked and took the printed picture from Ms. Dobson. "I'll keep you posted."

"Where's your buddy Grayson?" Hunter asked.

"Still at my brother's house." Her face flushed and Colton wondered if there was something going on there he didn't know about. She said, "He's extending his vacation." She turned on her heel and he saw a small smile curve Jillian's lips as she met the other detective's gaze. Katie sighed and marched from the room.

Colton looked at Jillian and raised a brow. She shrugged in silent communication and he took it to mean that he needed to mind his own business. Turning back to the video footage, he decided they'd gotten what they could. "Thanks for the help," he said to Ms. Dobson. "We appreciate it."

"Let me know if there's anything else I can do for you. We want this guy caught too."

Colton promised he would let her know. To Jillian, he asked, "Ready to call it a day?"

"Yes."

Blake had been studying the footage. He leaned in and pointed. "What's that?"

"A piece of paper?" Hunter murmured.

"Something fell out of his pocket?" Colton speculated. "Rewind it." Ms. Dobson did.

In slow motion, they watched the paper flutter to the ground from the man's pocket.

Colton looked at Hunter with satisfaction. "Fingerprints."

Hunter gave him a grim smile. "If it's still there."

They raced from the room with Jillian and Blake right behind them. Colton arrived at the area where they'd seen the paper fall from the shooter's jacket.

"You see it?" Colton asked.

Hunter grunted. "No."

Colton curled his fists in frustration, then stood still. "There's no wind. Not even a hint of a breeze."

"You think CSU picked it up?"

"Possibly. I'll call Rick and find out." Colton pulled his phone from his pocket and punched in the number for the head of the crime scene unit.

Rick answered with a growl. "I'm still processing everything, Brady."

"I know. I'm not calling for results yet. Chill."

"I'm just kidding. What do you need?"

"When you were processing the parking lot, did you pick up a piece of paper? It looked like it might be an invitation to one of the events going on in the hotel tonight."

Rick didn't say anything for a minute and Colton pictured the man thinking, his receding hairline exposing extra wrinkles in his tanned forehead. "I don't remember it, but maybe one of my team did. Let me check with them and get back to you."

"Thanks." Colton hung up and filled Hunter in.

"Nothing more to do here then."

"Yeah." He couldn't help the disgust. Finally a solid lead and they couldn't find it. "We just can't catch a break," he muttered.

Hunter shrugged. "No one's died yet."

Shame swept over him. "True. You're absolutely right. Guess God's got his hand on this and I'm not saying 'thank you' near enough."

Hunter clapped him on the back. "He knows. Come on, let's get Jillian back to the hotel room and call it a night."

Colton sighed. "I guess the next step in this dance is to talk to the Pikes."

Hunter nodded. "The Pikes and your uncle."

"I'll set it up."

"And I want to go with you," Jillian insisted.

"Of course you do."

THURSDAY

28

Colton activated his bluetooth as he pulled into the lake house drive. He was determined to check out his uncle's boat. Dominic's voice came on. "Alexia and I are still here. They had to take Dad back into surgery and it's touch and go right now."

"How's Alexia handling everything?"

"Fairly well. She's trying to be strong for our mom, but I can tell she's really battling to forgive the man." A heavy sigh came over the line. "I have to admit I'm in the same boat. But hey—there's no connection between Nicholas Tremaine and your uncle. At least none that I can find."

Relief darted through Colton. At least that was one positive. While Dominic talked, he walked around the side of his uncle's house to look out over the lake. Surprise rocked him back on his heels. "I don't believe this. It's gone!"

"What?"

"The boat is gone."

"Your uncle's?"

"Yeah."

"You think he moved it because he had it freshly painted?"

"How would he know—" He broke off as he remembered his

conversation with his aunt. "I asked Aunt Elizabeth if Frank had had the boat painted recently."

"You think she told him?"

Sorrow, regret, anger, and frustration swirled inside him. "What else am I supposed to think?"

"We need to talk to your uncle ASAP."

"Tell me about it." But one didn't just send a couple of uniforms to bring in a high-profile politician. He'd have to get the highest brass in the department and probably involve the feds too. No, he needed absolute, solid evidence before that happened. And he didn't have that. Was he even being objective about this? And how would he ever face his mom again? If he was involved in destroying his mother's brother, their already-strained relationship would most likely be severed. Colton swallowed hard as he processed exactly how this would affect his family.

His phone beeped and he looked at the screen. "Hey, let me get this other call. It's Rick. Just take care of your dad. We've got this covered."

"All right. Let me know when you find the boat."

Colton clicked over to the other line. "Hey, Rick."

"Colton, how would you like to know what we've got so far?"

"Lay it on me."

He listened as Rick ran down the evidence he'd finished processing. "Found your piece of paper from last night."

"What's on it?"

"It was an invitation. Right now I've got fingerprints of a woman by the name of Celia Brown, the one who mailed the invitations. Another partial print I haven't identified yet and a couple of smudges. Sorry, not much here."

"Well, we've got the guest list and everyone who showed up. We've got officers working those names." Colton rubbed a hand down his cheek as he thought about the time that would take.

"Good." Rick paused. "Your shooter seems pretty determined."

"I know. All these attempts. It's amazing she's still alive. God's really having to keep his protection around her."

Rick grunted. "Whatever the case, we haven't got much of anything that's going to tie us to the person after Jillian. Your best shot is the DNA sample of the blood on the drive. Get me a suspect to match it to."

Colton blew out a breath. "Right."

Rick hung up and Colton stared at the dock where the boat was supposed to be. He shook his head and rubbed his eyes. "What have you done, Uncle Frank?"

———■———

10:04 AM

Colton stepped inside his captain's office and sat down with a sigh.

"What's on your mind, Brady?"

Colton rubbed a hand down his face, then laced his fingers together in front of him. "I've got a problem."

"I don't like problems. I'm too close to retirement and I don't want any problems for the next two months."

"Yeah, me neither. But you're going to have to help me with this one."

Murdoch's silvery mustache quivered. "I'm not letting you out of going to Rick's seminar."

Colton blinked, then choked on a chuckle. "Ah. Right."

"Not even for a set of World Series tickets."

Colton froze and narrowed his eyes. "Who's the blabbermouth?"

"I have my sources."

Colton pressed his lips together to keep from laughing. Then Murdoch said, "All right, lay it on me."

Colton's frown returned. "I have a report from an eyewitness that our former governor didn't die in a car wreck ten years ago. She says she saw him murdered."

The captain barked a short laugh. "What psych ward did she escape from?"

Colton held the man's gaze. "I believe her."

Murdoch's eyes widened. Then hardened. "Go on."

Colton gave him the details. Before he was finished, the captain was pacing from one end of his office to the other. When he reached the far window, he spun and said, "You have any proof?"

Colton hesitated. "No, but I have a way to get it—only you're probably not going to like it."

"Why am I not surprised?"

Colton gave him a small smile and explained what he needed. In the middle of his captain's choking, Colton's phone buzzed. He stood and slipped it from his pocket. "Hello?"

"Hello, son."

"Uncle Frank." Surprise lifted his right brow. He hadn't checked the caller ID before answering the phone. "Are you all right after last night? You disappeared pretty fast after the bullets started flying."

"Security got me and the whole campaign crew out of there lightning fast."

"You've got a good team working for you."

"Indeed I do."

"But that's not what you called about."

A short silence echoed across the line, then his uncle said, "I guess we need to have a chat."

"I guess we do."

"It's not what you're thinking, Colton."

This time Colton was quiet for a few seconds while he debated whether or not he believed the man. "Then let's talk it out and you can tell me exactly what it is."

"I'd like the chance to do that."

"When?"

"Now?"

Colton hesitated. He wanted to see the Pikes first, get their story, before he talked with Frank. The truth was a slippery thing these days, and he needed every advantage. "I've got a stop I have to make first."

"Where are you going?"

"To question another witness."

"From last night?"

"No." Colton shifted. "Sorry, Uncle Frank, but you know I can't discuss this with you. Where do you want to meet?"

"My office?"

"At your house or the Capitol?"

"Never mind. It's about 10:30 now. How long will your appointment take?"

Colton thought about it. "I'm not sure. I have the stop to make. Then probably an hour, hour and a half, with the witness. Can you do a late lunch?"

"1:00 at The Blue Marlin on Lincoln Street?"

"See you there."

Colton hung up to find his captain staring at him. "Any other problems you need to let me in on?"

A sigh left him. "I'm probably going to have to take myself off this case."

His captain lifted a brow. "Why's that?"

"Because if the evidence points in the direction it seems to be pointing, it's going to be a conflict of interest for me to continue."

"How's that evidence pointing now?"

Colton met the man's eyes. "What do you think?"

"You have no proof indicating your uncle was involved in anything illegal?"

"Not a speck of it. Just . . . suspicions." And a missing boat.

"Then you don't have to recuse yourself yet, but the moment you do—"

"I know. As soon as I do, I'll remove myself, that's a promise."

"See that you keep it. I'll start your order."

■

Colton called the Pikes from the hotel. "I'll be there in about forty-five minutes."

Jillian walked out of her room and Colton blinked at the sight. He'd gotten kind of used to seeing her as a brunette. But he couldn't deny the effect she had on him no matter what she looked like. She had her blond curls pulled up in a scrunchy and was wearing a shirt he recognized as Serena's.

She planted her hands on her hips, wincing as her left hand made contact, and asked, "Where are we going?"

Colton sighed. "Jillian, please let me handle this."

"I am. But I can't be left behind. I *need* to go with you."

"It's too dangerous, Jillian."

"Colton . . ."

He stared at her when she stopped. "What?"

Her lips twisted and she studied him. "I'm sorry."

That caught his attention. "About what?"

Her eyes slid from his. "Everything. Leaving. Not getting in touch after I left, coming back . . ." She waved a hand as she ran out of words.

Colton felt the familiar shaft of pain he'd lived with for ten years. "I get it, Jillian. I don't like it, but you may have saved your life by doing what you did." He shook his head. "It's in the past. Let's leave it there."

She opened her mouth as though to argue—or say something else. Then she seemed to think better of it and said, "So, you're okay with me going to the Pikes'?"

Colton thought about it. "Maybe. I don't know. If you stay here, we'll need security at the hotel—which we have with Blake, and I can get Slade to come over. I don't like the idea of you going to the Pikes' house."

"You think I'll bring danger to them?"

"If whoever is after you sees you, yes, maybe."

She winced. "I definitely don't want to do that."

"Then again," Blake said from the door to the other bedroom, "if somehow whoever is after Jillian has discovered she's here at the hotel, he could just be waiting for you to leave to strike."

Colton lifted a brow. "So you think she should come?"

The man hesitated. "I think there's safety in numbers."

Colton shot a pointed look at Jillian's left arm. "He almost got her last night in a crowd of people."

"True." Blake ran a hand over his freshly shaven jaw. "He's getting desperate."

"Which makes him incredibly dangerous." He looked at Jillian. "I think you'd be safer here." He paused. "Then again, I thought you'd be safe at the lake house." He sighed and rubbed his eyes as he thought. "No," he finally said. "You have to stay here with Blake. We simply can't take the chance on you putting the Pikes in danger."

Jillian frowned. "Fine, but I don't like it."

Colton gave her a sad smile. "We're not in this to keep you happy, Jilly, we're in it to keep you safe."

29

After Colton and Hunter left, Jillian stared out the hotel window as she processed her racing thoughts. She'd slept little the night before, tossing and turning, dreaming about Meg falling into the hands of the people who were determined to kill her and keep her quiet.

But she'd told.

She'd shared her story with people who believed her, they just needed time to prove it. And that was the reason she knew she was still a target. She was the one who'd seen the murder. An eyewitness to something that had been covered up for a decade. And now she was here to shed the light, to expose the truth.

The other very serious truth she'd kept hidden also had to be exposed. She had to tell Colton about Meg and today was the day to come clean. Soon.

Dread centered itself in her stomach. She was more worried about telling Colton about Meg than she was being a target of a killer.

"Jilly?"

She looked over her shoulder. Blake stood behind her. The smirk on his face made her want to smack him. "It's a nickname from high school."

"I can't imagine you letting anyone get away with calling you Jilly."

"Shut up." She kept her tone mild.

He chuckled, then sobered. "That's why you picked the name Julie."

She spun. "What?"

"Julie. Jilly. They're not so different."

"They are too," she sputtered. "You're crazy."

"Liar. You like the name Jilly, because Colton gave it to you."

"Do not." She sounded like a three-year-old.

"Do too," he taunted.

A fraction of the tension left her shoulders and she burst out laughing. "Okay, maybe you're right." She threw up her hands. "Who knows what I was thinking during those first few days on the run." She sighed. "Maybe it was a subconscious decision." She narrowed her eyes at him. "But you may not call me that. Ever." His eyes sparked and she knew he'd call her that at some point. "I'm glad I never had any brothers. You're so annoying."

"I live to serve." He frowned. "So, what are you thinking about?"

"Everything. And it's all jumbled in my mind."

"Yeah. I know what you mean."

"Gerald Benjamin did the autopsy of Governor Martin."

"Right."

"Benjamin and Pike were friends who'd planned to get together to go fishing at a place Benjamin had sprayed for bees. And yet he was stung repeatedly, his epi-pen untouched in the unopened cooler."

"Murder."

"Definitely. And premeditated at that."

"And you think Senator Hoffman had something to do with that murder too?"

She sighed and turned back to the window. "I have no idea. I just know that I want this over with. I want my life and my daughter back."

"And you want Colton back."

Jillian flinched and kept her eyes on the window. Then shrugged. "Yes. I want Colton back."

Colton's phone rang and he answered it as he and Hunter walked up the steps to the Pikes' front door. "Hey, Katie, if it can wait, let me call you back."

"Sure. No problem."

Conrad Pike answered a few seconds after Colton rapped his knuckles on the wooden door. A handsome man in his early sixties with a full head of salt-and-pepper hair smiled. His blue eyes crinkled at the corners.

"Come in," he said and held the door open for them.

Colton stepped inside the spacious home and took in the details. Mr. Pike led them to a cozy den area that reminded Colton of his own house. A lot of wood and a deer head over the mantel. The brick fireplace held gas logs. Fortunately the air-conditioning worked well.

Once they were seated and introductions made, Conrad asked, "So ten years later you decide Gerald's death warrants looking into?"

Colton leaned forward. "Yes, sir. We've had some new evidence come to light that suggests his death wasn't an accident."

"I've said that all along. Just couldn't prove it." He narrowed his eyes. "Can you?"

"That's what we're working on."

The man's shrewd gaze drilled him. "What have you found?"

"An eyewitness. It appears we're getting too close for comfort for someone. We're not sure what it is yet, but it's obviously making someone nervous and he's made several attempts to kill her. She's in protective custody right now." Colton paused. "Did you receive any threats after Gerald died?"

That got the man's attention. "Threats? No. Why?"

"Because his wife did."

224

He leaned back with a heavy sigh. "Ah. Well, that explains a lot."

"She never mentioned them?"

Pike shook his head. "No, not a word, but every time I brought up Gerald's death, she'd get skittish and shut me down."

"Too scared," Hunter murmured.

"Where's Mrs. Pike?" Colton asked.

"Babysitting our grandchildren. We have two," he said as his chest puffed out a bit.

"Did Mr. Benjamin say anything to you about the death of Governor Martin?"

Mr. Pike flinched. "Harrison?"

"You were friends with him?"

"Yes." He shrugged. "Not best pals or anything like that, but we saw each other at a lot of social functions and I respected him as the governor. I thought he was doing an outstanding job. Harrison's death was a tragedy for our state."

"Did Gerald say anything about the autopsy?"

Mr. Pike frowned and thought. "Not that I recall. Why?"

"Did you notice any changes in his behavior after the governor's death?"

The man shook his head. "No." He paused. "Well, yes. He was stressed, but I think that was about the time his daughter was so sick. Needed a kidney transplant. I just figured that's why he seemed so out of sorts."

"But he never said anything that got your attention about anything he was doing at work."

"No. Nothing."

Colton sighed. This was going nowhere fast. He questioned the man about the day the ME died, and Mr. Pike's story matched the one they'd gotten from Gerald's wife. "Just one last question," Colton said. "Do you know where Gerald would have gotten the fifty thousand dollars he used to pay toward his daughter's kidney transplant?"

Pike lifted a brow. "Seems like he said something about borrowing it from his wife's parents." A shrug. "He died shortly after that." He rubbed his chin. "Such a shame. Two good men gone within weeks of each other." He narrowed his eyes. "You think there's a connection?"

"We're trying to figure that out. Can you give us a connection?"

Pike pressed his lips together while he thought, then said, "Gerald and the governor were high school buddies. I think they even roomed together in college for a year or two before Gerald went to med school. Gerald was devastated when Harrison was killed."

Colton's brain whirled as he processed everything.

Hunter asked, "When you found Gerald at the lake, he was already dead. Did anything stand out to you as . . . abnormal?"

"Other than the fact that my friend was dead? Stung by dozens of bees that never should have been in that area because he had it sprayed on a regular basis? And his epi-pen was still in the cooler?"

"Yeah. Other than that."

Pike rubbed his face and sighed. "No. Not really. But it didn't feel right. The whole thing was just . . . wrong. Everything—the email, the lack of communication with Gerald that morning. Everything. I took it to the authorities and they shut me down."

They talked with Pike a few minutes longer, but learned nothing more. After thanks and goodbyes, Colton and Hunter left.

Once in the car, Colton asked, "You get the feeling he knows more than he does?"

"No. You?"

"No." Disgusted, he cranked the car and turned the air-conditioning on full blast with a glance at the clock. "Maybe my uncle will have something enlightening to share with me. I'll drop you at the hotel to get your car and check on Jillian for me."

Hunter nodded. "You need backup at lunch?"

Colton pursed his lips, the fact that Hunter even felt the need to ask bothering him. "No. He wouldn't hurt me."

And yet the niggling of doubt he heard in his voice made him wonder if he believed that anymore.

———■———

Colton approached the restaurant, his eyes darting, watching, being careful not to assume anything anymore. Would his uncle set him up? Tell him he'd meet him for lunch, then have someone waiting to take him out?

A sigh slipped from him. Paranoia didn't feel good, but he couldn't seem to help himself. His uncle's reaction at the hotel, then his utter shock at seeing Jillian, convinced him the man knew something, even if he wasn't directly responsible for the governor's death. But Colton still didn't have any proof either way.

Inside the restaurant, he flashed his badge. "I'm meeting Senator Hoffman. Do you mind if we use your back room?"

"Of course." The waitress smiled and grabbed two menus. She led the way and motioned to him to pick his seat. He did. Back to the wall, in full view of the door.

She handed him the menu and placed the other at the seat opposite him. "Someone will be with you in just a moment."

Colton waited ten minutes before he started to wonder if his uncle was going to stand him up. He called Katie as he waited.

She answered on the first ring.

"What do you have?"

"The fifty grand deposited into Gerald Benjamin's account did come from the Vances, but Mr. Vance finally broke down and told me the truth."

"What's that?"

"Gerald gave the couple fifty thousand in cash. Told them it was to pay for Tracy's kidney, but he couldn't have the money traced back to him as cash. He asked if they would deposit the money from their retirement fund into his checking account, and if anyone asked where the money came from, he would say his in-laws."

"And they just accepted that?"

"No, but when they asked questions, Gerald wouldn't tell them anything, just said that if they cared about Tracy, they'd do it."

"So they did."

"Yeah. Everything was totally legit on the surface. They just put that fifty thousand in cash back in the bank a little at a time over the next six or seven years so as not to arouse any suspicion."

Colton blew out a sigh. "Just another confusing piece in this crazy puzzle. All the pieces go together, I know they do, I just can't figure out where to place them so they make sense."

"I'll keep digging."

Frank entered the room and made his way toward the table.

Colton said, "I've got to go. I'll talk to you later."

Katie hung up and Colton stood to greet his uncle. "Thanks for coming."

Frank ignored his outstretched hand and slipped into the chair. "What's this all about?"

Colton lifted a brow. So that's the way it was going to play out. Frank looked rough. Deep grooves had etched themselves on either side of his mouth. His forehead had extra creases and dark circles rimmed the man's eyes. Colton decided to be blunt. "You look horrible. You sick?"

Frank barked a short laugh and placed his napkin in his lap. "No, I'm not sick. I'm stressed."

"The campaign?" Colton decided to play along.

"Yes. The campaign. Among other things."

"Like being accused of murder?" So much for playing along. Frank froze.

The waiter chose that moment to enter the room and the men fell silent. After receiving their glasses of water and placing their orders, they were once again alone. Colton waited.

Frank met his gaze. "What was that?"

"You heard me."

"Why would you even say that? Whose murder?"

Time to play again. "Governor Harrison Martin."

"Harrison?" His uncle laughed, then sobered. "You're joking, right? The man was a good friend of mine and he was killed in a car wreck."

"Jillian says she saw you shoot him."

"And you believe her?"

"I don't know what to believe. Why don't you tell me what she saw that night."

"Exactly what night would that be?"

Weariness hit Colton. "Ten years ago. June 6th, 2002."

"Son, I have no idea—" He cut himself off. "Wait a minute. I was in the hospital that night with a mild heart attack."

"I know. But you didn't get there until after two in the morning."

Frank lifted a brow. "Checking up on me?"

"Yeah. And neighbors reported a gunshot in your neighborhood that night."

Frank scratched his chin. "I remember that. Cops knocked on the door right after the party. Told them we didn't hear anything. It ended up being some car backfiring or something."

Colton ground his teeth, then said, "Then why would Jillian lie? She said you shot him and then fell. You saw her and raised the gun." He leaned forward, letting the intensity of his emotions show.

Frank slapped a hand on the table and rose to his feet. "Enough. I won't sit here and listen to this nonsense."

Colton stood too. "Then tell me the truth! Stop pretending nothing happened and tell me the truth! What did Jillian see if you didn't kill him? Why else would someone want her dead?"

His uncle's jaw worked, then tightened as he sank back into the padded chair.

Their food arrived, but the waiter, sensing the thick tension between the men, didn't linger.

"The truth, Uncle Frank, or I take you downtown and we look at all the evidence against you."

That snapped his head up. "What evidence? You don't have any evidence because there's none to be found."

"Did you have your boat painted recently?"

Frank's eyes shuttered. "What does that matter?"

"Give me a straight answer. You're being evasive and it doesn't inspire my confidence in you."

Frank rocked back against his chair and Colton softened his tone. "It matters because the crime scene unit found a slip of material at the scene of Serena's bombed house. That material had boat paint on it. I asked Aunt Elizabeth if you'd had your boat painted. She didn't know. I go out to the lake house to look and the boat's gone." Colton leaned in. "What am I supposed to think?"

"Maybe that I'm being set up! Maybe you should be trying to prove my innocence rather than my guilt. Why aren't you asking your father these questions? He was at the house that night too."

Colton narrowed his eyes and refused to follow that thread. He knew when someone was trying to distract him. "Then you can tell me about that later. Where's your boat?"

"Getting painted."

"Why?"

Frank shrugged. "It was time, Colton. I usually have it painted every other year. You know that."

Despair, hurt, fury . . . and fear mixed together inside Colton to produce a certainty that he was going to have to recuse himself from this case. But before he did, he had to make sure Jillian was safe and find out if her accusations had any merit. The sick feeling in his gut said they did. "You never have it painted this early. If you won't talk to me, I'll have someone pick you up and take you downtown." He slapped a fifty on the table and rose. There was no way he would be able to swallow a bite. "Lunch is on me."

He started for the door.

"Colton. Wait."

Colton stopped and spun back to face his uncle. The look on the man's parchment-white face drained some of Colton's fury. "What?"

"I didn't . . ." As before, Frank sank back into the chair. His right hand grasped his left arm and he grimaced. But he looked up at Colton. "The night is fuzzy, I can't remember everything. I guess I had a little too much to drink, but . . . I—" He gasped and panted. "I . . ."

Colton reacted. He pulled out his cell phone and dialed 911, then got his uncle on the floor and loosened the man's clothing while he barked orders at the 911 operator.

"Sir? What is it?"

Colton looked up to see the waiter's anxious face. "See if you can find me some aspirin." The man spun and bolted out the door. Colton looked down at his uncle's pale face. Sweat glistened on his forehead. "Help's on the way, Uncle Frank."

"I didn't . . ."

"Here." The waiter held out two tablets. "Is he going to be all right?"

Colton gave one to Frank. "Chew it up. Gets in your system faster."

Frank chewed and time passed at a snail's pace.

Paramedics finally arrived and Colton stepped back to give them room to work. As they rolled his uncle toward the ambulance, Colton ignored his heavy heart and dialed his captain's number.

30

Colton paced the hallway of the hospital, waiting for someone to give him an update on his uncle. He'd called Jillian and Blake and told them what happened. They'd reassured him that Jillian was staying put.

Aunt Elizabeth and Carmen, followed by Elliott Darwin, rushed through the sliding doors. He held his hands out and Elizabeth slipped her cool, dry ones into his.

"Well? How is he?" she asked.

"Hanging in there."

"What happened?" Elliott asked. His pinched face betrayed his worry for his longtime friend. Friends. Elliott would be crushed when Colton had to break the news about his uncle's possible involvement in a murder. Not to mention how it was going to affect Elliott's career. How it was going to affect the careers of all of the people who'd put their trust in Frank Hoffman. Tamping down his emotions and digging out his cop facade, Colton recapped the lunch, leaving out most of the details.

Carmen shifted, her perpetually bored expression sliding into place.

Elizabeth frowned. "He's been under so much stress lately with the campaign and all. Something is really stressing him out."

"More than just the campaign?"

She shrugged and Colton looked at Elliott. "Do you have any idea what's going on with him?"

"No, but she's right. I've noticed it too."

"Any pressure from the senate about voting a certain way?" Colton asked.

They both shook their heads. Elizabeth said, "I haven't heard him mention anything. Then again, like I said, he's been . . . not himself lately."

Elliott's phone rang. He looked at the screen and his lips tightened. "I need to take this."

"Sure." The man stepped away and Colton looked at his aunt. Her usually smooth features were drawn into a frown, a thoughtful look in her eyes.

"What is it?"

She jerked and her face smoothed. "Nothing."

Carmen let out a sigh. "It's probably those letters he's been getting and hiding in his desk drawer."

His aunt's face suddenly paled. Colton grabbed her arm and led her to a nearby chair as she swayed. She sank into it, never taking her eyes from her daughter. "Carmen, what are you talking about?"

The girl shrugged. "I went looking for some cash so I picked the lock on his desk." Something flickered in her eyes. "I found the letters in an envelope. I think he's stressed about those threats."

"They were threats?" Colton asked.

"Yeah. Apparently my dad did something he shouldn't have and someone's threatening to tell."

Colton drilled his aunt with a look. "I need to see those letters ASAP."

She looked away.

He sank to his haunches in front of her. "Did you know about those letters?"

"Yes."

"Why didn't you say anything?"

"Because I . . . I just found them the other day." She shot a look at Carmen. "Carmen's not the only one who knows how to snoop." She bit her lip, then firmed her jaw and met his gaze. "But I had to know why he was being so secretive. He kept locking himself away in that office and I—" She broke off and swallowed hard.

"You what?" Colton asked, keeping his voice low.

Her eyes shot to Carmen's, then slammed back into his. "I thought he was having an affair."

Carmen snorted and shook her head. "Figures."

At Colton's sharply indrawn breath, she cast her eyes to the left, then the right, and lowered her voice even more. "Well, he wasn't, but what else was I supposed to think? The secretive phone calls, the dash to the mailbox, the working at home when he would usually be at his office? I didn't know what to think, so I searched his desk and found them."

"What do they say?" He looked between his cousin and his aunt, waiting for one of them to tell him.

His aunt's eyes darted. "Not here. Come to the house later after Frank's stable and I'll show you. You're a detective. Maybe you can get to the bottom of it."

"Fine."

Colton gestured to the nearby waiting room. "Do you want some coffee?"

"No, not from this place." She gave a delicate shudder.

A toddler got away from his mother and ran on unsteady legs to fall at their feet. Before Colton could react, his aunt swooped down and lifted the little one up. She held him until the weary woman could claim him, and Colton almost smiled.

A snob to the core with a heart of gold.

Carmen had settled into a nearby chair and shoved the earbuds to her iPod into her ears. Already, the whole idea of her father possibly dying and the threatening letters was being drowned out by whatever she listened to. She had her eyes closed, head back against the wall.

A doctor appeared from the hall, his eyes scanning the waiting area until they landed on Elizabeth and Colton. Colton touched his aunt's arm and nodded. She rose and approached the man in green scrubs, blue booties, and white lab coat. Carmen stayed tuned out and Colton left her that way. He followed a few steps behind his aunt. The doctor didn't look like he had tragic news to deliver.

As they shook hands, the man said, "I'm Dr. Cordell, Senator Hoffman's cardiologist."

"How is he?" his aunt asked.

The door swooshed open and Colton sighed when he saw the media headed their way. "Is there someplace private we can talk?"

He didn't have to ask twice. Colton got Carmen's attention and motioned for her to follow. She gave a sigh and got to her feet. Dr. Cordell led them down the hall to a small room with several chairs. They each took one and the doctor said, "Right now, he's stable. The emergency surgery went well, but he's had another heart attack. I've got his chart from the one he had ten years ago. That one was a warning. This one is a bit more serious."

"How serious?"

"He's going to have to take it easy. Get rid of some of the stress in his life."

Elizabeth raised a delicate brow. "Good luck with that."

"He's got to. Or he's going to die."

Colton looked at the floor and reached up to rub the back of his neck. He felt a twinge of guilt. Had his accusations at lunch caused the heart attack? And if he was arrested for murder . . . Colton felt sick.

And now he'd learned his uncle had been receiving mysterious letters. "We'll talk to him."

A knock on the door brought his head around to see his mother enter the room. His father followed two steps behind.

Elliott Darwin slipped in behind them. His mother walked over and gave him her "I'm-happy-to-see-you-even-though-you've-disappointed-us-terribly" hug. A weak squeeze with a sad look that was supposed to send him into throes of guilt. Fortunately, it didn't work anymore.

He kissed her forehead. "Hi, Mom."

"Hello." She stepped back.

Colton's father shook his hand. "Colton." Then turned to the doctor. "I'm Zachary Brady. This is my wife, Sonya. How is he?"

Colton sighed. At least he'd gotten a handshake.

The doctor repeated his earlier statements, then stood. "I've got to get back in there. He'll be in ICU for at least the next forty-eight hours and will be in an induced coma for now. I'll have another update for you soon."

Colton said, "I've got to get back to work. Keep me updated on Uncle Frank, will you?"

His aunt nodded. "I will."

Colton's phone buzzed and he pulled it from his pocket as he started to leave the room.

"Colton, wait—" At his mother's voice, he turned.

"Let the boy go, Sonya," his father huffed. "You heard him. He has to get back to work."

His mother wilted against the chair, her defeated posture rousing his ire toward his father. But he knew if he said anything, it would just make the situation worse. "I'll talk to you later, Mom."

She nodded and Colton left. He'd missed the call from his captain. He hit speed dial. The man answered with a gruff, "Where are you?"

"At the hospital. My uncle had a heart attack while we were eating lunch."

Captain Murdoch's tone changed. "Oh hey, sorry about that. He going to make it?"

"He's stable right now. What do you have for me?"

"A court order and the widow's agreement to exhume the governor's body."

Colton sucked in a deep breath. "All right." He paused.

"What is it, Brady?"

"I think it's time I recused myself from this investigation."

"I see. Who's the best person to take it over?"

"Hunter Graham."

"I'll call him."

31

Jillian sat in the car beside Mrs. Martin as Governor Martin's body was exhumed. "I'm sorry," she said without taking her eyes from the proceedings.

Mrs. Martin turned quizzical eyes toward Jillian. "Whatever do you have to be sorry for?"

With a small shrug, Jillian said, "This. Everything."

Mrs. Martin took a deep breath and turned to watch the coffin slowly emerge from its resting place. "It's time for the truth to come to light. Harrison was very much about justice. This is a good thing, I promise you." She gave Jillian a small smile. "Why do you think I had him interred in a climate-controlled area? I prayed for this day to come. If his body holds any evidence, your ME should be able to find it." The whir of the machine stopped and everyone went silent. A moment of respect for the man and his wife.

Workers moved the coffin into the waiting hearse. Security was tight and numerous around the area.

Jillian asked, "Do you plan to come to the morgue?"

"No. I don't suppose I will. I've signed all the papers." She let her gaze fall on the disappearing hearse. "Harrison's not in that box."

"No, ma'am, I know he's not."

"God had a reason for allowing Harrison to die when he did. I don't know what it was and I've managed to gain peace with that over the years. But," she drew in a deep breath, "if you can prove he wasn't killed in a car wreck, I think that would add a new layer of peace. You know what I mean?"

"I know."

The woman offered a gentle smile and Jillian felt her throat clog as she thought about the families affected by that night ten years ago. Good families. God-fearing and loving people who probably hadn't done anything to hurt anyone.

She straightened her spine and firmed her jaw as Colton and Hunter walked toward them.

She'd made the right decision.

5:15 PM

Jillian stared out the window and watched the hearse leave, escorted by several police cruisers. Now that it was over, she was stunned by how fast it had happened.

"You all right?" Colton asked as he slid into the seat beside her and shut the door.

She shrugged. "Antsy. Anxious. Anticipating."

"You got a thing for A words today?"

"When they're A-ccurate."

He gave a mock wince and she found a small smile on her lips as she buckled her seatbelt. Within twenty minutes they were pulling up to the morgue entrance. Blake and Colton never dropped their guard as they ushered her in. Hunter and Katie pulled up the rear.

Jillian allowed herself to be escorted through a door that reminded her of a garage door. When it settled closed behind them, Serena stepped around the corner and motioned them back. The coffin rolled in on the gurney and the team opened the lid. Jillian held her breath while Serena looked inside. She grimaced. "He didn't die a pleasant death, did he?" She continued her perusal. "I will say as bad as he's burned, he's very well preserved."

"His wife did that on purpose." Jillian looked at Colton. "She knew his death wasn't an accident so she put him in a climate-controlled grave."

"How very insightful. Lucky for us."

He paused as he thought and watched Serena. "When she got the report from Gerald that there was no sign of foul play, she probably didn't know what to do after that. She trusted him—it would be hard to question his findings."

"So she prayed and waited."

He looked at her. "She didn't know it at the time, but she was waiting for you to come home."

"Maybe."

After Serena and her assistant, with the help of two other morgue workers, got Governor Martin onto the table, she went to work. Jillian watched her make the Y-incision over the previous one. Her stomach churned. Not at the sight of the autopsy, but at the thought of this man being murdered and his family being threatened. Would justice finally be done?

Please, Lord, Jillian whispered her silent prayer.

She heard Colton's phone buzz. He looked at it and said, "My aunt is calling. I'm just going to step outside and see what she needs."

She turned pained eyes on him. "I'm sorry," she whispered.

"Yeah. Me too. Especially since it looks like you're right about everything."

"I wish I wasn't."

His jaw clamped. "What matters is the truth." He nodded toward Governor Martin's body. "Truth and justice for him. For all the people involved—"

"Well, I can tell you one more thing," Serena said.

Jillian whipped her head around. "What?"

Even Colton tensed and ignored his still-buzzing phone. Serena looked up over her mask. "I haven't examined his head yet—he may have died from blunt force trauma as the original report states, but he was also shot." A clink sounded. "And there's the bullet."

Jillian gasped, felt her knees buckle. Colton's strong hand gripped her arm. She caught herself and looked up into his face. Now that the truth stared him in the eye, he was devastated.

And she'd caused that.

"Something else is pretty interesting," Serena went on with a sympathetic glance in Colton's direction. To Jillian she said, "You said the senator pulled the gun and shot the governor. Was the governor facing him? Or leaving the room?"

Jillian frowned. "Facing him. He shot him in the chest."

Serena's glance went back to the body, then to Colton and Jillian. "I thought that's what you said." She pushed her mask up and bit her lip. Worry danced in her pretty dark eyes.

"What is it, Serena?"

"That's not what happened, according to the governor here."

Stunned, Jillian asked, "What do you mean?"

"I mean, this man was shot in the back."

32

Frank opened his eyes into a squint and tried to figure out where he was. An annoying beeping echoed in his left ear. Disinfectant teased his nose.

A hospital.

What happened?

He grunted and tried to move.

"He's coming around, Doctor."

Frank blinked again, but his eyes wouldn't stay open.

"Frank, Senator Hoffman, can you hear me? You had a heart attack. You've had surgery. We've taken you off the respirator and you're breathing on your own."

Memories swept over him; the stress returned. Frank winced and decided he liked the blackness better. No pain, no thoughts, no dead governor to haunt him.

The doctors and nurses fussed over him and he just wanted them to go away and let him think. He'd had a heart attack and surgery. Well, what did he expect? Colton's accusations from their lunch together swept to the surface. Cold fear surged. He needed to talk to Elliott. A sharp stab of pain hit him in the chest and he gasped.

"Just a moment, sir. I've got something for that pain, right here. Do you feel any nausea?"

Did he? "No."

"Good. And here you go." The nurse injected something into the port and Frank felt himself swimming off again. But first he had to know.

"What's today?" he heard his voice croak.

"Thursday. You came in earlier and went immediately to surgery."

Thursday. And Saturday was the reunion. He drifted, welcoming the darkness, the escape from the weariness that had become his life. No, he had a good life. A great life. One where Jillian could point her finger and declare him a murderer. Panic set in. Suffocating him.

He couldn't let that happen.

Only he was trapped in a body that had betrayed him.

Think!

But he couldn't.

The drugs worked fast and soon he returned to the blackness.

——■——

Colton stood in the three-car garage and stared at his uncle's boat. Jillian and Hunter stood beside him. He'd thought about leaving her to ride back to the hotel with Blake, but he felt better off knowing she was with him.

One fact remained. His uncle was unconscious in the hospital. He wouldn't be issuing any murderous orders today. If that's what he'd been doing. And staring at the boat, he now had no more doubts, no rationalizations, excuses . . . nothing.

The smell of fresh paint assaulted him and sadness nearly crippled him. He looked at Hunter. "Guess you need to get a sample of that paint to compare to the cloth that Rick has."

"Yeah." Hunter's voice was subdued, but he'd come prepared. He pulled out a small camera and took pictures. Once he finished with the pictures, he took out a tool and started scraping the paint into a small vial. "Want me to call Rick and have him come haul the boat?"

243

"Yes. He'll need to go over it and see if there's anything in there that can connect it with Serena's house bomb." Colton felt a muscle jumping in his jaw. He stood back and let Hunter do all the work. No sense in him messing up the investigation. He couldn't work this anymore. At least not in an official capacity. Hunter and Dominic would have to keep him informed. The fact grated, but it had to be that way. Jillian hadn't said a word since they'd arrived to find the boat in the garage.

And yet, he reminded himself, none of the evidence pointed to his uncle. Not yet.

If the paint on the boat came back a match to the paint on the cloth, then yes, there were some serious questions about his uncle's involvement in the attempts on Jillian's life.

Hunter made the call to Rick. When he hung up, the three of them turned to find Ian watching from the door. "Everything all right, Colton?"

"We're going to find that out, Ian." He took a deep breath. "Hunter's gotten a warrant. Someone is going to come get the boat. It's evidence in a case. Hunter's going to stay with the boat until it's hauled away."

Ian lifted a brow and nodded without saying anything else, but Colton could read the questions and concern in the man's eyes. Unfortunately, Colton couldn't answer them right now.

While Hunter waited with the boat, Colton took Jillian by the arm and entered the house. He made his way through the sunroom, then out onto the porch where Jillian had said his uncle had murdered a man. He felt her stiffen and draw in a harsh breath. "Are you all right?"

"No."

Her strangled answer worried him. "You want to leave?"

"Yes. No."

"Okay."

"Just let me stand here a minute." He watched her glance toward the hall in the direction of his uncle's office, then back to the sunporch. "It's just like I remember."

He tried to imagine the scenario like she'd originally described, but couldn't picture it. Serena's revelation that the governor had definitely not died in a car wreck but had indeed been shot had shaken him. The fact he'd been shot in the back had surprised them all.

That was a fact that didn't jibe with Jillian's story.

So what did he believe?

He could hear his aunt talking on the phone in the den, so he waited. He did not want to tell her everything he was going to have to tell her.

He waited five minutes. Then ten. Finally, he heard her footsteps coming toward him. "He's still unconscious," his aunt said from the doorway.

Colton turned and nodded. He'd expected as much.

His aunt eyed Jillian curiously. "Hello."

"Hi," Jillian said, her voice a bit breathless. "I'm Jillian."

The phone rang again. His aunt sighed and closed her eyes for a brief second. When she opened them, she said, "That thing hasn't stopped ringing since Frank went in the hospital. I hate not to answer, it might be the hospital." She bit her lip as she eyed Jillian, then looked back at Colton.

He said, "It's all right. Jillian knows almost everything about . . . everything."

The phone demanded attention. His aunt drew in a breath. "All right. The notes are in his office. Why don't you wait there? I'll try to just be a minute."

"Okay." Colton took Jillian's small hand in his and strode down the hall to slip inside his uncle's sanctuary. He almost felt guilty, like he was trespassing and bringing a traitor with him.

But no, his uncle was the traitor, not Jillian.

He stepped to the side and studied the room that had been tastefully decorated by his aunt. She'd created a man's space.

A heavy cherry desk dominated a large portion of the area. A leather couch lined one wall. A matching leather chair was behind the desk. Pictures of Frank with well-known people dotted the credenza behind the leather chair. The place was neat to the point of immaculate.

Colton walked to the credenza and picked up a picture.

"Nice office," Jillian said from behind him.

"Yeah." Colton frowned.

"Your aunt decorated it for him, didn't she?"

He lifted a brow. "Yes."

"I can tell." She took a seat on the couch.

Hunter walked in and Colton asked, "Did Rick get here that fast?"

"No. Katie's there supervising. I figured you might need some moral support."

Colton gave his friend a sad smile. "I won't turn that down." Hunter didn't have to say it, but they both knew it would be best to have another detective with Colton at all times. Just to keep everything aboveboard.

He studied the photo in his hand.

Frank, decked out in his Army uniform with his buddies from his unit around him, stared back with a slight smile and narrowed eyes. Special forces. His uncle had been trained to fight. To kill the enemy. And now Jillian was the enemy and his uncle was after her. Colton wondered if he too was considered an enemy. Would his uncle decide to get rid of him now that he knew Colton was a threat? A chill swept through him, followed by a wave of nausea. He couldn't believe what he was thinking.

He put the picture back. Deciding to wait on the couch beside Jillian, he took a step toward it, then stopped. A small piece of paper lay just under the wheel of the leather chair.

The scrap stood out in the neatness of the room. Colton leaned down. The words made his heart skip a beat.

I KNOW WHAT YOU DID. TELL. OR I WILL.

Without a word he showed it to Hunter, who lifted a brow. "Who's that from?"

Another chill shuddered through him as he read the words again. "I don't know."

Jillian? Would she do that? He looked at her and she looked just as confused as the rest of them. No. Surely not. But if not her, then who? Who else knew what happened that night and wanted the senator to know it? His gut twisted.

Aunt Elizabeth returned. "That was Carmen. She was at a friend's house when I called. She's on her way back to the hospital now."

Colton nodded. "Is this one of the letters?" He pointed to it.

She read it and swallowed hard. "Yes."

"There's more?"

"Yes."

Elizabeth swiped her palms down the front of her khaki pants, a nervous gesture Colton had never seen from her before. She looked at Jillian again. "Do you mind waiting in the hall?"

Jillian started, then shrugged. "Sure."

She left the room and Colton frowned. He didn't like her out of his sight.

Elizabeth walked to the desk and slid her hand under the drawer to pull out a key. She looked at Colton. "He keeps the drawer locked but taped the key to the bottom of it. Frank could never keep track of keys."

Colton lifted a brow, but made no comment on his aunt's actions. While he didn't agree with the way she went about searching for evidence against her husband, obviously his uncle had given his wife a reason to doubt him. He felt a pang of hurt for the two of them. She slid the key into the lock and Colton heard the low click.

He opened the drawer and Elizabeth reached in to pull out a manila envelope. "I don't need to read them again." She motioned to the leather chair. "Have a seat."

Colton's eye caught a name written on a piece of paper in the desk. "Wait a minute. What's this?"

Hunter pulled on a pair of gloves and reached in to grasp it. "It's a name. Jillian's name with a bull's-eye drawn around it."

He looked at his aunt. "Uncle Frank thinks Jillian Carter is sending these notes?"

"I don't know. Like I said, he's never mentioned the notes or her to me." Her brow creased. "Is Jillian Carter the girl in the hall?"

"Yes."

"Then let's ask her."

"In a minute." Colton opened the envelope. Then closed it. "This is evidence." He handed it to Hunter. "You need to process it."

She frowned. "Evidence? Evidence for what?"

Colton's heart beat with a painful thud in his chest. He was going to have to tell her his suspicions. "Aunt Elizabeth, I need to talk to you about Uncle Frank."

Wariness flashed in her eyes. "All right."

"Someone has accused him of murder."

She froze. Then lifted a brow and gave a cool little laugh. "Well, that's just silly. Who's making these accusations?" She paused and flicked her gaze toward the envelope still in Hunter's hand, then toward the hall. "The person who sent those notes? This Jillian Carter girl? If she sent those notes, I want her out of my house. Don't you understand what this has done to your uncle? And you dare bring her here?"

Her outrage cut through him, bringing a surge of guilt along with it. "I'm not sure if it's the same person or not. I'm thinking not. I know Jillian and it's not her style to send threatening notes, but we'll let the lab see what they can find on those letters."

"Find something like what?"

"Prints, for one. They'll examine the kind of paper, the ink, everything."

"And you'll be able to track the person that way?"

"Possibly, if it's a special kind of paper."

"Then—" She stopped and waved a hand in dismissal. "That's not important right now. Who is he supposed to have murdered?"

Colton glanced at Hunter, who nodded. "Harrison Martin."

"Harrison?" She gaped at him.

"I know it sounds crazy, but . . . yes."

"If someone has made this accusation against Frank, what's going to happen?"

"Right now, there's no proof." Except some disturbing coincidences.

"So what's going to happen?" she asked again. Anxiety pulled her brows into the bridge of her nose. He noticed the fine lines around her eyes for the first time.

Colton rested his hands on her shoulders. "Nothing for now. There's still no proof that he's done anything wrong." Other than there was a bullet in the governor. A bullet Jillian said his uncle put there. And as soon as ballistics finished the report, he'd know if it was an antique bullet. Colton glanced at the gun collection on the wall. Which one?

Elizabeth fussed with the necklace at her throat. "What about the media? Do they have wind of this yet? That he's been accused of murder?" She lifted a shaking hand to her lips. "Oh, this is just awful."

Colton's heart thumped in sympathy for his aunt. "No. Nothing about that yet. And we're going to do our best to keep it that way." At least until Frank was arrested. The thought sickened him, but it also felt inevitable. The pieces were slowly coming together. Soon, they'd have the big picture.

"Oh, he'll be horrified. It'll ruin his chances in the election."

"That's why we need to get to the truth before that happens." He paused, then asked, "What can you tell me about the night Governor Martin died? June 6th, 2002."

"Oh good grief, Colton, that was ten years ago. How am I supposed to remember what happened that night?"

"It was the night of the fundraising party for Frank. You and my parents came to my graduation that afternoon and then you had the party that night. Do you remember the men arguing?"

She rubbed her forehead. "I don't recall any arguing. No. What time did all this happen?"

"It would have been later, after everyone had left, but before Uncle Frank had his heart attack scare."

"I . . . I'm sorry. I just don't . . ." She sank into a nearby chair. "I remember being at the hospital with Frank, of course. He went to bed and woke up around 1:30 or so complaining he couldn't breathe. I woke Ian and we called 911 and got Frank to the hospital. We were there the rest of the night and for two days after that."

"It was also the night the police came to the house asking if you'd heard a gunshot?"

She blinked. "I do remember *that*. I was upstairs and thought I heard something. But it turned out to be a car backfiring, I think." She rubbed her hands together. "I really think I need to get back to the hospital. I want to be there with Carmen." Her lips tightened. "Especially if the media show up."

Colton nodded. How could she not have heard the argument? If there'd been one. But Jillian had described it in detail. He pursed his lips. "I'll be there as soon as we're finished here."

"Should I stay?"

"No, not unless you just want to."

"I'll stay a few more minutes, then I need to go. I feel like I should probably be with Frank. I only came home to show you those letters. I didn't expect this to take so long." She fretted with the crease in her pants, then smoothed her palms down the front of the material. She pointed a finger toward the hall. Toward Jillian. "If she's the one that's caused this mess, then I want her gone."

33

Jillian's stomach growled as she paced outside the office, waiting for Colton and Hunter. She wasn't sure why Elizabeth Hoffman hadn't wanted her in the room, but that was fine. She needed to think. They'd found the bullet. But the governor had been shot from the back, not the front. How was that possible?

She'd replayed that night over and over in her mind and nothing had changed. She'd seen the senator shoot the governor, the governor facing the senator. She'd *seen* it.

Or had she?

Colton came out of the office and motioned her in. She followed him inside and took her seat back on the couch. Elizabeth's glare pinned her and made her want to squirm. She turned her attention to Colton.

He handed her a plastic-encased note. "Have you ever seen this before?"

Jillian read it. "I KNOW WHAT YOU DID. TELL. OR I WILL." She felt herself weaken. "No."

He studied her a minute, then nodded. Relief filled her. He believed her.

She asked, "So who wrote it?"

"I don't know. Aunt Elizabeth doesn't know either." He shifted and looked at Hunter. "You'll have to question my uncle about the letters."

"I know. When the doctor says it's all right."

Jillian bit her lip and said, "I want to reenact that night."

Colton lifted a brow. He and Hunter exchanged a glance. Hunter gave a slow nod. "I think that's an excellent idea."

Elizabeth jumped up. "What on earth are you talking about? Nothing happened that night except for the fact that my husband almost had a heart attack." Her flushed cheeks told Colton he may have pushed the woman too far.

"Aunt Elizabeth, Jillian was here that night. She saw Uncle Frank shoot Harrison Martin."

Elizabeth's fingers curled into fists as though imagining Jillian's throat trapped within them. "How dare you?"

Colton stood to run interference. "Aunt Elizabeth, please. Just hear her story."

"I won't. Get out of my house."

Jillian stood. "I *didn't* send those notes. I *did* see your husband pull a gun on the governor and pull the trigger." She frowned and bit her lip. "But the governor was shot in the back and I . . ." She looked at Colton and Hunter. "I *didn't* see that."

"Get out now." The woman's cold voice sent shivers up Jillian's spine. She nodded and headed for the door.

"No, wait."

Jillian stopped and turned at Colton's command. He said to his aunt, "I need you to let her do this. For me."

"No."

"Aunt Elizabeth," his voice hardened, "Uncle Frank is being accused of murder and the evidence looks pretty grim. With your help, we might be able to prove he didn't do it. But I need your cooperation. They've already taken his boat as evidence. Now are you going to help me or not?"

Jillian could see the no forming on the woman's lips. Then she clamped them together. After a tense five seconds, she gave a short nod. "Fine."

Colton pulled his phone from his pocket. "Serena called." He looked at Hunter. "Can you give her a call and find out what she wants?" He paused and tucked his phone back in his pocket. "And Rick too. If Jillian's going to re-create this, we might as well have forensics out here. They can help us get a better picture." He rubbed a hand over his eyes. "I have to keep reminding myself I'm not on this anymore."

Hunter started making the calls while Colton led Jillian out of the office. Aunt Elizabeth stayed right on their heels.

At the door to the sunroom, Jillian stopped. Colton saw her swallow hard but square her shoulders.

"You want to wait on Rick?" he asked.

"Yes." Each time she pulled in a breath, she nearly choked on the thick tension.

As they waited for Rick and his team, Jillian watched Elizabeth Hoffman get antsier by the minute. She finally said, "I'm going to the hospital to be with Frank and Carmen. Do whatever you have to do here."

Colton nodded. "I'm sorry, but we really need to do this."

She straightened her shoulders. "Frank didn't shoot anyone. So prove it before his career is done."

"Yes, ma'am."

She drilled a hard stare at Jillian. "Who *are* you? Why do you hate my husband?"

Defensiveness welled up in Jillian. She simply said, "I just want the truth."

For a moment, the woman didn't say anything else. She gave an abrupt spin on her heel and left.

Jillian looked at Colton, who sighed and shook his head. "If this turns out the way I think it's going to, I'll make sure she has support and someone with her."

"Yeah, that would probably be a good idea." She bit her lip, then said, "If the governor was shot in the back, that means there was another person here."

"I know. You're sure you don't remember seeing anyone else?"

"No one. But I wasn't looking for anyone else. The only people I was aware of were Frank Hoffman and Harrison Martin."

Colton nodded. Hunter joined them and said, "Katie's on her way back here with Rick. They'll work with us on reconstructing the scene."

Five minutes later, Rick entered the sunroom. Katie followed him, along with a young woman in her late twenties whom Jillian recognized to be Hunter's younger sister, Christina Graham.

Hunter looked a little surprised to see her. "You're working in the field now?"

She smiled. "Yep."

"Cool."

Jillian got the impression they'd be discussing how that came about at a later time.

Rick looked at Jillian. "I hear we're reconstructing the scene."

"Yes."

"I'll need every detail you can remember."

She nodded. "That won't be hard. I remember everything about that night."

Colton pulled back to the side to watch and Jillian missed his presence next to her. It was obvious now that he'd officially recused himself and handed over responsibility for the investigation to Hunter. The realization of what it meant brought mixed emotions . . . waves of hope that this would soon be over—and sadness for Colton.

Jillian told what she'd seen. "Then the governor laid the gun on the desk and told Frank to take some time to cool off. He walked out of the office and toward the sunroom. Frank came storming out with the gun. They went through the sunroom and out onto the patio. The governor turned and Frank had the gun on him. They argued some more. Frank lifted the gun, stumbled, and pulled the trigger. And they both fell."

"Okay," Rick said. "I think I have a pretty good picture of how that played out. So let's do some role playing here. I'm going to need some help." He started pulling tools out of his bag. "How tall was the governor?"

"He was six feet one inch and weighed a hundred ninety-five pounds," Colton said. Rick lifted a brow at him and Colton shrugged. "I read the original autopsy report."

Rick eyed Hunter. "You'll do. Stand where Jillian says the governor was standing when he was shot."

Jillian positioned him so his back was to the copse of trees, his left side almost touching the side of the sunroom. "No, wait a minute. He'd backed off the porch onto the gravel walkway." She urged him back farther.

Rick nodded to Colton. "I know you're not working this investigation anymore, but you can be used for a moment, can't you? Jillian, place him where Senator Hoffman was."

Colton moved and Jillian took his hand to show him where to stand. His fingers clasped hers and she felt a shiver dance up her arm. When this was over . . . "He was right here, past the table and chairs, near the edge. The gun was in his left hand."

He held his thumb and forefinger like a gun and pointed it toward Hunter.

Jillian stepped back and swallowed hard. The memories rushed over her and she couldn't help the tremor that washed through her. "They argued some more. The senator lifted his gun and pointed it. Then stumbled and pulled the trigger."

Colton acted it out. Hunter fell to the ground and Jillian pushed Colton down to the concrete. She stood back, held her hands to her face, and tried to stop the shaking.

She gathered control as best she could and said, "That's what I saw." She frowned. "But that's not what Serena said happened."

"Okay," Rick said. "I've got it. I've also got the dummies and the lasers. Let's set them up and we'll run through it with the real stuff."

By the time they got everything set up, Jillian felt like she'd been hit by a truck. So much drama and trauma in one day.

Rick looked at her. "Are you sure you didn't hear more than one shot?"

Jillian frowned. "No. It was just one."

Rick motioned to Katie. "And you're sure the senator's gun fired?"

"Yes."

Rick nodded. "Okay, I think I might know what happened. Get one of the lasers and go stand in that area of the trees along the walking path." Katie cocked her head like she wanted to ask questions, but didn't. She walked over to where Rick indicated. Rick then handed Colton one of the lasers. "Point it at Hunter and see where it lands."

Colton did. It hit the dummy in the left shoulder.

Rick said, "He was shot in the upper right side of his back."

"How?" Jillian whispered. "I know what I saw."

"I suspect you saw exactly what you say you saw. I think the senator did fire the gun at the governor. Only he missed." He walked over and studied the brick wall behind the dummy's left shoulder. "It's chipped. My guess is the bullet from the senator's gun hit the wall."

"What?" Jillian stared, incredulous.

"And the person standing where Katie is now," Rick went on, "is the one who actually shot the governor. In the back."

"But there was only one gunshot."

Rick shook his head. "There were two. Fired simultaneously to sound like one shot."

FRIDAY

34

Jillian headed for the coffeepot in the small but efficient kitchen next to her room. After yesterday's stunning revelation, she hadn't known what to think.

So Senator Hoffman hadn't shot the governor.

Then why did he want her dead?

Or—what if it wasn't him? What if it was the real shooter? A sinking sensation swirled in the pit of her stomach.

She poured the coffee and took a sip.

Blake sat on the couch, staring at his phone. He hadn't said a word to her as she'd walked into the room. "Hey, you okay?"

He looked up and she went cold as she saw his panicked expression. Rangers didn't panic. Ever.

She'd only seen that look on him one time before—when the doctors had given his wife three months to live. "What?" she demanded. He covered his panic with that blank look she hated and couldn't read. "Don't look at me like that. What?"

He sighed and ran a hand across his lips. "Mom texted me. She was on her way back to her friend's house when Tony called her and told her there'd been a break-in at the ranch. He said the place was trashed."

She knew immediately what that meant. "They tracked you to

the ranch. For real this time." Her stomach twisted as nausea rose in her throat.

"I'm sorry, Jillian." His tortured eyes told her how sorry he was. It wasn't his fault. She hadn't told him everything. He said, "My buddy realized what that meant and headed straight to the airport."

"The airport?" The words squeaked from her suddenly tight throat.

"Meg's on her way here. She lands at Columbia airport in a little under thirty minutes."

"What!" This time the word was a cry of distress and sheer terror. "He sent her here? She can't come here!"

"What is it?"

Jillian whirled to face the man she'd once loved with all her heart. He held a green and white bag that indicated he'd made a donut run.

He'd slipped into the suite without her hearing. But there was no way Blake hadn't known he was there. Blake had let Colton overhear the exchange. She shot him a betrayed look and saw the guilty flush that darkened his cheeks. He didn't apologize.

Fury—and a certain weird gratefulness—warred within her.

It was time.

She took a deep breath and let it out slowly. "I have to tell you something," she whispered. "And this is *not* how I wanted to do it."

His brows drew together. She sensed, more than saw, Blake slip from the room. Wariness invaded Colton's eyes and she drew in a fortifying breath. *Oh sweet Lord, please give me the words . . .* "I have a daughter. A nine-year-old daughter. Her name is Meg and she's in danger." She watched the words register. He swallowed hard, then blinked.

In a voice so soft she had to strain to hear, he asked, "A daughter?"

"Yes."

"And she's—nine?"

"Almost ten," she whispered. "Christmas Day. In four months."

He nodded and his jaw worked for a good three seconds before he managed, "Almost ten. So . . ."

He looked away, then back. She was sure he was doing the mental math. She could see the question stamped in his eyes before he forced it out.

"She's mine?"

A sob slipped from her lips. "I'm so sorry."

"So she's mine." A statement this time. A strangled three-word sentence that nearly shot her to her knees.

"Yes, she's yours." Jillian bit her lip, refusing to try to find words to justify her actions. It would be a futile search.

He spun away from her. She knew better than to push him for a response. Instead, she waited. And silently prayed. He turned back to her, his eyes shuttered, chilled. "You're sure?"

The cold question knocked the breath from her as the pain lanced through her heart. Okay, she could give him that one. He deserved it. "Yes. I'm sure. You're the only one—"

"Where is she?"

"On her way here." She repeated what Blake had just told her. "She lands in about twenty minutes." Anxiety tugged at her. "We need to go, *now.*"

His nostrils flared, his eyes fluttered. He pulled his phone from his pocket. "Then we're going to need some reinforcements."

Colton couldn't seem to catch his breath as they raced to the car. Blake offered to follow behind to make sure no one tailed them. Colton absently agreed.

Even while his mind reeled with this latest shock, it was also in cop mode. He wanted to rush from the room and find a quiet place to process the fact that he had a daughter, yet he wasn't to have that luxury. They climbed into the car and sped toward the airport.

As he drove, he tried to force his mind to work. And all he could hear was Jillian's shaky voice telling him she'd borne his child. A child who'd existed for almost ten years. A child who had his blood running through her veins.

Aware of the woman sitting next to him, he ignored her, dividing his focus between driving and praying. Silently, he begged, *Oh God, I need some help with this one. What do I do? What do I say? What do I even pray?*

He'd called in reinforcements to make sure Meg was secure the moment the plane touched down. He'd done his duty as a cop.

How was he supposed to act as a father? Resentment threatened to smother him. Anger with Jillian threatened to evolve into full-blown hatred. How could she have kept this from him? They had loved each other. She was supposed to trust him.

A small voice whispered the thought: *She'd just seen a murder.* Was she supposed to trust an eighteen-year-old kid on the outs with his parents?

Part of the fury faded. A small part.

"Colton?"

Her whisper tore at him. He looked at her, her face ravaged by her guilt and terror for her daughter. Their daughter. Colton felt the anger buzz anew and snapped his gaze back on the road. "You came looking for me at the party to tell me you were pregnant, didn't you?"

"Yes."

"So you *were* going to tell me."

"I was."

"And then Uncle Frank shot the governor. Or at least you thought he did . . ."

"And he saw me."

Colton paused. "I became a cop to find you, you know. As a cop, I had more resources available to me." His lips twisted as he shot her a sad look. "But you were too good for me. I still couldn't find you."

"Only because I had Blake to help me disappear."

Yeah. Blake . . .

His phone buzzed and he forced himself to check the number. Dominic. "Hello."

"I've got security on high alert at the airport. We've been in contact with the pilot of the plane and Blake's buddy who's been taking care of Meg. Everything should be fine. Once she's on the ground, Jillian will meet her at the gate."

Some of the tension in Colton's shoulders eased. But not much. "Thanks, Dominic."

"Anytime."

"How's your father?"

A low sigh came through the line. "Fading fast."

Colton winced. "I'm sorry."

"Yeah, well . . . I'm just worried about his eternal destination."

"What does your mom say?"

"She just shakes her head and says what a good man he used to be. Her pastor came by and talked to him when he was having a lucid moment. He looked at mom and mouthed the word, 'Sorry.'"

"Wow."

"Yeah. Alexia left the room at that point, but she was praying, I could tell."

"I'll be praying too."

"Thanks. You okay?"

"Sure. Why would you ask?" He couldn't help the sarcasm.

"You're under enough pressure to crack the strongest man right now."

He kept his gaze from slipping to Jillian. He couldn't look at her. "I'll be all right. Thanks."

He tightened his grip on the wheel . . . then released.

He needed time.

Space.

He needed to think and pray.

And he needed to see—meet—his daughter.

35

Jillian thought her heart might just break in two. In fact, she was quite sure it already had, because she'd never felt a pain like this before. This kind of pain stemmed from being the cause of *another's* pain and it hurt to even breathe.

When Colton's phone rang, she jumped.

He looked at her. "It's Dominic again."

"Put him on speakerphone? Please?"

Colton did. "Yeah?"

"We've been doing background stuff on your uncle and those close to him. Those especially involved in his campaign. We keep coming back to one name."

"Who's that?"

"Elliott Darwin."

"Elliott?" Colton rocked back. "He and my uncle have been friends forever. Elliott's like another uncle to me."

"Elliott was also in the same unit with Nicholas Tremaine. They were in the Navy together."

Colton went still and Jillian stared at him. "The man who tried to kill me at the airport?" she whispered.

"Yeah." He told Dominic, "We'll be at the gate in a few minutes. As soon as I know she's safe, I'll call you back. But text me updates if you have any."

Jillian heard Dominic say, "They're looking for Darwin now."

"Try my uncle's hospital room." Then Colton pulled into the parking lot at the airport.

Jillian shook her head. "I can't believe Blake's buddy brought her here."

"Too late to worry about that now," Colton said.

She sighed. "I know. Let's just get her and keep her safe."

———————

8:16 AM

Jillian followed Colton into the airport. His phone rang as they walked into the building. He snatched it. While he talked, Jillian's eyes searched the boards for her daughter's flight. Relief coated her nerves as she found the ON TIME status at 8:22. Then her breath hitched as it changed to DELAYED. She rushed to the counter. "Why is flight 2327 delayed? Is something wrong? Did something happen on the plane?"

The attendant peered at Jillian over the top of her glasses. "No, ma'am, everything is fine." She clicked a few keys on the computer. "We just have several flights arriving at the same time. Some are having to circle for a few minutes until we can get everyone on the ground."

Jillian sagged. "Okay, thanks." She looked at the board again and saw the time now said 8:31. She could handle that short delay.

Blake hung back and she knew he was watching for anyone and anything suspicious. Colton hung up, spoke to security, and flashed his badge to everyone who got in his way. Jillian stayed right behind him, her goal to get to the gate and gather her child in her arms.

She finally made it to the gate and could go no farther. Her eyes darted, her nerves tingled.

Please, God, let her be fine.

Her arms ached with a physical pain that only the feel of Meg would soothe. Jillian's heart thumped and her adrenaline flowed.

She glanced around, her eyes bouncing from one person to the next. The man in the hoodie. Was he waiting for Meg? Waiting to snatch her and hold her as leverage against her mother? Or was it the innocent-looking blond with the Coach purse and high heels?

Get a grip, Jillian. She took a deep breath and felt Colton's gaze on her. He'd hung up the phone, but his tight lips and narrowed eyes said the news wasn't good. Either that or his response was due to the fact that he was going to meet his daughter for the first time. Her stomach dipped and swirled and she thought she might be sick from the nerves and fear alone.

But the senator was in the hospital. There'd been no more attempts to kill her since the day before.

Colton's hand squeezed her shoulder. "She'll have security all around her. Blake's buddy is with her. She'll be fine." Even after what she'd done to him, he still offered her comfort. Emotion swept over her, tears rising to the surface. She loved him. She'd never stopped.

What a relief to admit it.

"I don't know what she looks like," Colton said as he looked at passengers. The raw pain in his voice nearly shattered her.

When she could speak again, she whispered, "She looks like you."

Jillian felt the fine tremor that shook him.

Time passed at a snail's pace. She glanced at the clock on the wall, then at the door Meg would come from. Colton paced, and while Jillian knew he should be distracted by the thought of meeting Meg in just a few minutes, she noticed he never stopped scanning the area, never let his guard down just because they were in an airport with extra security. And neither did Blake.

The flow of people picked up. The plane had landed and was now unloading.

Jillian tensed as she watched each person. She examined the face of every child.

Where was Meg?

36

"There!" Jillian gasped and pointed as she grabbed Colton's arm. "There she is."

Colton honed in on a slender young girl with reddish gold hair and long skinny legs extending from her green shorts. He felt frozen, unable to move.

"Mom!"

The child's high-pitched cry reached his ears as Meg hurled herself down the rest of the steps. Blake's friend, a tall man in his late twenties with a shiny bald head, hurried after her. Colton's eyes darted from one face to the next, looking for anything that represented danger to her. Only when Meg flung herself into Jillian's arms did the tension in Colton's shoulders relax a fraction.

"Oh Meg, I missed you, baby." Jillian buried her face in Meg's neck.

"I missed you too, Mom. Now can you let me go? You're smashing my nose."

She looked like a young Liliana Mumy. He waited.

"Uncle Blake!" Meg flew from her mother's arms into Blake's waiting ones. He lifted her easily from her feet by her biceps and brought her eye to eye with him. "Hey, Spunky."

She kissed his nose. "Let me down."

Blake put her on the floor and reached out to shake Meg's escort's hand. "Tony."

"Blake."

"Thanks for keeping her safe."

"No problem. She kept me on my toes." He shook his head and said, "Give me a tour in Iraq any day, it's easier."

Colton also shook the man's hand. "You need a place to stay?"

"Naw, I got a buddy here who's been asking me to come visit. He's waiting on me now unless you need anything else."

"I think we can take it from here."

Meg and Tony said their goodbyes, the little girl giving him a neck-crushing hug. Colton saw the man smile. Not such a hard heart after all.

Colton continued to assess the area as did Blake now that Meg was safe and Tony was gone.

And then the little girl was standing in front of him, eyes wide, mouth open. He offered her a smile. "Hello, Meg."

She reached out and touched his hand. It felt like she'd singed him with a match. "You're real."

Confused, he squatted so he was eye level with her. "Of course I am." With his forefinger, he tapped her on the forehead. "Just like you are."

"No, I mean you're . . . you."

Colton's eyes sought Jillian's. Tears stood there, trembling on her lashes, fingers pressed to her lips. Meg had recognized him. His heart thudded. "Who do you think I am, Meg?"

A grin spread across her lips, exposing a deep dimple in her left cheek. "My dad." She pulled a locket from beneath her shirt and opened it. Then she turned it around so he could see it. His high school senior picture. "Mom gave it to me and said I needed to know what you looked like when I met you one day. I been waiting a lo-o-ong time."

Colton felt the air in his lungs simply leave. The knot in his throat made it hard to swallow. It was a good thing Blake was there to watch for any trouble because Colton was simply unable to function at the moment. Somehow he found his voice. "She told you about me, huh?"

"Sure. She told me all kinds of stuff about you. She said you were the best thing that ever happened to her, next to me of course, and that you loved me even though you never met me." Another grin and a flash of her dimple and Colton was lost.

"Well, she was right about that."

"Good. Cuz that makes it easier to love you even though I never met you." She giggled, then stepped forward to wrap her slender arms around his neck. Colton hugged her back and tried to get a grip on his roller-coastering emotions. The transparency of a child. What you saw was what you got. If only everyone could be that way, unfettered by appearances and what people thought of them.

Holding his daughter next to his heart, there was one thing he did recognize. Now that he knew about Meg, there was no way he wasn't going to be a part of the rest of her life. He lasered a look toward Jillian. She had her lips pressed together to keep them from trembling. A few stray tears streaked her cheeks.

She nodded. "I know, Colton."

Colton looked at Blake and the security surrounding them. One man had tears in his eyes. Colton stood and cleared his throat, a tad embarrassed at the display. "Okay, let's get out of here." He thanked those who'd acted as his daughter's bodyguards. "Appreciate the extra measure."

"No problem . . . Sure thing," came the replies.

Colton's phone rang. A glance at the screen told him he wanted to take this one. "Hey, Dominic, can you give me ten minutes?"

"Yeah."

Colton, with Blake's help, ushered Jillian and Meg toward the waiting vehicle. They'd parked in police parking just outside.

He looked at Blake. "Keep your eyes open for anything. I doubt we've anything to worry about until we get on the highway, but just in case . . ."

Blake nodded and moved closer to Jillian. Colton had moved in front, keeping Meg between him and Jillian.

The airport was active, but not terribly busy. He glanced to the right, then left. Then right again.

"Clear."

He opened the rear door and helped Meg into the car. Jillian slid in next, her hand already reaching for the seatbelt to help Meg fasten it. Colton rounded the car toward the driver's side.

Blake pulled open the front passenger door and leaned in. "I'll follow you—" He stiffened and swiveled his head to the left.

Then Colton heard it.

A roaring engine, growing louder under the cover of the waiting area.

He hollered, "Get in!" as he jumped into the driver's seat.

Blake dove into the front seat and slammed the door. "Get down, Jillian! Cover Meg!"

In the rearview mirror, Colton saw Jillian act. He pressed the gas pedal and shot from the parking space. Already security was in action.

"It's a motorcycle, Blake."

The bike blasted past and came to a stop at the curb. Security followed. The driver of the bike pulled his helmet off and grinned at the woman beelining toward him.

"Idiot," Colton muttered under his breath but some of the tension left him as he pulled the car over to let Blake get out.

"What was that all about?" Jillian asked.

"Just a guy showing off for his girlfriend. Security's blasting him."

His phone buzzed in answer to the next question on his mind. Dominic said, "Just got off the phone with the team going through Darwin's home. Nothing yet, but I'll keep you posted. You have Jillian and Meg?"

"I've got them." He could still feel Meg's sweet arms around his neck.

"Stay safe, Colton."

"Yeah." He knew he sounded short; he was just too full of emotions to talk right now and he needed to keep his wits about him in order to obey Dominic's order to keep Meg and Jillian safe.

"Right."

"Hey, sorry."

"You don't have to apologize to me."

"How's your dad?"

"We've said our goodbyes."

Colton winced. "Stay in touch."

"You know it."

Jillian held on to Meg as they pulled into the hotel parking lot. The child had been quiet, as though sensing the tension running through the car. She'd only had a small backpack with her and Jillian knew Blake's mother had acted quickly. She just prayed the woman would stay in hiding for a little while longer. At least until she received word from Blake that this was all over.

Oh please let it be over soon, she prayed.

Blake and Colton ushered them into the hotel while Jillian hovered over Meg, determined that if someone was going to take a shot at them, Meg wouldn't be the target.

She noticed Colton covering *her* back.

Inside the lobby, she breathed a sigh of relief. Meg kept her hand snug inside Jillian's, no doubt still feeling some of the tension. Colton didn't say much on the short ride up to the room, but Jillian caught him shooting glances at Meg.

Blake opened the door and Meg stepped inside. "Wow, nice place you got here."

Jillian smiled. "Thanks." She pointed to her bedroom. "You're in there with me." She looked up in time to see Blake nod at Colton and slip out the door.

Meg bounced across to the room and pushed open the bedroom door. She tossed her backpack onto the bed, then spun around. "I'm hungry. What's a girl got to do to get some food around here?" She grinned and planted her hands on her hips.

"I'll call room service," Colton said. "What do you like?" Jillian noticed his jaw tighten as he waited for Meg's answer. He didn't like that he had to ask that last question.

Meg said, "I like anything. Eggs and bacon mostly. With toast. And orange juice. And those little hash brown potato things if they have them. And a hot chocolate. And—"

"Okay," Jillian broke in. "I think we can stop at the hash browns."

Meg gave a small pout, then grinned. "Never hurts to try." She spun back into the room and attacked her backpack with that energy Jillian always envied. Meg pulled out a blue-and-black one-piece swimsuit. "So, when are we going swimming?"

Colton couldn't seem to take his eyes from the girl. Jillian figured she'd give him some room to process everything. "We'll be right back, okay?"

He nodded. "Sure. Yeah."

She crossed into the bedroom and shut the door. "Meg, honey, why did you bring your swimsuit?"

Her daughter shrugged. "Grandma Jo said we were staying in a hotel, so I figured, why not?"

Jillian rushed over to gather the girl in a tight squeeze. "I've missed you."

Meg tightened her arms. "Not as much as I've missed you."

Jillian ignored the knot in her throat. "Well, we can't go swimming yet, I'm afraid."

Meg pouted. "Why not?"

How much should she tell her? Jillian didn't want to scare the child to death, but she wanted her to be on guard nevertheless. "Because there are some really bad people after me and I have to be very careful where I go right now."

Meg frowned. "Why is someone after you?"

"Because I saw something and these people don't like that I saw it."

"So they want to take you out so you can't testify?"

Jillian rocked back. "What? Where on earth did you learn that kind of talk?"

She shrugged. "Grandma Jo likes *NCIS*, you know that."

She did know that. She just didn't know Grandma Jo, Blake's mother, was allowing her impressionable daughter to watch it. "I'm going to have to talk to Grandma Jo. In the meantime, I need you to keep your head down and stay with an adult at all times."

"Can one of those other adults take me swimming? Like my dad?" She chewed on her lip. "He's really my dad, isn't he? For real?"

Jillian's heart thudded. "Yes. For real."

Meg cocked her head and studied Jillian. "I'm glad." She picked up the swimsuit and shook it at her mother. "I still want to go swimming."

Colton backed from the door where he'd been shamelessly eavesdropping. It sounded like Jillian was a good mother. Not that he really had any doubts. She and Meg shared a strong bond in spite of the circumstances of her birth.

He glanced at his watch and wondered how his uncle was doing. He hated being out of the loop, but for now his priority was keeping his girls safe.

His girls. A tremor raced through him. He liked the sound of that.

Colton pulled his phone from his pocket as he headed back to the couch. He dialed Hunter's number.

"Hey," Hunter answered.

"Hey. You got anything newsworthy?"

"I've been meaning to call you, just haven't had a chance. I've been working this other case that dropped in my lap earlier this morning and it's taken up a lot of my time."

Colton winced. He had managed to delegate most of the cases sitting on his desk, but not all of them. His captain was a good one, not a micromanager as long as he was kept in the loop. But even Captain Murdoch had his limit and would have to tell Colton to get busy on his other cases. Colton was running out of time. "So what is it?"

"We got a search warrant for Darwin's home. So far he hasn't turned up. Wasn't in your uncle's hospital room either. We've got someone on the house. We'll get him if he comes home."

"Good."

"One interesting thing. We did find a shirt in the neighbor's trash that looked like it had the same pattern as the scrap of material found at Serena's. Be glad trash pickup isn't until Monday."

Satisfaction zipped through him. "About time we had a break."

"I know." He paused. "Rick's working on the boat."

Something in Hunter's tone clued Colton in. "What did he find?"

"A line-throwing device."

"That tells me nothing. What's that?"

Hunter snorted. "It's a shotgun with a device that goes into the barrel. It has a large soft pad on the end and a rope attached. It's used at sea to 'toss' a line between vessels over long distances. Distances that are farther than can be thrown by hand."

"So all this guy had to do was replace the pad with the explosive device and—"

"And boom. It had the same chemicals on it that were found in Serena's house."

He got the idea. "That's the device used to launch the bomb into Serena's house."

"Exactly."

"Smart. So where is this guy?"

"We're still working on that."

"Keep an eye on my uncle's hospital room. He might show up there."

"Will do. When you have some time, Serena said she had something to show us."

Colton looked at his watch. "Can she bring it over here?"

"I'll ask her."

37

Jillian distracted Meg with one of her favorite Disney shows on the television in the bedroom. She walked into the main living area in time to see Colton hang up the phone. She held back, unsure of her welcome anymore.

He looked at her. "It's going to take some time."

Jillian swallowed hard. "I know."

"I'm angry. And hurt. And . . ." He shook his head. "I don't even know what else."

"I understand."

"And . . ."

She tensed. "What?"

"After hearing all you've been through, seeing the attempts on your life with my own eyes . . ." He paused and rose to stand in front of her. "I can't deny you had a very good reason for doing what you did. I just wish—"

"I shouldn't have done it. I should have told you." Tears leaked and slid down her cheeks. "I wish I'd done it all different, but I . . . I was eighteen and scared and . . ." She couldn't form the words.

"We can't go back and change it. And if we could, I don't know that it would be the best move."

She sniffed. "What?"

"You kept her alive. You kept both of you alive. Back then, we were kids. Young and probably more stupid than we remember. My gut tells me if you hadn't run, you'd be dead."

Relief at his ability to look at things objectively, even when his emotions had to be running crazy, slid through her. "Our guts agree then," she whispered.

"There's just no way to tell." He drew in a deep breath. "I have a decision to make."

"About what?"

"Whether to hold on to my bitterness and anger at missing out on the first ten years of Meg's life . . ."

"Or?" Hope blossomed.

"Or let it go and grab on to what I have now with both hands."

A tear slipped down her cheek. "I know what I want you to do."

He pulled her into a sudden hug, then leaned down to capture her lips. Emotion swelled and she kissed him back with everything in her. When he pulled away, he leaned his forehead on hers. "I've never stopped loving you, Jillian."

Her throat clogged on her response. She managed a nod and a smile.

He gave her another tender kiss. "I want to see what we can have together. The three of us."

"Me too." All she could do was whisper.

"So does this mean y'all are getting back together?"

They both jumped at Meg's impish question.

Because Jillian still hadn't found her voice, Colton answered, "Time will tell, Meg."

"Well, just want you to know, it's okay with me if you do." She fingered her necklace. "I'm tired of wearing you around my neck and just hearing stories about you. I want to be able to give you hugs every day."

A quiet sob escaped Jillian and she thought she saw a sheen of tears in Colton's green eyes. He nodded and held out a hand to his daughter. Meg joined them and Jillian sucked a breath in at the small circle they made.

Finally, there was a chance they could be a family.

"So will I ever get to go swimming?" Meg asked.

A knock on the door disrupted the little reunion before she or Colton could answer her question.

Colton pulled away and stepped to check the peephole. "It's Serena."

He let her in.

Serena took one look at Jillian and asked, "Are you all right?"

"Yes."

Serena's gaze bounced from Meg to Colton to Jillian. "Really?"

"Really." Jillian placed her hands on Meg's shoulders and said, "Meg, I want you to meet one of my very best friends. This is Serena Hopkins."

"Hello, Ms. Hopkins." Meg held her hand out for a shake. "You're pretty and tall. Are you a model?"

Serena grinned. "I like this girl," she said to Jillian. To Meg, she said, "I'm a medical examiner."

"Oh cool!"

"Thanks."

Jillian steered her child back to the bedroom. "Finish your show, hon, okay?"

"Sure, sure. Send the kid to the bedroom so y'all can do your grown-up talk. I get it."

Jillian smothered a smile. Her baby could always make her smile. "Thanks."

Meg quirked a brow at her, looking so much like Colton it took her breath away. Meg turned back. "I'll stay out of your hair, but you owe me."

"Add it to my tab."

"Of course." Meg disappeared into the room and shut the door.

When Jillian turned back, Serena had a piece of paper in her hand. Blake came from the other bedroom and the four of them sat.

Serena said, "This is a copy. The original was buried with the governor."

Jillian gasped. Colton grunted. Blake looked interested. "What is it?"

"A letter. Now sit back and listen." She took a deep breath and read, "'If you are reading this, then you've exhumed Harrison's body because you've found something amiss in his death. You are right. He did not die in the staged car accident that burned the majority of his body. He died from a gunshot wound to the back. The small caliber bullet that caused the wound was right to left, back to front, and downward and diagonally piercing the heart and lodging in the lower 10th floating left rib.'"

Colton leaned forward as Serena continued. "'The body came to me. I was in the process of doing the autopsy when I received an anonymous phone call telling me to falsify the autopsy report or my family would die. If I agreed to falsify the report, I would receive the money needed to pay the hospital and my daughter would receive the kidney she couldn't live without. The caller demanded an answer at that moment. He described my wife and two youngest children, noting what each one was wearing. He also knew that my oldest daughter, Tracy, was at the hospital getting dialysis. He went on to say that if I did not agree to falsify the report, they wouldn't make it home from the movie. It went against everything I believed in, but I agreed. I would receive instructions on where to pick up the cash and how to make it look like a loan from my in-laws and my daughter would receive her kidney. As I write this, I don't know if this will come to pass, I just know I have to protect my family at this moment. I don't know who the caller was. I don't know the details of why these people wanted the shooting covered up. I just know that my good friend is dead and I've done him a horrible injustice by calling his death an accident. I've prayed for the Lord to forgive me and I pray that one day the murderer will be brought to justice. Sincerely, Gerald Benjamin, M.D.'"

Colton blew out a breath when Serena stopped reading. "Well, guess we know why the man was so agitated the last few weeks of his life."

"What a choice," Jillian muttered. "I don't know that I wouldn't have done the same thing given the circumstances. Still . . . couldn't he have gone to the authorities after the fact?"

Colton shrugged. "He probably had no proof. He'd still done something illegal . . . I don't know what would have happened. But from what his wife said, it sounds like he was overcome with guilt and was going to tell."

"And they knew it," Jillian said. "They were watching him and knew it."

"So they killed him."

"Who could set something like that up?" Serena asked.

Colton rubbed a hand over his face. "My guess is this person after Jillian has military training. The bomb at Serena's, getting into the lake house with the tranquilizer gun—everything is very professional, precise."

"And I'm still alive." She looked at Serena. "We all are. Any more attempts to get to you?"

She shook her head. "I was followed to work yesterday. Dominic was with me and noticed the tail. I still have Chris, my bodyguard, and if the person following me was planning to try anything, he was scared off."

"And Alexia?"

"No. Nothing."

"Probably because I'm here," Jillian said. "I'm the one they've wanted all along."

Serena yawned. "Well, I'd better get back to work before I decide to go home and take a nap."

Colton stood. "I'll walk you down."

"No need. Chris is right outside the door."

They said their goodbyes and Serena left, Chris at her side.

Colton turned. "Why don't you get some rest while you can? I'll entertain Meg."

Jillian bit her lip and he smiled.

"Come on, Jilly, I want to spend time with her."

"All right. I am exhausted. Maybe I'll take that nap since Serena can't."

"Great." Glee entered his eyes. "Hey Meg, you want to play charades?"

Meg came to the door and crossed her arms. "Any chance I can talk you into a swim?"

Colton motioned the little girl over. "I promise, when all of this is over, I'll take you swimming."

Meg released a heavy sigh. "I don't get it. We'll be inside and you'll be there. You won't let anything happen to me."

"Which is why we're going to play charades."

Another dramatic sigh ensued. She turned back into the room, and Jillian was just about to reprimand the child for being rude when Meg came back into the room with a deck of cards.

"Can we at least play something fun like Texas Hold 'em?"

"Meg!"

Meg shrugged and gave them an innocent look. "What?" Then giggled. "Okay, how about Hearts?"

SATURDAY

38

Jillian opened her eyes—to an empty side of the bed. She reached out a hand to run it over the shallow indentation left by Meg's head.

Then frowned as she looked at the clock.

What was Meg doing up so early? Especially when her body was on California time, which would be 5:30 in the morning. Usually when she had the chance to sleep in, Meg did so. But it was a new place, a strange situation. Maybe she couldn't sleep.

So where was she?

Shoving her tangled curls from her face, Jillian sat up and swung her legs over the side of the bed. She heard the suite door click as she stumbled into the bathroom.

Empty.

Maybe Meg and Colton were having breakfast. Jillian dressed in a pair of shorts and a yellow T-shirt. She stepped into the main living area and stopped. Also empty. Now the worry kicked in. "Meg? Where are you?"

Colton came from the other bedroom, freshly shaven, eyes alert. "What is it?"

"Is Meg with you?"

"No." He frowned. "I thought she was sleeping in there with

285

you." He walked to the balcony's sliding door and looked out. "She's not out there."

The knot in Jillian's stomach doubled. "Where's Blake?"

"He's doing a routine safety check of the hotel. You know, the stairwells, the elevator . . ."

Her blood hummed as her pulse picked up speed. "All right. Meg's gone. Blake's gone. He wouldn't have taken her with him, would he?"

Colton's jaw went rigid. "Not if he has any brains." He pulled out his phone and she knew he was calling Blake. She raced back into the bedroom and slipped her feet into the flip-flops Alexia had provided.

Back in the living area of the suite, Colton stood by the door. "Blake doesn't have her. He's looking for her now."

Jillian's fingers curled into fists. "I can't believe this. She slipped out of the room."

"If she's not here, it's the only explanation."

"But why? When I get my hands on her . . ."

She started toward the door and he said, "Wait a minute. You can't go out there. This might be some kind of trap to get you out of the room."

"Or it might be a way to get me alone in the room with no one to help me fight back."

He grimaced. "Yeah."

He pressed his eye to the peephole, then opened the door. They slipped into the hall. She noticed he kept his hand on his weapon even though he hadn't pulled it. Yet.

She stopped and said, "I heard the door click."

"When?" They walked toward the elevator.

"Just a few minutes before I came in the living area looking for her. I thought it was you or Blake coming back with breakfast or something."

"Blake was gone at least thirty minutes before that." They stepped onto the elevator. "We'll check the lobby."

286

Jillian swallowed hard. "She did leave on her own then," she whispered as frantic fear spread through her veins. "We have to find her."

"We will."

"The pool."

"What?"

"I didn't check to see if her suit was missing, but I'm guessing she went to the pool."

"Then that's where we'll check first."

Hysteria welled. "What if he's watching the hotel?" She managed to control the quiver in her voice. "Can you call Blake and tell him to check the pool?"

Colton dialed the number. "No answer."

The elevator dinged, indicating they'd arrived on the first floor. Colton held her back when she would have dashed off. He stepped out, looked both ways like he was crossing the street, then motioned for her to follow him.

Jillian hurried after him. "The pool's that way."

"I know."

Together, they headed toward it.

As they drew closer, Jillian heard a scream that shot terror straight to her heart. "Meg!"

———■———

Colton bolted in the direction of the scream, his heart pounding. He rushed into the pool area. A woman stood staring at the emergency exit and she spun at his entrance.

Her eyes widened as she saw his gun. He flashed his badge and she pointed to the door. "He took her! Just grabbed her and went out the door." Colton didn't have time to waste. He hollered to Jillian, "Stay with me!" He shoved his phone at Jillian. "Call 911!"

"I already did," the woman called.

Jillian stayed on his heels, her breaths coming in panicked gasps as she tried to keep up while dialing. "I'm trying Blake."

He burst through the exit into the sweltering outdoor heat.

From the corner of his eye, he saw movement, heard Meg's scared cry. Feet pounding against the asphalt, he raced toward them. "Police! Freeze!"

And the man did. For a split second.

Blake appeared on the opposite side of the would-be kidnapper. "Let her go!"

Meg hollered and kicked back into his shins. He flinched, but didn't loosen his grip.

Jillian rushed up. "Let her go! She's just a little girl!"

"Let me go!" Meg screamed. "Mom!" Her eyes landed on Colton. "Daddy, help me!"

Colton felt his heart slam into his chest at her words. Daddy . . .

The man spun, Meg still clutched against him, his face covered with a black mask. "Get back! Get back now or she's dead!"

Colton felt Jillian's presence behind him, her terror making the air vibrate around them. Blake caught his eye and pulled his weapon. Colton said, "Meg, be still. The man is going to let you go."

His small daughter in her blue-and-black bathing suit ceased her struggles, her gaze locked on his. Colton felt the trust in her eyes leap out and grab him by the throat. He couldn't fail. "Let her go!"

"I can't do that. She's my ticket out of here. Now back off!" One hand gripped Meg, his superior strength no match for the scared nine-year-old. Colton saw the flash of a weapon in the other hand.

Sirens rent the air and the kidnapper froze. His eyes changed, his body language signaled his intent to run.

Blake stepped forward just as the man turned and spotted him.

"Back off! Back off!" He raised the gun to press the muzzle against Meg's temple and backed toward the waiting vehicle.

Colton immediately saw his plan. As soon as he was between the car and the trees, he'd be almost home free.

"Don't move! Drop the weapon!"

Officers yelled.

Blake moved closer.

"Blake, get back!" Colton yelled.

Meg's scared cries broke his heart and filled him with determination to save his child.

Blake said, "Let her go."

"I'm leaving. Just let me go and I'll drop her somewhere safe. Somewhere you can find her."

"Not going to happen," Blake spat.

The kidnapper whirled, lifted the gun, and fired.

Blake dropped.

Jillian screamed as he fell. Meg's frightened cry echoed hers. "Blake!"

While the circle of blood pooling on Blake's chest grew larger, the man in the mask yelled, "Does that let you know I'm serious?" He started backing toward the car. "I'm getting out of here!"

"Hold your fire! Hold your fire!" Colton ordered the other officers.

Jillian knew Colton wouldn't let them take a chance on hitting Meg. The little girl was an effective shield.

Jillian, heart pounding, looked up to see the man's eyes on her. She shivered. She'd recognize those eyes anywhere. Eyes from the lake house. The gun in his right hand lifted. "Get over here."

"No," Colton said. "She's not going anywhere."

The gun pressed against Meg's temple and the little girl cried out.

Her mother's heart slammed inside her chest and she moved forward. Colton jerked her back.

"Let me go."

"You can't go and give him two hostages."

She kept her eyes on the man who'd terrorized her and her family for the last ten years. "I'm going for my daughter. But be ready."

She jerked away from him, and before he could grab her back, she moved out in the open toward the man who held her heart in his hands.

"Faster! Get over here or I'll shoot her!"

Jillian shuddered at the look in his eyes. He'd do it. Her blood thundered in her veins, the gun a deadly reminder that she would only have one chance to escape. One chance to get it right.

Meg saw her coming and squirmed, reaching for her.

"Jillian!"

She ignored Colton's angry shout. Her baby needed her. As soon as she rounded the car and was within range, the man transferred the gun to her temple and she winced. "Get in!"

Jillian pulled Meg to her and hunched as best she could, covering her child with her body, praying his finger wouldn't twitch and blow a hole in her head.

"Go, go!" the man yelled. "Get in the car!"

Jillian knew the minute they got in, they were dead.

Cops hollered, Meg cried, Colton yelled. Jillian did her best to block it all and focus. Remember what Blake had taught her.

"Go!" the man yelled again.

The gun slipped away from Jillian's head as she opened the car door and shoved Meg in. Then to her captor's surprise, she slammed the door and whirled, bringing her arm up to jam her elbow into his exposed throat. He gagged, spewed. The gun fell to the ground. Jillian kicked out to catch him in the stomach.

A shot rang out, followed by two more, and he dropped like a rock.

39

Jillian looked down at the bleeding man who'd caused her and those she loved so much misery. Before Colton could stop her, she ripped the mask from his face.

He howled his outrage even as he gripped his bleeding shoulder. Stunned, she simply stared. "Elliott Darwin?" She spun to see Colton, weapon still trained on the man, approaching. He looked shell-shocked and she could easily read his thoughts.

First his uncle, now Elliott?

"He has a vest on," Colton muttered. "No wonder he wasn't too worried about being shot."

EMS had just arrived, and Jillian grabbed Meg from the car and bolted over to her wounded friend. "Blake!"

One of the desk clerks sat next to him, holding a towel over his chest. "He's still breathing, but I think his pulse is getting weaker."

Jillian pointed to the curb and said to Meg, "Sit there and don't move. Got it?" Without a word, eyes wide, mouth trembling, Meg sat. Jillian squatted in front of her and softened her tone as she stroked Meg's hair. "I'm not mad, baby. It's all right. I'm going to get help for Uncle Blake, all right?"

Meg nodded. "Hurry."

Jillian waved down one of the EMTs. "Over here."

She noticed Colton hovering as paramedics worked on Darwin. After she made sure Blake was getting the attention he needed, she motioned for Meg to join her.

She marched to Darwin and shoved a palm against his wounded shoulder. He hollered and slammed back against the gurney. "That's for scaring my daughter." Colton grabbed her and pulled her back, but not before she got another punch in. Darwin hissed and writhed with her added agony and Colton looked like he wished he'd been the one to take the swing. Like he was thinking real hard about it.

He refrained.

Jillian asked, "What was so important that you were willing to help someone kill me? Kill people who didn't even have anything to do with that night!"

Elliott's jaw firmed and he lasered her with intense green eyes. Hard as emeralds, no remorse. Jillian met him stare for stare with thoughts of what this man had put her and her friends through the last three months. He rasped, "You have no idea what you've done." He winced and laid his head back against the mattress.

"I'll tell you what I've done," Jillian hissed. "I've taken a killer off the streets and exposed at least two murders." She narrowed her eyes, grateful Colton was giving her this moment. "Did you shoot the governor? Was it you on the gravel path that night? Did you hear them arguing and decide to get rid of the problem?"

A genuine frown pulled his brows down and puzzlement showed in his eyes. "What?"

"Did. You. Shoot. Him."

"No."

"Well, guess what? Frank Hoffman didn't either."

Elliott froze, his entire being went still. He pushed the paramedic away, his wound apparently forgotten. "What are you talking about?"

Colton stepped forward. "Governor Martin was shot in the back. If you didn't shoot him, who else was there?"

"Shot in the back?" Confusion rippled across his features.

"What happened that night?"

Jillian saw another set of paramedics whisk Blake to the next ambulance. She left Colton, keeping Meg next to her. The child stayed close, still traumatized over everything that had happened.

Hunter and Katie pulled into the parking lot. Hunter looked stunned when he saw Elliott Darwin on the gurney. "Him?"

"Him," Jillian muttered. She looked at Meg. "Honey, sit in the policewoman's car for a minute. I don't need you disappearing again."

Again, without a word, Meg obeyed. Jillian frowned, worried at her daughter's silent compliance. Then turned her attention back to Elliott and Colton.

One of the paramedics waved Colton away, insisting they needed to get him to the hospital. Colton hopped in the back of the ambulance and Jillian knew she would have to wait for her answers.

Relief filled her. It was over.

She'd proven the governor was murdered. She'd done what she'd come back to do.

Only one thing niggled at her.

"Who shot him?" she murmured.

———■———

Colton rode to the hospital with Elliott, determined to get whatever information out of the man that he could. Even while the paramedics monitored him, Colton questioned. "What were they arguing about that night?"

"Drop it, Colton. What does it matter now?"

"What matters is the truth! I want the truth!"

Elliott grimaced and Colton felt nothing but fury for the man who'd been part of a murder cover-up.

"Tell me," he hissed.

Elliott stared at the roof of the ambulance for a good three minutes. Colton thought the man was just tuning him out. Then he spoke. "I guess I can answer my own question. It doesn't really matter now, does it?"

"No. It doesn't. Why don't you go for reduced charges? I'll tell them you cooperated. But talk fast, it's only a five-minute ride."

"Cooperated, huh?" A huge sigh slipped from the man. "I was in the Navy for twenty years, you know?"

"I know."

"Your uncle was my best friend. Saved my life during one particularly nasty joint mission."

"Yeah."

"When we got out, he decided to go into politics and asked me to help him. He was born a politician. The people loved him. I was pushing him to think about the Oval Office."

"Until Jillian threw you a curve ball."

Elliott's eyes hardened once again. "Jillian," he spat. "All she had to do was stay gone."

"She tried that and you still went after her, remember?"

"She was the one thing that could spoil it all."

"All this time you thought Frank shot the governor? Were you there that night?"

"Yes."

"So you heard the argument and saw what happened?"

"I heard the argument, but I . . . was being discreet. I stepped out of the office and let them have at it. Later, I heard the gunshot. I went running and found Frank clutching his chest with one hand and a gun with the other. The governor was dead."

"And Jillian?"

"I saw her, but she didn't see me."

"Where was my aunt? And Carmen? Surely they would have heard the shot."

"Everyone had left by this time. The clean-up crew wasn't supposed to be there until the next morning. Your aunt came running and I managed to stop her and convince her it was just a car back-firing. She left and I started to help clean up the mess."

"What about Ian?"

"I don't think he was in the house. Frank had given him the night off if I remember correctly."

Colton looked up as they turned into the hospital emergency entrance. He was running out of time. "What was the argument about?"

"Jobs."

"Tell me."

The ambulance stopped. Elliott's breathing had become more labored and the paramedic's frown said he didn't like it.

Colton just wanted the truth.

Elliott stared at him and then said, "Your uncle owned some property he was going to sell, the old textile plant over on Cort Road. He had a very generous offer from a real estate company who wanted the land to put up some condos."

"I remember that."

"Frank was in a bind. He needed money." Elliott shifted and grimaced, his face paling a shade lighter. "He was going to sell and that was that. Harrison didn't like it at all and tried to get your uncle to wait, see if he could get another business—and jobs—on the property. Frank said no."

"And that was it?"

"He thought so. I guess at the party, it came up again."

"Boy, did it ever," Colton muttered. He looked at the impatient paramedic. "All right, you can have him."

Elliott shot him a regretful look. "We were headed to the big time, Colt." A weird smile crossed his lips. "You think you've won, don't you?"

"Won? This wasn't a game, Elliott."

"No, it wasn't. But it could be now."

Colton frowned. "What are you talking about?"

"I suppose if I can't make a name for myself from Washington, then Columbia, SC, will do." His eyes hardened once again. "And I will be remembered."

"Yeah, having your face splashed on national television for helping cover up a murder will do that to a person."

Elliott smiled easily. His eyes fluttered closed, then back open. "Tell Jillian it's her fault. It will all be her fault."

"What?"

Before Colton could question him further, Elliott passed out. What had he meant by that last statement? Was it drugs talking?

Colton climbed from the ambulance and followed them into the building.

He still didn't know who pulled the trigger.

40

Jillian paced the floor of Colton's living area. Megan sat on the couch watching a Disney show with Bert curled up on her right and Ernie on her left. The dogs looked blissfully happy.

So did Meg for that matter. The trauma of the morning seemed to be put behind her for now.

Jillian turned back to her two friends. Serena and Alexia watched her with frowns on their faces. "You're really going?"

"Why not?" Alexia asked with a shrug.

"What about your dad?"

Alexia's mouth hardened. "There's been no change. Mom will call if she needs me."

"What about Dominic?"

"He's going too," Serena said.

Alexia snorted. "He and Mom went round and round about it, but she has a good point. Dad could linger for another few days or weeks. We have our cell phones if she needs anything." She stood up and placed a hand on Jillian's arm. "They got the guy after you—us. We all need a night of fun. Seeing old classmates will take our minds off stuff."

Jillian sighed. "I can't believe it was Elliott behind everything." She looked at Alexia. "He was the one that convinced Lori to try and kill you." She looked at Serena. "And you. He wanted to kill you and make it look like the work of a serial killer. He knew all these people. Lori had been in love with him since their military days and he knew she was mentally ill. But the whole serial killer stuff . . ."

Serena nodded. "He and Drake, the Doll Maker Killer, and Frank, were all in college together. The relationship wasn't obvious, but once Dominic was able to search specifically, he found it." She paused. "But you're right. We still don't know who shot the governor."

"And we might never figure that out," Alexia said.

Still Jillian persisted. "And who sent those letters? Someone else who knows exactly what happened that night."

Serena's forehead crinkled. "Do the letters even matter now?"

"Yes. I think whoever was sending him those letters was actually the shooter."

"How did you come up with that?" Colton asked from the door to the den.

Jillian spun to stare at the man she'd loved so long ago. The man she loved still. "Because it's the only thing that makes sense. The shooter's the only other person who knows what happened—and the one who wants to keep your uncle believing he's responsible." He took her breath away. She needed a distraction. "I need to call and check on Blake."

He smiled. "I just did. He's going to be fine."

"And your uncle?"

"Right now he's stable."

She bit her lip. "Good, I want to see him."

Colton frowned. "Why?"

"I just . . . need to."

Jillian saw Alexia and Serena exchange a puzzled look, but she didn't have the words to explain it. She just needed to.

Colton glanced at the clock on the mantel. "The reunion starts in an hour."

298

"I know. Maybe this won't take long." Jillian looked at Meg, hating the thought of making her go.

Alexia spoke up. "She can stay with us if you're really wanting to do this."

Jillian nodded. "I think I have to. He's haunted me for so long that . . ." She took a deep breath and let it out. "This is going to sound weird, but I need to see him . . . weak, without that smile he always portrays to the world." Maybe then the dreams would stop.

Colton rubbed a hand down the side of his face. "All right. I'll take you." His phone buzzed and he looked at the screen. "Carmen's been going through a hard time. I invited her to come tonight. She can help us keep an eye on Meg."

Jillian nodded. "That would be great."

Alexia said, "Just meet us at the gym. We're going a little early to hang out with Christina before everyone else gets there." She gave a quirky grin. Alexia looked at Colton. "We'll make sure Carmen feels comfortable."

After giving Meg a hug, Jillian and Colton took off for the hospital. Jillian's nerves wound tighter the closer they got.

"We're going to have to tell my parents and your dad about Meg at some point."

"I know." She swallowed hard. "I called my dad last night and he finally answered. He was glad to hear from me." Tears threatened. "I was afraid he wouldn't be."

"He loves you."

"Yeah. He does." She bit her lip.

"What is it?"

"What do you think your parents are going to say?"

His knuckles whitened as he gripped the steering wheel a little tighter. "I don't know. I think Mom will be thrilled."

"But your dad will be upset?"

"Maybe. But I'm hoping he'll get past that." He reached for her hand and squeezed it.

"Why were you able to forgive me so easily for keeping Meg from you?"

He gave a small, humorless laugh. "Oh, it wasn't easy, but I can't stop thinking that my lack of self-control is one of the reasons we have her. How can I throw stones?"

A tear slipped down her cheek. She whispered, "Thank you."

"And as for what my parents think, I care, but it's not going to dictate my life. And I'm definitely not all about covering things up or lying just for appearance's sake."

"Me either."

"So," he said. "We'll pray, tell them, and what happens will happen. We'll just make sure Meg is protected no matter what."

She smiled at him and nodded, unable to force any words past the lump in her throat.

Colton stepped into his uncle's hospital room. The man appeared pale, but better than the last time he saw him. Frank looked up and Colton's heart ached at how much the man had aged in such a short time. But he'd brought it on himself. Still, he couldn't stop thinking about the man who'd always been there for him. "Glad to see you're feeling better."

"I am."

Should he tell his uncle all that had transpired since his entrance to the hospital? Would it lead to another heart attack? Colton glanced at the television. Better do it now before the man felt good enough to see it on the news. "We . . . uh . . . caught Elliott Darwin trying to kill Jillian. He's been shot and is in this hospital under arrest."

Frank's pale features whitened even more. The heart monitor blipped a little faster. His throat convulsed and his eyelids fluttered. But he didn't have another heart attack. "How?"

Colton told him the story and just sat there while his uncle digested everything. "I see."

300

Colton waited, but the man didn't say anything else. Colton sighed. "I found your boat. The paint matched up to the piece of fabric we found when Serena's house was bombed. Found the line-throwing device too. It contained traces of all of the chemicals used to make the bomb."

Frank shuddered. "I don't know how that's possible."

Of course he didn't. Colton shook his head. He'd let the man stew on the information awhile before he told him he was to be arrested as soon as he was released from the hospital. The thought hurt.

He cleared his throat. "So anyway, I have someone who wants to see you. She's waiting in the hall." He went to the door and motioned for Jillian to enter.

Frank's brow lifted as Jillian stepped inside. Then stiffened as he realized who she was. "What are you doing here?"

"I came to . . . see you. I just needed to see you."

Frank blinked and Colton thought he saw the man relax a fraction, but the wariness in his eyes didn't fade.

The door opened once again, interrupting them. A nurse entered. "Hello, Senator, I just need to take some vitals and give you this." She handed him an envelope. "It was delivered yesterday, but every time I brought it to you, you were sleeping."

Frank stared at it like it was a viper poised to strike.

Colton took the envelope. "Another note?"

He nodded. "The handwriting is the same."

Colton opened it and read, "'CONFESSION IS GOOD FOR THE SOUL. YOUR SOUL IS A BLACK PIT THAT NEEDS REDEMPTION. CONFESS.'"

Frank looked like he would be sick.

Colton folded the letter and put it back in the envelope. Delivered yesterday. Great. No chance to chase after the delivery person. "We'll deal with this later." Colton nodded to Jillian.

She took a deep breath and let it out slowly. "I know that what

I thought I saw that night . . . wasn't what happened. You didn't shoot the governor."

Frank, gaze still on the note in Colton's hand, froze. Colton watched the heart monitor. Frank tried to speak, but the shock seemed to render him unable to find the words. Finally, he managed, "I didn't?" Then he caught himself and sputtered, "I mean, of course I didn't."

Jillian glanced at Colton and he nodded. "Go on."

"I saw you shoot *at* him. Only you didn't hit him. You hit the brick wall of the sunroom. Another person was behind him and shot at the same time you did. That person hit him. In the back. I thought it was you."

Frank flinched and twisted the sheet between his fingers. He looked at Colton. "What? I don't understand. What are you saying?"

Colton picked up the story. "Someone was on the gravel path that leads to the pond. It was dark out there. But the person could see you clearly. After studying all the angles and going over what happened that night—"

"Not to mention the autopsy of the governor's exhumed body," Jillian added.

"All that adds up to proving you didn't shoot Harrison. Ballistics did find a bullet in him when they dug him up, but it wasn't from one of your guns. It was from a .357 Magnum."

Frank sucked in a deep breath. "What?"

Colton tilted his head. "Why? You have one of those?"

"No. No, I don't. I just . . . didn't . . . expect . . . I didn't . . ."

"You thought it would be one of your antique bullets, didn't you?"

"N-no. No." He closed his eyes. "I think I need to rest now."

One other thing had been nagging at Colton. "You can rest in a few minutes. Look at me."

Frank opened his eyes, brows furrowed. "What?"

302

"When Elliott was spilling his guts in the back of the ambulance, he said he'd be remembered. He said to tell Jillian it was her fault. That all their deaths would be her fault. What did he mean by that?"

Frank's eyes widened, then shuttered. "I don't know."

The door opened and Colton turned to see his aunt enter the room.

She pulled up short when she saw him—then Jillian. "Oh. I didn't know you were here. I thought you were both at the reunion." Elizabeth looked scattered and unkempt.

"We decided to pay Uncle Frank a visit." What would his aunt do when his uncle went to jail? What would his mother do? The thought sent shards of pain through him.

"I was downstairs in the cafeteria and saw the news. What's this about Elliott being arrested? Please tell me that's not true."

She looked worn out, very un-Elizabeth-like. Her distress pierced him. Anger at his uncle's criminal actions made him want to punch some sense into the man. Colton knew he was guilty. And yet . . . there was no evidence of anything against him other than the boat. And a good defense attorney could explain that away with no problem. Unless Elliott talked, his uncle might get off scot-free.

Colton stood and took her hand. "I'm sorry, Aunt Elizabeth. Elliott's been the one trying to kill Jillian and her friends. He knew she had seen what happened that night and did his best to shut her up. And Uncle Frank—"

"Elliott?" Elizabeth gasped and pressed a hand to her chest. She stared at her husband. "Frank? What's this all about?"

"Nothing, Elizabeth." He glared at Colton even as he lifted a trembling hand and pointed toward the door. "I think it's time you left."

"Fine." He would have to break the news about his uncle later.

His aunt's shell-shocked features twisted the knife of anger with his uncle several inches deeper. As Colton nodded to Jillian and they turned toward the door, his aunt jerked from her stunned stupor.

"Oh. Wait." She opened her purse and pulled out a cell phone. "Could you please give this to Carmen? She left it. I was . . . going to take it to her myself, but since you'll be seeing her shortly, do you mind?" Elizabeth patted a hand over her hair. "I'm just going to freshen up a bit. I . . . I . . ."

"Carmen?" Frank asked, his voice low and shaky. "Why would they be able to give that phone to Carmen?"

Elizabeth frowned. "She's at the reunion. Colton was kind enough to invite her."

"No," he whispered. "No, no, no." His throat convulsed and he shut his eyes. His white face turned a deathly gray. "Get her away from there."

Colton stepped back next to the bed. "Why?"

To Elizabeth, Frank said, "Call her, now! Tell her to leave immediately!" He looked at the phone in Colton's hand. "No, you can't call her. Call someone she's with. Tell her . . ." His breathing came in pants.

Colton leaned in. "Tell me it's not what I'm thinking. You're targeting the reunion?"

Frank simply rolled his head back and forth on the pillow. "Get her out now!"

Jillian gasped. "What do you mean, Colton? Is Meg in some kind of danger?"

Colton clenched his fists. "What is it, Uncle Frank? Another bomb?"

Elizabeth shrieked, "A bomb?"

Jillian swayed and Colton reached out to grab her arm. To his uncle, he said, "Would you let your own daughter die?"

"No," the man moaned. "It wasn't supposed to happen like this."

41

"Yes," Frank whispered. "Yes, it's a bomb. The plan was to take care of all three of them at the same time." His eyes pleaded. "Get Carmen out of there."

Jillian felt her knees weaken. She shot a horrified look at Colton. "Meg," she whispered. Colton's white face said he was thinking about her.

Colton whipped out his phone, punched in a number. "We've got a bomb threat at Spring Valley High School. Need an immediate evacuation and bomb squad there ASAP."

As soon as he hung up with dispatch, he called Hunter. Jillian paced to the door. "We've got to go," she pleaded. "You can do that while we're walking."

When Hunter answered, Jillian could hear the music from her stance at the door. Colton yelled into the phone, "Hunter! Evacuate the building! There's a bomb!"

He listened a moment, then strode to the door and placed his hand on the handle. "Come on, come on, hurry up," he muttered.

"What is it?" Jillian demanded. She wanted to scream that they needed to get moving to the high school.

Colton looked at her. "Hunter can't hear over the music. He's stepping outside."

A vein throbbed in his forehead and she thought she heard him give a growl of frustration. She stayed close to him, hoping to be able to hear the conversation. "Put it on speaker."

He did.

Finally, the background noise ceased and Hunter came back on the line. "What'd you say?"

"Get everyone out of the building. There's a bomb!"

Hunter didn't ask questions. "Got it! Heading back in there. What do you know?"

"Just that there's a bomb. It's probably near the gym area. I've got the bomb squad on the way."

"There are kids in there!" The music blared once again.

Jillian stepped outside the room and motioned for him to come on. Elizabeth stared at him with a blank expression. He nodded to Jillian and they bolted down the hall. Colton kept the phone on speaker as they hurried to the elevator.

Jillian felt as though someone had reached and grabbed her lungs to squeeze every last bit of air from them. She couldn't breathe, couldn't think through her terror. "Oh Meg." *Oh God, please, please let them get out in time.*

The music ceased as they hit the door. She heard Hunter say, "I need everyone to exit the gym, please. We've had a report of a gas leak and we need to get it checked out. So if you'll just move to the parking lot away from the building, we'll get this taken care of and get back to our party."

Colton hung up.

She burst through the glass door and headed for the car parked in the police parking space. Colton clicked the doors open and she slid into the passenger seat. Urgency pounded through her.

"Alexia and Serena will take care of Meg," Colton said as he jammed the key into the ignition and cranked the car. With a squeal of tires, he pulled from the space and hit the siren.

Jillian knew this was true and it was the only thing keeping her from totally freaking out.

His phone rang. Jillian snapped her gaze to him as he answered. When his face paled and jaw clenched, she knew it was bad news. "What is it?" she whispered.

"They can't find Meg."

Colton pressed the gas even harder as he whipped around three cars that had pulled to the right to let him pass. He couldn't spare a glance at Jillian to see how she was faring, but he could feel her panic thicken the air in the car.

"We'll find her. The bomb squad's already there."

"Hurry, Colton."

"Try Serena's phone."

"I did. It went straight to voice mail."

Within minutes, he was flashing his badge to law enforcement already in the parking lot. Former classmates milled, well away from the gym should it blow.

Jillian bolted from the car, looking for a familiar face. She spotted Alexia standing with Carmen Hoffman and rushed over. "Where is she? Did you find her?"

"No." Alexia gripped Jillian's hands. "Hunter and Dominic are still in there looking for her and Serena. I came out here to wait on you."

"Where is Serena?"

"Serena took Meg to the bathroom about the time Hunter got up to announce we needed to evacuate. We haven't seen them since."

"If they were in the bathroom, they wouldn't have heard the announcement—and might not have a signal."

"Which would explain why she wouldn't answer her phone. The bomb squad and our guys are in there looking for them."

"And so is Colton," Jillian whispered as she watched him push into the building. She raced after him.

———■———

Colton's heart slammed into his ribs. He'd just found out he had a daughter, he wasn't about to lose her now.

"Colton!"

He heard Jillian scream his name and turned to see two police officers holding her back. "I'm going to find her, Jilly, stay back!"

He didn't have time to see if she obeyed. Hopefully the officers could keep her back. "Megan!" he yelled as he ran down the hall.

Hunter came out of a side door. "Clear in there. Alexia said Serena took Meg to the bathroom, but there's no one in there."

"Where would they have gone?"

"I can't figure it out."

"Another bathroom?"

"Possibly. Especially if Meg couldn't wait and the bathrooms were crowded."

Colton whirled and lifted a hand to his head as he thought. "Where's Dominic?"

"He went back to the bathrooms." Hunter shook his head. "I don't know why. They're not there."

"Desperation," Colton murmured. *Think!* He paced the floor.

Dominic came from the bathroom, saw them in the hall, and waved them over. "In here!"

Colton bolted toward him. "You found them?"

"No, but listen."

They entered the bathroom. At first Colton didn't know what he was supposed to be listening for. Then he heard it. A faint *clink, clink, clink.*

He looked up at Dominic. "They're above us?"

Dominic rushed through the door. "Only one way to find out."

Together, they raced down the hall to the door that led to the steps. "It's locked. I don't understand."

Dominic stopped and listened to the earpiece. His face paled.

"Guys, they found the bomb. Says we have less than five minutes before it goes off. They're working on disarming it, but we've got to get the girls and get out of here."

"Step back and plug your ears." Colton lifted his weapon and fired at the lock. Three quick shots. Since he hadn't been able to protect his own ears, his rang. Hopefully it wouldn't be permanent, but getting to the girls was priority.

Hunter pushed the heavy metal doors open and they bolted for the stairs.

Up the first flight. Hunter stooped and grabbed something. Colton didn't bother to stop and see. He rounded the landing and took the next set of stairs two at a time right behind Dominic. They burst through the door with Dominic in the lead.

Down the hall.

To the women's bathroom.

Dominic banged on the door. "Serena, get Meg and get in a stall now. We're going to have to blow the lock. Hurry, there's a bomb in the building."

"Dominic?" Serena's husky voice came through the door. "Oh thank you!" Five precious seconds later, her voice came much fainter. "Do it!"

Once again Colton lifted his gun. Stopped up his ears as best he could with a handkerchief Dominic handed him and tissue Hunter had found in the stairwell. They'd planned ahead. He pulled the trigger.

Hunter kicked the door in.

Serena and Meg came from the stall. Serena stared, white-faced. "We came up here because all the other bathrooms were packed. I didn't know the door—Did you say bomb?"

Colton scooped Meg into his arms and bolted back toward the exit. "How much time do we have?"

"Less than two minutes!" Dominic hollered.

"What's that about a bomb?" Serena asked as she ran as fast as Dominic, his hand gripping hers. They hit the stairs.

"Tell you when we get out," Dominic promised.

Meg's featherweight didn't slow Colton down. If there'd been another way out of the building, he'd have chosen it, but the only way out was back the way they came. At the bottom, they raced behind the bomb squad. Not a good sign.

They hadn't been able to diffuse it.

Not for a lack of skill, but for a lack of time, he was sure.

"Twenty seconds!" Hunter hollered.

Jillian prayed and paced, paced and prayed. She'd chewed her right thumbnail to the quick and was working on the left when the gym doors flew open.

Her heart stuttered as she saw everyone racing in mass exodus from the building. The bomb squad.

Where were—

"Oh thank you, Lord!" Alexia squealed as Hunter came into sight. Dominic and Serena ran. Colton, with Meg in his arms, brought up the rear.

"Nine seconds!" Hunter yelled. "Everyone duck!"

The seconds ticked down as each person did their best to put as much distance as they could between themselves and the gym. Colton stumbled, caught himself, and swept Meg behind the nearest brick pillar of the football stadium.

Dominic and Serena made it to the next one. And Hunter leapt the fence to roll down the hill.

A rumble shook the ground beneath Jillian's feet and a loud explosion caused her to clasp her hands over her ears. Debris started falling, but thankfully she was far enough away that none reached her.

Fear clenching her insides, she squinted through the haze of smoke to see if Colton had gotten far enough away. *Please, God.*

"Meg! Colton!"

She got a lungful of smoke and coughed. Pulling her shirt up over her nose and mouth, she raced toward where she'd seen Meg and Colton disappear.

When she was halfway there, they emerged from behind the pillar.

Whole.

Safe.

Alive.

Frank watched the news. Again. Columbia, South Carolina, had made national news and the only channel Frank was interested in was the one that showed the footage.

Spring Valley High School's gym had exploded. A bomb was suspected, but fortunately no one had been hurt.

No one had been hurt. He found himself glad for that. Especially that Carmen was safe.

It was over.

Elizabeth had left the room as soon as she realized her husband was guilty of the horrible accusations made against him.

And for doing the unforgivable.

He'd endangered Carmen.

Frank glanced at the television screen again, pushed away the food tray, and thought about what this meant. There was no real evidence other than the boat that he'd had anything to do with the attempts on Jillian's life. He had admitted things to Colton under pressure, but he hadn't been Mirandized. There was no recording of his admission to knowing about the bomb. Elliott had talked, but had no proof.

Maybe there was a way out of this after all.

Hope stirred for the first time as he started to envision the press conference that he would call upon his release from the hospital.

"I had no idea about the evil side of Elliott Darwin. He was my good friend for many years—" Here his voice would choke a little, maybe a few tears as he took a moment to compose himself.

Yeah, it might work.

The door opened and surprise held him still for a moment. "Elizabeth. You're back."

She entered slowly, as though not sure she wanted to be there. She carried a cup of coffee and Frank's mouth watered as she sat in the chair next to his bed. "I had to make sure Carmen was safe."

"She is. No one was hurt."

Her mouth thinned. "No thanks to you."

He swallowed hard. "I'm sorry, Elizabeth. You know I never would have put her in danger. You know that."

Elizabeth studied him, the hard look in her eyes not encouraging him. She sipped the coffee and Frank reached for it. "Do you mind? I haven't had any caffeine since I've been in here."

She pulled the cup away and frowned. "That's probably for a reason."

"Oh come on, just a sip."

She sighed. "It's bitter. Let me get some milk and sugar."

When she returned with a cup of water, a carton of milk, and two packets of sugar, his brow rose. Wariness stood out. "Why are you being so nice to me?"

She set the cup in front of him and opened the sugar. He poured in the milk and took a sip. Then another. She took the water and settled into the chair. "I'm being nice because I don't want a divorce."

His hand stopped, delaying his third sip. "I don't want one either."

"I found the papers, Frank."

He stilled. "Did you see the date on them?"

"Yes."

"That was ten years ago. I couldn't go through with it, obviously."

"Why? Because you didn't want to divorce me? Or because of the way it might have hurt you politically?"

He sighed and closed his eyes. His hands tingled and he flexed them. "Probably a combination of both."

She sat silent for a moment and Frank opened his eyes to find her staring at him. He couldn't read the expression there, but it made him uneasy. "Elizabeth?"

She blinked. "I don't know what to do now."

Frank studied her. "Do you want to go to counseling?"

She seemed to consider that. "Possibly. If you think that would help. But we would have to be careful, I wouldn't want anyone to know." She rubbed her forehead. "The only problem is, you're probably going to be in jail. There's an officer posted outside your door right now."

Frank fiddled with the coffee cup. "There've been no charges brought against me."

"I know. But I think they're coming."

Just the thought sent shudders racing through him. He gulped more coffee, hoping the caffeine would settle his nerves. "Maybe not."

She lifted a brow. "What do you mean?"

He told her his thoughts. "So even though I knew about the bomb, I can plead ignorance, say I had no idea Elliott was doing what he was doing." He waved a hand. "I'll come up with something."

Elizabeth stood and paced. "You really think it would work?"

"Maybe. Only if you're on my side and we can present a united front." He sighed. "Where did it all go wrong?"

Her lips tightened. "Let's not think about that."

He shook his head. "I was too greedy, wasn't I?"

"Greedy?"

"I wanted it all. And I didn't care what it took to get it." He sighed. "I was a fool."

She lifted her glass of water to tap his cup of coffee. "I'll agree to that."

Frank finished off his coffee with a grimace and considered staying with this woman he had no love for. He pushed aside that thought.

Minutes passed as they discussed possibilities for the future. The nurse came in and took his vitals. She frowned. "Your heart rate is very slow and your lips have a blue tint to them. I think we need to call the doctor."

Frank tried to take a deep breath. And couldn't. He looked at her and Elizabeth. "I can't breathe."

Pain shot through his chest and he cried out, tried to lift his right hand and couldn't.

Darkness pulled at him. He resisted. Weights held him to the bed. He couldn't move!

Alarms sounded and he knew no more.

SUNDAY

42

Colton sat across from Jillian and Meg in the fast-food booth, delighting in getting to know his daughter. She'd already downed three pieces of pizza and played four video games in between bites.

"Thanks for doing this. She's having a blast." Jillian leaned against his arm and he kissed her nose.

"My pleasure. You know I want to—" His phone rang and his brow shot north when he saw the number. "Hi, Mom."

"Colton, I have some bad news."

Concern hit him. "What is it?"

"Frank died about an hour ago."

"What?" His shout echoed through the restaurant. He finished the call with his mind in a fog.

Jillian stared at him. "What's wrong?"

He told her, shock still running through him. "I can't believe it."

"A heart attack?" she guessed.

"Yeah."

She reached out and grasped his hand. "I'm so sorry."

Colton forced a small smile and said to Meg, "Come on, kiddo, I've got to go visit my mom."

"I'm sorry your uncle died," Meg told him, her brow furrowed.

"Yeah, me too."

She wrapped her arms around his neck. "You can cry on my shoulder if you need to."

A lump formed in his throat. "Thanks, Meg. I might need to take you up on that."

Jillian held his hand all the way to the hospital and he found himself grateful and full of love for the woman beside him.

Grief welled as it sank in. Frank was gone.

"It's okay to grieve for him."

Colton shot her a look. "How did you know I was feeling guilty about that?"

"It's only natural. You loved the man like a father for a long time. He was good to you and was there for you when you needed him."

His jaw tightened. "He also had a whole other side to him that I never suspected was there."

Her fingers squeezed his. "That side probably developed over time."

"I don't understand. He's the one who encouraged me to go to church, to be involved in the youth group, to go on mission trips. He even paid for a couple."

She stayed silent for about a minute, then said, "I think some people can start out having a passion for God, but if that passion isn't flamed, discipled, or encouraged, it can—" She stopped as though searching for a word.

"Fizzle out?"

"Yeah. Don't you think? I mean, having a relationship with God still takes work on our part. If you ignore it long enough, it will wither and die. I'm talking about on the human end, not God's."

He thought about that as he drove. "That makes sense. And when one person ends the relationship, the only way to restore it is for that person to come back and apologize." His words slowed as he got to the end of the sentence. "Kind of like what happened to us, huh?"

Tears stood in her eyes. "Yes, kind of like that."

"And if Uncle Frank was constantly ignoring God, then do you think it's possible he just got to the point where he couldn't hear him anymore?"

"I do."

Colton nodded.

"And if you're not listening to someone, eventually they just stop talking to you," Meg piped in from the backseat. "That happened to my friend Chrissy and me. I talked and talked, but sometimes she would just walk off like she didn't want to hear what I was talking about." Indignation tinted her tone. "I finally decided I didn't want to talk to her anymore and I got a new best friend. She listens to me all the time."

A smile curved Jillian's lips and Colton choked on his emotion. "Exactly," he said. "So if Uncle Frank quit listening to the one who told him the right choices to make, he was bound to make some wrong choices."

Meg grunted. "Like I did when I went down to the pool. Boy, was that a dumb choice. I knew I wasn't supposed to do that, but I decided to listen to the part of me that wanted to go." In the rearview mirror, Colton saw her lip quiver. "I'm sorry."

"And you're forgiven. You're fine and you won't ever do something like that again, right?"

His daughter stayed quiet.

"Right, Meg?" Jillian asked.

She sighed. "Well, I want to promise I won't. But I'm only nine. I've got the teen years coming, you know."

Jillian broke up laughing, and in spite of his grief over his uncle, Colton felt his heart lighten and thanked God for bringing Jillian and this little girl into his life.

———■———

Jillian still had a smile on her face as they walked into the hospital. She'd missed Meg and her sassiness over the past week.

As they rode the elevator, her smile faded and nerves kicked in. She clutched Meg's hand. What would Colton's parents say about her and Meg coming? *Please, Lord, let this go well.* She paused, then added, *And please don't let Meg say anything too outrageous.*

The elevator door opened and they made their way down the hall to the small family room not far from the surgery waiting room.

At their entrance, conversation ceased.

Colton didn't seem bothered by the awkward moment as he walked over to his aunt and offered her a hug. "I'm sorry."

She sniffed and nodded. When her gaze landed on Jillian, she stiffened, but said nothing.

Jillian then noticed Colton's parents staring at Meg. Both looked a little shell-shocked as their gazes went between the little girl and Colton.

Finally his mother said, "Colton, is she . . . ?"

He nodded. "This isn't exactly the way I wanted to introduce you, but," he took a deep breath, "Mom, Dad, meet Megan. My daughter." Colton placed a hand on her head. "Meg, I'd like you to meet your grandparents, Zachary and Sonya Brady."

Meg stood silent for a moment longer, head tilted to the right as she studied the older couple. Then she grinned. "Cool. I like old people. Nice to meet you."

A strangled choke escaped Jillian. "Meg . . ."

She saw Colton smothering a grin as Mrs. Brady lifted a brow. Even Elizabeth had a small smile on her pale lips.

A snort slipped from Colton's father and Jillian tensed, waiting, ready to defend Meg if he said anything that might hurt the little girl.

To her shock, a belly laugh escaped the man and he knelt in front of Meg. "Well, we old people like little girls named Megan. Pleased to meet you too." He held out his hand and Meg slipped hers into his. "Would you like to see if we can find a snack in the restaurant downstairs?"

She looked at Jillian. Jillian looked at Colton. Colton simply looked speechless. Jillian cleared her throat. "Uh, sure. Go ahead. I'm sure she'd love that."

"Excellent," Mr. Brady said.

"Do you think they have ice cream?" Jillian heard Meg ask as they walked out the door. She missed the answer but had a feeling Meg would get her ice cream.

Colton still stared at the door. She nudged him and he blinked.

Then the doctor came in, followed by a red-eyed Carmen, and the mood changed.

Elizabeth took a deep breath. "So, what happens now?"

Colton felt his throat tighten. "We bury my uncle."

WEDNESDAY

43

Colton saw Rick coming and smothered a grin, exchanged a hopeful look with Hunter, and took a deep breath. Bending his head, he pretended to be involved in paperwork.

Rick dropped into the chair beside him. "This better be good."

Colton looked up. "Hey, thanks for coming."

"You said you had some evidence of a case you're working on? What were you so busy with that you couldn't just bring it to the lab?"

Colton reached into the top drawer to his right and pulled out a plastic bag. "This."

Rick snagged it and looked. Drew in a deep breath and looked again.

"Are these real?"

"Of course."

"Two tickets to the World Series?" Rick breathed, his tone reverent.

"Just for you."

Rick looked at him. "I don't understand. Why would you do this for me?"

Colton shrugged. "I overheard you talking about wanting to go one day."

Rick's gaze returned to the tickets. "They must have cost a fortune."

"They did. But it was for a good cause. Trust me."

A frown formed and Rick looked up with narrowed eyes. "This is for the same weekend as my seminar."

Colton pasted a concerned look on his face. "I know, man, I really hate that. I mean, if you don't want the tickets I'm sure I can sell—"

Rick snatched them to his chest. "You win."

"What?"

"You did it. The seminar is canceled."

Colton grinned, then frowned. "There's just one string attached to these."

"Of course there is," Rick grumbled. "I've canceled the seminar, what else do you need?"

"You have to take Captain Murdoch."

Rick lifted a brow and started to argue. Colton reached out as though to take the tickets. Rick huffed out a breath. "Fine."

He turned to leave. Colton met Hunter's gaze and stood. They did a midair high five as Rick turned back to give him a wicked grin. "This is only one weekend you know. That leaves fifty-one during the year." He scooted for the door.

Colton sat down. "Hey! Those tickets should be good for a lifetime of canceled seminars!"

Colton shook his head and swiveled in his chair to glare at the computer screen, willing it to give him the information he'd been looking for before Rick had interrupted.

Captain Murdoch had given Colton the good news this morning. He was a candidate for captain. Satisfaction filled him even though his computer wouldn't cooperate with him.

Dominic walked in. "What are you doing here? I would have thought you'd be with your family."

"I've had enough of the well-wishers with their nosy questions."

The media had covered Frank's funeral and someone had leaked the fact that Frank may have been involved in the former governor's death. Of course that had been a whole other story. One the media

326

now speculated about endlessly. "I'm doing my best to ignore every-thing, but it isn't easy. Frank's dead. Wish they would just let it go."

"They won't."

"I know."

Colton took a second look at the grim look on Dominic's face. "What is it?"

Dominic sat across from him and looked at the paper in his hand. "I did some digging."

"Yeah? On what?"

"On all of the people that could possibly be the shooter that night."

"We already did that. Ran background checks and everything on everyone in the house that night."

"Everyone but two."

As Dominic's meaning sank in, Colton's breath left his lungs. Colton took a deep breath. "All right. What'd you find?"

"I think I found who the .357 Magnum could belong to."

Jillian stepped out of the car and walked up the steps to ring the doorbell. The man she remembered as Ian answered.

"I'm Jillian Carter. I'd like to speak with Mrs. Hoffman if she's available."

"Do you have an appointment?"

"No. This is kind of a spur-of-the-moment thing."

His eyes narrowed. "You're the one, aren't you?"

She didn't have to ask what he meant, she heard it loud and clear. *You're the one who came back and stirred up trouble. You're the one who changed my world.* "I'm the one."

He inclined his head. "Come in. I'll see if Mrs. Hoffman wishes to speak with you." His cool tone indicated Jillian shouldn't hold her breath. She stepped inside and he motioned for her to follow him. "If she wants to see you, it will be in her charity room."

"Charity room?"

He smiled slightly. "She doesn't call it an office, but it's where she does all of her charity work." He led her down the hall past Senator Hoffman's office and into a small room off the den. Ian waved a hand toward the couch and Jillian sank onto it. He left and she waited.

Maybe Elizabeth wouldn't talk to her. But Jillian had plans to be in Colton's life for a long time and she knew he planned to be there for his aunt and cousin now that Frank was dead. She would do what she could to ease the pain.

Jillian glanced at her watch, then at the desk. Pictures.

She got up and moved to see if there were any of Colton. She spotted one when he must have been about seven. He held up a nice-sized fish in one hand. His uncle Frank stood beside him with an arm around his shoulders. Jillian's throat tightened. Things could have been so different if the man had just appreciated what he had instead of being so greedy for more. So concerned about appearances.

She pushed closer to the hutch behind the desk where more photos had been positioned. Colton had been a cute kid. Meg was a female version of him.

As she moved, her hip bumped the table. The computer came out of hibernation mode and the screen lit up.

She gaped at the words she'd just inadvertently revealed.

"Confession is good for the soul. Your soul is a black pit that needs redemption."

Her breath became entangled in her lungs and black spots whirled before her eyes. Then her investigative reporter instinct kicked in.

She glanced at the papers next to the keyboard.

Divorce papers. Quickly she scanned them. And looked at the date.

May 15, 2002.

"Miss? Are you all right?"

Ian stood in the door. Jillian had to get out of here, had to get to Colton. She pulled in a deep breath and put a smile on her face as she felt her phone vibrate in the back pocket of her shorts. "I'm . . . fine. I was just looking at pictures of Colton when he was a child." She hoped she sounded more convincing than she thought she did.

"Mrs. Hoffman was on a phone call. She'll be right in to see you."

Jillian moved from behind the desk. "That's all right. I'll just come back later when she's not busy."

"No, she's coming. Just have a seat."

Jillian's stomach curled. What should she do? If she rushed out, would that look suspicious?

Ian turned and left the room.

Jillian stood in thought for another thirty seconds before deciding to slip out.

Then she froze. She had no evidence. She bit her lip and turned back to the computer.

"Looks like I'm going to be a little busier today than I'd planned."

Jillian whirled to see Elizabeth Hoffman holding a weapon. A .357 Magnum, if she wasn't mistaken.

Elizabeth said, "I see you've managed to snoop your way into a bit of trouble here."

Colton shook his head. His aunt owned a .357 Magnum? He couldn't believe it. He'd never taken her for being interested in guns. In fact, she'd always expressed such disdain for her husband's collection.

He looked up at Dominic. "I'm stunned."

"I thought you might be."

"So who had access to this gun that night? Someone must have gotten ahold of it and . . ."

"What if it was Elizabeth, Colton?"

Colton let out a small laugh of disbelief. "That's crazy." He rubbed a hand down his chin. "I don't know which way is up anymore, man."

"Why don't we head over there and ask her about it?"

Colton stood. "All right. Sure. Let's go." He looked at his watch. "I need to call Jillian on the way. We were going to have lunch together. Looks like we may have to make it dinner."

———■———

Gathering her shocked and scattered wits, Jillian managed to corral her fear and say, "Is that the same gun that you shot the governor with?"

A smile curved the woman's lips. Unfortunately, her eyes remained chips of ice. "Indeed."

"Why?"

"It was a mistake. He wasn't the target."

Jillian let her gaze fall to the papers. "Right. You were aiming for your husband, weren't you?"

"Yes." Her mouth tightened. "A stupid, momentary lapse of self-control."

Jillian licked her lips. "It couldn't have been too impulsive. You had the gun."

"Well, true. I'd been thinking about it. Every night, Frank would take a walk down to the pond and stand on the dock. It was his quiet moment for the day. Something he looked forward to and needed like the air he breathed. I knew as soon as the party was over, he would be there."

"And you would be waiting."

"Only it didn't happen like that. I got tired of waiting on him and came back to find them arguing. And then when I came up the gravel path, I could see them. Harrison was my friend," she whispered and her cold facade momentarily softened with grief. Then hardened once again. "He asked Frank what I would think about what he was doing." She lifted the gun. "And do you know what Frank said?"

"What?"

"He laughed, then said I would think whatever he told me to think. Then he lifted the gun like he was going to shoot Harrison and I fired. We both did. Only Harrison moved to dodge Frank's bullet and ran right into mine. It happened so fast, so incredibly, crazy . . . fast." A groan escaped her.

Jillian glanced at the man standing silently behind Elizabeth. "You're in on this too?"

"I'm not 'in on' anything. I'm simply the one person Elizabeth knows she can rely on."

Jillian looked back at Elizabeth. She seemed lost in the memories she was talking about. "Why did Frank think he shot him?"

"Because he pulled the trigger. And I'd drugged him pretty good."

Jillian blinked. "Drugged him?"

"Yes. I slipped something in his drinks." She smirked, the grief at having murdered the governor gone now. "He had me bring them to him so I would look the attentive wife. Appearances, you know."

"Right."

"I kept adding a little to each drink hoping he would finally just keel over."

"Were you really going to shoot him?"

She shrugged. "I don't know if I was going to or not. The thought made me feel better. Holding the gun made me feel powerful. And then . . . everything happened. Harrison was dead and . . . " She frowned, then a small smile lifted the corners of her mouth. "Then Frank woke up moaning about killing Harrison. I let him believe it. It's tortured him for years."

Jillian shuddered at the pleasure the woman found in the thought. "So he knew you knew?"

"Oh no. Ian was the only one who Frank thought knew his little secret—other than you, of course. And Elliott. Ian kept me out of it."

Jillian stared at Ian. "So you helped arrange the car wreck and set it on fire?"

He sniffed. "I did."

"Why would you do that for them?"

"It's a little thing called loyalty."

Jillian would never understand that definition of loyalty. "Why the divorce papers?"

Elizabeth frowned. "I found them that afternoon before the party." She licked her lips and shifted the gun. "I couldn't believe it. He was going to kick me to the curb and take Carmen."

"But he didn't."

"No, I found out just recently that he'd decided not to go through with it. It was all about appearances, you know. If he divorced me, there would have been scandal. Only at the time, I didn't know he wasn't going to follow through with it. And besides, after that night," she gave a smug glance back toward Ian, "Frank wasn't sure what I knew and he wasn't about to ask me. Ian just played stupid. But let Frank know that if the subject of divorce came up again, the authorities would find irrefutable evidence of what really happened that night. Well, what Frank *thought* really happened that night." She swallowed hard. "I kept waiting for the police to knock on my door and arrest me."

Ian leaned over and whispered something in Elizabeth's ear. Her face shifted and she motioned with the gun. "Let's go. Enough talking."

"Wait a minute. What about Gerald Benjamin?"

"Frank set all that up. He and Elliott thought the only way to cover up the murder was to blackmail Gerald. Only Gerald couldn't live with what he'd done and was going to tell, so Elliott got rid of him."

Jillian shuddered. "Was Frank's heart attack really a heart attack or did you do something to him?"

The woman blinked. "What made you ask that?"

"I don't know. The thought crossed my mind more than once that the person who pulled the trigger the night of the party might not want Frank to live much longer now that everything was being investigated."

"Think you're pretty smart, don't you?" She tilted her head and studied Jillian. "Okay, yes, I slipped enough potassium chloride into his coffee to kill him. Another heart attack. One that would finish the job this time and no one would question it. I took a chance and got away with it."

Jillian shuddered at the woman's lack of remorse.

Elizabeth glanced at the clock on the wall over Jillian's head. "Let's go."

"Where?" Jillian asked, her mind clicking, searching for a way out. *Please, God, get me out of this.*

"You're going to disappear again. After all, you've done it once, what's to keep you from doing it again?"

"Because I'm not hiding a secret anymore and Colton knows I wouldn't leave him. Not now. How can you do that to him?"

Pain flickered briefly. "Hurting Colton is just an unfortunate turn of events." A cruel smile twisted her lips. "Who knows? He may even thank me when he gets full custody of that cute little girl he's grown so fond of."

Nausea threatened. Her mind raced. What was she going to do? If it was just Elizabeth, Jillian had no doubt about her ability to overpower the woman. But add Ian into the picture and that made things a little more tricky. She needed a way out and fast.

The phone on the desk rang and they all froze. Then Jillian dove for the phone as Elizabeth lifted the weapon.

44

Colton listened as the line picked up and waited for the greeting.

A gunshot echoed through the line and he flinched, nearly dropping his phone. "Hey!"

Dominic shot him a sharp look as the car swerved onto the shoulder of the road before Colton jerked it back under control. He flipped the siren on and hit the gas pedal. To Dominic he said, "That was a gunshot!"

Dominic called it in, requesting backup.

Colton drove fast, but carefully, senses alert, eyes darting to make sure he saw anyone not paying attention. He pressed the gas harder and figured it would take him about another ten minutes before he could be at his uncle's home.

Jillian hunkered down behind the desk. She'd managed to knock the old-fashioned handset off the hook onto the desk. She just prayed someone heard the shot and called the police. "Elizabeth, stop! I have a child!"

"And so do I. If I go to jail, she'll have no one."

"She's twenty years old! Meg's nine!" Jillian couldn't believe she was arguing about this. But as long as the woman kept talking, she wasn't shooting.

"I'm not going to jail," Elizabeth fairly growled. "Come out from behind that desk."

Jillian looked for a weapon. Any weapon.

Elizabeth huffed as though tired of the game. "Ian, get her out from behind there. This is crazy. Carmen's going to be home shortly and I need to have this mess taken care of."

"I'm a 'mess' to take care of?" Jillian demanded. "Really? I'm a human being, Elizabeth! How can you just kill me so easily?"

A dark-shod male foot stepped to the edge of the desk and Jillian rose to come face-to-face with Ian. The menace in his eyes didn't bode well for her. He reached for her and a number of self-defense moves flipped through her mind. But Elizabeth still had the gun. She held up a hand. "What do you want me to do?"

"Follow me," Elizabeth barked.

Ian shoved her hand aside, wrapped rough fingers around her upper arm, and pulled her from behind the desk. Jillian didn't bother to struggle. Yet. She had to get out of the confines of the office.

Elizabeth led the way, looking back over her shoulder every once in a while. And still Jillian couldn't act in the narrow hallway, even if the gun wasn't pointed at her right this moment. And then they were through the sunroom and out onto the porch where Elizabeth had murdered the governor.

Ian kept going. Onto the gravel walkway toward the wooded area beyond. Where were they taking her? Then she remembered the large man-made pond just ahead and fear gripped her by the throat.

Colton swung into the drive and stared at Jillian's car. "What's she doing here?"

He and Dominic bolted from the vehicle and raced to the front door. Colton checked it to find it unlocked. He pushed it open and stepped inside with Dominic on his heels. "Jillian? Aunt Elizabeth? Carmen?"

The foyer echoed back at him.

He walked toward the kitchen. "Empty."

Dominic cleared the den.

They met back in front of the sunporch.

"Look," Dominic said. "The door's open."

The door leading from the sunroom to the porch stood wide. "Come on."

———■———

Jillian stumbled on the gravel, her ankle twisting slightly. Elizabeth had moved behind her and now jabbed her with the weapon.

The pond loomed, the edge of the dock only two feet away. She stopped and whirled. "What are you planning? To shoot me and dump me in the water?"

"Works for me. Now move."

Ian gave her a shove. Jillian stepped onto the dock, her brain whirring. No way was she just going to go quietly to her death.

"Mom?"

Elizabeth froze and turned as though in slow motion toward the gazebo. Carmen lay stretched out on the bench. She sat up, eyes narrowed. "What are you doing?"

"She's planning to kill me," Jillian blurted.

"Shut up!" The woman looked horrified, petrified that Carmen had seen her. To Carmen, she stammered, "It's nothing, darling, just, um . . . some business—" She broke off at Carmen's look of disbelief, her pointed stare at the weapon her mother had on Jillian.

Carmen walked toward them, her eyes bouncing between her mother, the gun, Ian.

"Carmen, go on up to the house and forget you ever saw this," Ian said.

"How?" Tears shimmered in the girl's eyes. "Like I had to try and forget what happened the night my mother shot the governor?"

Elizabeth gasped. "What? You saw?"

"Oh, I saw all right."

Jillian moved toward the edge of the dock, her eye catching movement at the tree line. Hope rose as she tried to see who was there, but Carmen stood between the movement and her mother.

"Put the gun down, Elizabeth!" Colton yelled.

Jillian's pulse leapt. She might survive this after all.

"No!" Elizabeth screamed as she spotted her nephew and Dominic. "No! No! No! It's not supposed to be this way!" She turned back to Jillian. "This is all your fault!"

"Carmen, move!" Colton hollered.

The girl froze.

Elizabeth aimed the weapon and Jillian heard the crack of the gun as the water rushed up to meet her.

———■———

Colton yelled, "Drop the gun, Aunt Elizabeth! Do it! Do it now!"

Sirens finally sounded and grew closer. Backup had arrived, but it might be too late to save Jillian. Fear choked him as he kept the weapon on Ian. The man stood with his hands in sight. Carmen stayed in front of her mother.

Dominic glanced at Colton and shook his head. No shot. Agony coursed through him. "Carmen, move!"

She caught his eye and shook her head.

"Ian! On your knees, now!"

Ian dropped to his knees, hands still above his head.

To Dominic, he said, "I'm going to get Carmen out of the way, then get Jillian out of the water. You take care of the rest." He paused. "I can't shoot her, Dom."

"But she might shoot you."

"I don't think she will. It's a risk I'm going to have to take. We're running out of time for Jillian."

Dominic nodded. "Get Carmen, leave the rest to me."

Colton moved, heart in his throat, his worry for Jillian nearly smothering him. As long as he kept Carmen between himself and the gun, he knew his aunt wouldn't shoot. He raced out into the open, changed his mind at the last minute, and shot past a stunned Carmen. He tackled Elizabeth before she had a chance to do more than let out a ragged scream. He wrenched the gun from her hand.

Dominic approached at a rapid jog, weapon still trained on Ian. He hollered, "Get Jillian!"

Elizabeth lay wilted against the ground, the fight gone from her. Carmen knelt beside the woman, weeping.

Colton passed the gun to Dominic and hit the dock full speed ahead. Then he was in the water, which was only about six feet deep. Frantic, he looked for her. "Jillian!"

He ducked under and opened his eyes. Silence surrounded him. Murky, cloudy water hit his vision. He waded back and forth, panic building as he looked and found nothing. He came up, sucked in a deep breath, and readied himself to go back under.

"Colton!"

The air whooshed from his lungs. "Jillian! Where are you?"

"Here! Under the dock."

He spun to see her in the water, but just under the edge of the dock, one hand raised to hang on to one of the wood crosspieces holding the dock together.

Colton swam to her and pulled her into a fierce hug. "Are you all right?" His gaze swept over her. Blond hair plastered to her face and blue eyes wide, but she was alive.

"I'm fine. The bullet missed."

"You jumped."

"Yeah."

"I thought so, but I wasn't sure. You scared me."

"I was pretty scared myself."

He gave her a quick, hard kiss, then said, "Let me check on Dominic."

Jillian nodded and together they swam to the ladder at the edge of the dock and climbed up. He reached down to help her up, then he looked up to find most of the Columbia Police Department surrounding the area, along with Hunter and Katie, holding their guns on part of his family.

He shuddered. His mother would be devastated all over again. But he'd be willing to bet she'd take in Carmen.

Poor Carmen.

She sat on the ground next to her mother, who now had her hands cuffed behind her back. Carmen's arms were wrapped around the woman's stooped shoulders.

Ian was gone.

"Where's Ian?"

"In the back of a squad car with two officers on him," Dominic said. "I wanted to wait on you to see if you would help with your cousin. She's not letting Elizabeth go and I didn't have the heart to pry her away."

Colton sighed and Jillian gave him a gentle push. "Go to her, she needs you."

He approached Carmen and sat beside her. "We have to take her in, you know."

"I know." Her words were muffled against her mother's shoulder.

"Come on, Carmen, let her go."

A sob shook her. "I saw her that night. I saw her shoot the governor and I never said a word. It's eaten me up inside."

Elizabeth didn't move, her eyes empty, vacant. She'd retreated somewhere within her mind.

Colton rubbed a hand down Carmen's back. "You're going to have a long journey, dealing with all this. We'll be there to walk with you. I promise."

Another sob ripped from her and she let go of her mother to throw her arms around his neck. He looked up at Dominic and nodded. Dominic came and hooked a hand under his aunt's arm and helped her to her feet. She moved obediently, yet with no expression on her face.

Carmen clung to him, apparently not caring that he was soaking her. "I couldn't say anything about that night. If I told the police the governor didn't have an accident, then I would have to admit my mom shot him—even though she didn't mean to. And I couldn't do that because my dad was never around and if my mom went to jail, what would happen to me?" She looked up at him, eyes pleading. "I'm sorry. I'm so sorry."

Colton held her in a hug. "It wasn't your fault, Carmen, you were just a kid." He held her awhile longer as he processed what she'd said. She'd known all along. "Come on, let's get this over with."

He looked up to see Jillian dripping tears and water, standing beside Hunter. He took Carmen by the hand and wrapped an arm around Jillian's shoulder. Together, they made their way back up to the house.

EPILOGUE

SIX MONTHS LATER

Colton smoothed his sweaty palms down his suit-clad thighs. Him. With sweaty palms. He never would have imagined it.

The last six months had been heartbreaking—and amazing. His aunt had gotten a thirty-year prison sentence. Colton ached for his cousin, but frankly didn't feel the sentence was long enough. He knew his aunt would probably die there, but she'd gotten off easy in his opinion. He would continue to try to visit. Maybe one day she'd let him see her.

Dominic and Serena's Christmas wedding was followed by Alexia and Hunter's Valentine's Day nuptials.

Dominic and Alexia's father had passed away the last week in September, and it looked like their mother and her pastor might tie the knot before much longer.

Grayson had taken a job with the Columbia PD and word had it that he and Katie might make a go of it.

Colton breathed a laugh and shook his head.

As for Jillian and Meg, he loved them more and more each day. Which brought him to the sweaty palms.

Jillian and Meg would be there shortly.

Bert and Ernie watched him pace, their eyes following him back and forth. Colton stopped in front of them. "Okay, guys, just like we practiced for the last four weeks, right?"

Bert yawned and Colton groaned.

The knock on the door made him flinch and his heart flip into overdrive. "Showtime," he whispered.

—■—

Jillian waited for Colton to answer the door. Meg shifted from one foot to the other. "Can I go down to the creek with Bert and Ernie?"

"Maybe in a little bit. Colton said he had a surprise for us, so let's find out what it is, okay?"

Meg sighed. "Okay, but if it's a dorky surprise, can I go?"

"*May* you go?"

"Why are you asking me?"

Jillian groaned as the door opened. Her groan turned to a gasp. "Why are you so dressed up?"

Colton grinned at her. "Because I had been looking forward to our reunion dance and it kind of got blown up. So, I decided to re-create it here."

Jillian looked down at her winter boots and jeans. "I'm not exactly dressed for it."

"Me either," Meg said.

"Come right this way, ladies."

Jillian and Meg followed him down the hall into one of the bedrooms. Another gasp escaped her and even Meg was impressed. "Wow."

Two sparkling gowns graced the bed. Colton smiled. "Will you?"

"Colton—"

"You bet we will," Meg said as she placed both hands on Colton's stomach to push him from the room. "We'll be just a few minutes."

Colton's laughter echoed even after Meg shut the door. Jillian laughed. "What is he up to?"

"Who cares? Get changed."

"Yes, ma'am."

Fifteen minutes later, they emerged from the bedroom. Jillian had on a green silk gown with pearl beading. Meg's dress was a long-sleeved pale yellow velvet with a sweetheart neckline. Her gold locket necklace, white tights, and white shoes completed her ensemble.

Colton had his head next to Bert and Ernie's and appeared to be in a deep conversation with them. Meg's laugh caused him to turn. His eyes went wide and his jaw dropped. Jillian walked up to him and tapped it shut.

Colton clicked the remote and music filled the room. A slow, bluesy tune without any lyrics. He placed a light kiss on her lips, then looked at Meg. "May I have this dance, Miss Carter?"

Shyness seemed to overtake Meg and she ducked her head even as she held out a hand. Colton took it and led her in a dance around the room.

Jillian watched, hands clasped in front of her, heart filled to overflowing with love for the man who had taken the time to get to know her all over again—and allowed her to get to know him.

Added joy had been watching him win over his daughter's heart.

Meg pulled away. "Your turn, Mom."

Jillian slipped into Colton's arms and nestled her head against the base of his throat. She felt him kiss the top of her head.

After they finished their spin around the room, Meg said, "What's Bert got in his mouth?"

Jillian pulled back as Colton dropped to his knee and clicked the dog over. "Here, boy." Bert padded over and Colton held out his hand. The dog dropped the object into his palm, then sat, tongue lolling. Jillian couldn't see what it was the dog had given Colton and shifted for a better look, but she was too late.

Colton made a sweeping motion with his hand and Bert bolted over to lie down beside Ernie in front of the fireplace.

Colton stayed on his knees and waved Meg over. Curious, Jillian watched as Meg crossed to stand next to her. "What is it?"

He looked up at Jillian and held up his hand. She gaped at the ring staring back at her.

Meg laughed. "Wow! That's huge!"

Jillian clapped a hand over her daughter's mouth. "Colton . . . it's . . ."

"Gorgeous," Meg mumbled against Jillian's palm.

"Gorgeous," Jillian repeated. She dropped her hand and stared at the man in front of her.

He said, "I've had this ring for over ten years now. I was going to give it to you the night of graduation." He glanced down at it. "It's not exactly your style now, but I couldn't . . ." He stopped and bit his lip. "Back then I thought you needed a huge ring. I . . . I thought that I had to prove how much I loved you by how big the ring was. Only now . . ."

"I would have loved it."

"Would have? What about now?"

"What about now?"

"What kind of answer is that?"

Meg sighed. "You haven't asked the question yet, Dad."

He blinked. "Oh." Back to Jillian, he asked, "Will you marry me?"

Jillian choked out a strangled "Yes." She looked at Meg, who nodded. "Yes. We will."

The relief in his eyes almost made her laugh. He slipped the ring out of the box and onto her finger. A beautiful square-cut diamond. "If you want something different, we'll go shopping—"

She laid a finger over his lips. "It's perfect. Thank you."

Meg squealed and clapped her hands. "We're getting married!"

Colton laughed and said, "Yes, it appears we are."

"But you forgot one thing," Meg said.

"What's that?"

"You haven't kissed her. I imagine when people get engaged, they gotta kiss."

Colton turned his green eyes back to Jillian. "I imagine they do."

He lowered his head and covered her lips with his, and Jillian reached behind her to cover Meg's eyes as she kissed him back with every ounce of love she had in her.

When he raised his head, he asked, "Short engagement?"

Breathless, Jillian nodded. "Definitely."

"Okay, now that we got this mushy stuff taken care of, can I go to the creek?"

Colton laughed. "Sure. Take the dogs with you."

"And change your clothes first," Jillian said.

Three minutes later, Meg was out the door, the dogs on her heels, and Colton had Jillian back in his arms. "I love you, Jillian Carter."

Emotion made it hard to force the words out, but she managed a strangled, "And I love you, Colton Brady."

"For a lifetime?"

"A whole lifetime. Whatever time God gives us." She wiped a stray tear and sniffed.

"Well, he sure has gone to a lot of trouble to reunite us. I figure we've got a good fifty or sixty years left."

"Sounds like a plan to me," she said.

"Yep, no plan B needed," he agreed.

Jillian threw back her head and laughed.

ACKNOWLEDGMENTS

Thank you once again to Jim Hall, police officer extraordinaire. I appreciate so much your willingness to take the time to read each book and give me your expert feedback.

And thank you to Drucilla Wells with the D2L Behavioral & Investigative Consulting Services, LLC, and retired FBI Special Agent.

Thank you to my agent, Tamela Hancock Murray of the Steve Laube Agency, for all your work on my behalf.

Thank you to the crimescenewriters yahoo group for answering my numerous questions.

Thank you to Cara Putman, who took time out of her busy schedule to read and give me feedback. I appreciate it!

Thank you to the fans who buy the books. Without you, I couldn't do this!

Thank you to my family for your understanding and encouragement, for believing in me and letting me follow my dream.

But most especially, I thank my Lord and Savior, Jesus Christ, for giving me the best job in the world.

Lynette Eason is the award winning, best-selling author of several romantic suspense novels, including *Too Close to Home*, *Don't Look Back*, and *A Killer Among Us*. She is a member of American Christian Fiction Writers and Romance Writers of America. Lynette graduated from the University of South Carolina and went on to earn her master's degree in education from Converse College. She lives in South Carolina with her husband and two children.

Come meet
Lynette Eason at
www.LynetteEason.com

Follow her on

facebook.   Lynette Barker Eason

twitter   LynetteEason

Women of
JUSTICE Series